ELEMENTS
A TEAR OF GOD NOVEL

Cover design, interior book design,
and eBook design by Blue Harvest Creative
www.blueharvestcreative.com

ELEMENTS: A TEAR OF GOD NOVEL

Published by
Resonance Books

Library of Congress Control Number:
2016933575

ISBN-13: 978-1-943151-02-8
ISBN-10: 1-943151-02-4

Visit the author at:
www.bhcauthors.com

Visit the author on BHC Authors
by scanning the QR code.

ELEMENTS

A TEAR OF GOD NOVEL

RAYMOND HENRI

RESONANCE
BOOKS

Wilmington, North Carolina

WITH THANKS TO:

Angel, Flynn, Dave, Sherry, Rhianna, Aaron,
Erin, TiCie, Brandon, Jim, Amber

SPECIAL THANKS TO:

Mom and Dad for encouraging my self-expression.
My wife Alexandra for her tireless support and
always insisting on one more rewrite.

CHAPTER

1

NOTHING IN Mink's appearance stood out from any other sixteen-year old Elementalist. The more he tried to blend in, the less he suffered bullying. As things were, the daily violence he endured, especially from that rothead Lightning user Blin, was all he could bear. His dark eyes matched his wavy, shoulder-length hair, and though his skin was not the manliest shade of brown, average did call less attention, and he was glad enough for it. Even on warm days like this, he wore an oversized pocket jacket and long pants to disguise and soften his sinewy frame. They further concealed the physical damage of bullying well enough until a Body user, either Pulti or his mom, could heal him.

When his parents suggested this camping trip on Rift Ridge, Mink suspected it would turn into yet another well-intended attempt to finally determine his Elemental affinity. The location was so far into the wilderness of Georra that there was no risk of being spotted by anyone of the four nations, despite the lack of trees. That didn't make it any less embarrassing for Mink. At sixteen and failing to accomplish something typically mastered by a five-year-old, embarrassment fit like skin.

The view from Rift Ridge was amazing. Mink had never been this far out in the wilderness before, nor at so high an elevation. A steady breeze rose up to cut through the heat of the day. To the east below him, he could barely make out the jagged green horizon line of the Great Barrier Range. Thousands of years ago, the vast expanse before him was one of the largest oceans on Georra. Now its depths were awash in a sea of green grass waving with wind. Several miles away, a distinct line indicated where the grasses stopped trying to climb up the ridge.

Due to the lack of vegetation or shade, Mink thought it odd that his parents would pick this spot on the plateau to camp. A grove of hudlew trees grew a few miles to the north. For as long as it took Mink to go pluck some of their bright red fruit and bring it back to their campsite yesterday, he wished they were set up closer. His parents worried that being too near the trees would increase the risk that Reeks might find them. But the country of Harvest was far enough north into the permafrost, Mink thought they were being overly protective. This whole vacation had been so impromptu, and yet so specific, he knew something else must be going on.

Even more so, the tactics his parents resorted to these past couple of years were becoming increasingly more extreme, as any sane means of finding his Element had failed a multitude of times. Long gone were the days Mink could get away with simply practicing the chants of the different Elements in their various vocal styles. He wanted to know his affinity just as much as them, if not more, but his parents were starting to scare him. Now they had deliberately taken him to this remote area, far away from anyone's sight.

Mink backed away from the overlook and headed back to their campsite a hundred yards farther west. Juré and Nyam were still busying themselves with a pre-lunch straightening up. Seats were positioned around the Fire, boxes and bags pulled out of the tent, and ceramic pots arranged. His mom's cart was parked alongside the camp to cast whatever shade it could. For all Mink knew, lifetimes might have passed since anyone had last set foot in this part of the world, let alone camped here. He wasn't even sure it was legal. That only strengthened his gut feeling that they were about to employ some controversial means to reveal his latent Elemental affinity.

Mink's suspicions were confirmed as soon as he saw Juré, his dad, grab a yellow crystalline Star of Order from his bag near the tent. Two overlapping squares formed an eight-pointed star that demonstrated the relationships of the Elements represented by each point: Lightning, Air, Spirit, Water, Wood, Soil, Body, and Fire. Eight hateful little Elements that had been the bane of Mink's life as far back as he could remember.

Juré wheeled his slender arm in circles, trying to garner his son's attention. Mink ignored his dad's beckonings, walking slowly the rest of the way to the camp Fire. He let his hair fall over his face as his mind raced for any possible way to avoid the inevitable. He longed for normal family vacations that didn't make him feel like a cause, or a freak.

Mink understood that it had been difficult for them, too. After all, they were the parents of the only known person ever on the planet Georra who couldn't identify his Element. They tried a little too hard to support and encourage him in any activity that didn't rely on having an Element, going out of their way to show him he could still have a normal life. But this week-long vacation, roughing it far out on Rift Ridge, was becoming quite abnormal. Mink wanted nothing more than to be back in Floth with Dreh and Pulti, throwing back a few nutties and talking about how much better life would be after leaving home.

He couldn't argue that nothing had worked before. His parents would only be bold enough to go to these lengths if they had something new up their sleeves. They must believe they had developed a new way to kick start his affinity. He could try the maybe-I-just-don't-have-an-Element angle, but everybody had one. Even Machinists, who shunned Elemental powers.

Anticipation kindled inside of Mink as he started to wonder if their mysterious plan might actually work. This could be the end of the agony, of the name calling, of having to spend a few hours of each school day sitting at the only large desk in a room full of first-graders who looked down on him. He could start learning how to use his Element. Which one was it? He had to find out. Determined and focused, he turned to his dad.

"You just did something to me, didn't you?" Mink felt skeptical of his own sudden optimism. His dad's Element was Spirit, and Mink justifiably gave his father credit for any sudden u-turns in mood.

"Hm?" Juré responded, innocently enough. "Oh, no... I was just thinking this would be a good time for us to talk, if you'd like."

The desire for discovering his affinity reached a fever pitch. Artificially influenced or not, Mink readied himself to initiate the tests.

"Forget talk. Whatever you and mom have planned, let's get to it."

Juré indicated a cushioned blanket on the ground and smiled. "Okay, son. Sit comfortably, looking south."

As Mink sat, Juré fixed the Star of Order atop a short Wooden rod stuck into the ground, a few feet in front of his nose. The star was clear and golden, with a diameter about as wide as Mink's face. His father was an attractive man who few would guess was forty-nine years old. Lean and academic, he had somehow managed to avoid any physical ailments that often gave Spirit users away. His skin tone was a shade lighter than his son's, but they shared a strong family resemblence in hair, eyes, and Body type.

"I've already done this meditation an insane amount of times, Dad."

"Not like this... Well, sort of. You will be doing the meditation the way you've been taught, but I'll be... helping," Juré reassured, moving behind Mink.

On the other side of the Fire, Nyam busied herself with making lunch while fighting back her long, curly mahogany hair. Mink took it as a good sign that whatever his dad wanted to do probably wouldn't take too long. He stared through the center of the star to the lands in the south.

A lazy, clear river flowed out of the rift and into the forested foothills of the Federation of Animalist Nations. As he relaxed, he wondered how the Animalists tested for their Elemental affinities. The river's casual but persistant movement helped him ease into the meditation, arms resting on his knees, hands loose, and fingers downward. He imagined the river's current pulling all tension and thoughts out of his forehead through the center of the star and into its waters.

In a light, rhythmic voice, Juré began the Spirit Unification chant,

"I am one with my Element.
It passes through me and I it.
When combined, it is part of me.
My Spirit remains as in me.
My target and I can converse.
I can see as my target sees.
I can travel throughout the nerves.
Unify when I utter 'Mink.'"

He spoke his son's name and Mink immediately recognized the weight of his father's consciousness in the back of his head. It never failed to impress him how powerful this felt. He noticed this time his dad had added two specifications to the chant.

"Perfect. Your gaze is in just the right place," Juré said from inside Mink's mind. "Does it feel to you like you're favoring any one point on the star more than the others?" Mink had answered this same sad, standard question dozens of times before.

"Nope," he quipped casually. "Actually, it's more like they're all pushing my focus dead center. Could you double check my fingers for me?"

A pulsing energy ran down each of Mink's arms and pooled in his hands. Each finger represented a specific Element. Any one that bent closer to a thumb more than others when relaxed would be a good indication of Elemental affinity.

"Just like always," Juré admitted. "All fingers are exactly equidistant from the thumbs. Dammit." The energy shot back up Mink's arms and into the back of his head again.

"So, what was the new thing you wanted to try?" he asked telepathically.

"I'm going to divert your eyes to each Element on the star and see if they return to center. But this time, Mink, I need you to fight my movements."

"What?! That's impossible, dad. That level of control is theoretical." Mink tensed in anticipation of what his dad had in mind. No one had controlled movements of living people before, nor was doing so legal by any stretch.

"It's a chant I need to say while in your occipital lobe. I've managed to test it successfully several times before." Juré recited in the slow, light way of a Spirit user,

> "Your eyesight controlled by my will.
> I already see what you see.
> Your vision and my vision unite.
> I move the muscles of your eyes.
> I am focusing your vision.
> Sight understood by consciousness.
> Our spirits inside control the
> Muscles that move and focus eyes – "

As Juré continued to chant in Mink's mind, he feared his dad might actually be serious. The longer the chant, the more powerful the effect, and this one was already going long. This method was disturbingly similar to the Reeks' animation of their puppets after a ritualistic murder, which scared Mink to his core. Juré continued on,

> *"Your eyes, my will, your will, our sight.*
> *Your control will not be foregone.*
> *My control will not be overrode.*
> *The wind in our sight is my strength.*
> *Each breath empowers my Spirit.*
> *Vision is light carried by Air.*
> *Anointed Eternsa's agent.*
> *Control is mine when I say, 'See.'"*

He implemented the effect by saying, "See." At once, Mink's vision all but went black. He could tell where the Star of Order was, but could no longer make out the river in the distance. His eyes burned. The muscles all around them cramped. Objectively, Mink marveled that his dad may have broken a historical barrier.

"Whoa, Dad. Where did you come up with this?"

"Your uncle Durren worked on it with me."

Mink's Uncle Durren was a Senior Advocate in the Main Cameral building at the Capitol, and a very busy man. It was equally flattering and embarrassing to have such investment in the discovery of his Element. Yet again, Mink felt he had become a cause.

CHAPTER

2

OKAY, MINK, I'm going to move your eyes to each of the points, starting with Lightning," Juré explained telepathically. "Resist me as much as you can. When you feel me let up, relax. If your eyes don't move back to center, then that should be your Element. If they do go back to center, we'll go to the next point. Got it?"

"Yeah. No problem. Thanks, Dad." Mink had no idea what was going on.

"Sure. I'm starting now."

Mink's eyes started moving upward on their own. He tried to resist and felt the muscles rip.

He screamed. "Stop, stop, stop!"

"It's going to hurt, Mink. Just do the best you can to resist."

"No! It feels like all the muscles in my face are being torn apart!"

"I know. I'm sorry, son. Your muscles must be disabled so that they don't prevent your eyes from favoring your Element."

"But, without muscles my eyes are just going to go limp and fall down to the Wood Element. That doesn't mean I'm a Wood user."

"No, your soul will take over after your muscles are gone. This method has proven accurate several times."

"Uncle Durren let you do this to him?"

"A few times, yes. Okay, relax."

As his eyes rose involuntarily up to the Lightning point on the Star of Order, Mink fought as best he could against the excruciating pain of his father's control. He was beyond relieved when the pressure stopped, and his eyes dropped back to the center of the star.

"Well, it's not Lightning," Juré casually observed. "Next we'll try Air."

The sharp pain shot through Mink's face again as he resisted his father moving his eyes up and to the right. He hissed through his teeth and moaned horribly. He hoped to God that Air was not his Element. Juré often remarked that he would like to have a child with an Air affinity to augment his own Spirit Element. Mink was quite disinclined to give any support to his father at this time.

"Relax," Juré encouraged.

Mink's eyes quickly settled back into the center. "Yes, yes, yes! Thank you, God! Yes!" he thought spontaneously.

"Okay. Moving on." Juré's tone turned cool in response to his son's momentary lack of restraint. "Maybe you're Spirit, like me."

That was highly unlikely. Were Mink a Spirit user, his mom's Body effects wouldn't work on him, and he would show the scars of all the abuse he took from other students at school. His eyes moved to the right with enough force and pain to make Mink realize just how much his dad had been going easy on him. He could scarcely resist the force. Not wanting his father to think him a total wimp, he strained hard against the pull. A hot pain engulfed his face.

"Seriously, Dad! I'm going to go blind! I think I just felt something pop."

"Good. Your muscles have finally broken. Took longer than I would have liked. You can stop resisting now. You won't be able to."

In a surreal shift of sensation, Mink's eyes felt nothing, as if he were now the observing consciousness in his dad's head. His eyes moved on their own back to the center of the star, traveled down and to the right toward Water, held for a second, and then moved back to center. Oh well.

The test turned to Wood, the lowest symbol on the star. Mink was surprised his broken eyes actually managed to lift back up from Wood to center. Too bad. Wood was the most coveted Element, after all. Augmented by both Soil and Water, mitigated by none, and only canceled by Lightning.

The exercise continued through Soil and Body, both times returning to center. One last Element remained: Fire, which had its own seductive quality. It wasn't an especially strong Element, but did prove quite useful in many situations. Everyone liked having a Fire user around. Being Fire could definitely improve Mink's social life. Not to mention he would be able to augment his mother's Body Element. His eyes drifted up and to the left. They paused twice as long, giving Mink a sense of Juré's own anticipation. Released, his eyes floated back down and to the right, all the way to dead center of the stupid star.

Juré said nothing. Mink couldn't think of anything to say either. He felt his father's energy move back down each arm. Juré spent a long time in Mink's hands, but he knew the situation without his dad's report. None of his fingers had moved any closer to his thumbs. No Elemental affinity revealed here. Juré returned his energy to Mink's head.

"I'm sorry it didn't work out, buddy. Thank you for letting me try."

"Don't worry. I'm sorry, too. I can tell you went through a lot of trouble for this. Hey, at least you invented a new effect."

"Yeah," Juré responded unenthusiatically before chanting his Dispel effect, Unthink,

> *Eternsa undoes the effect.*
> *Take back the power which you gave.*

Mink had expected his eyes to relax, but they remained fixed in the center of the Star of Order. The throbbing, warm pain was no worse than before his eye muscles tore. In fact, his vision had otherwise returned to normal. He turned to face his parents and his broken eyes rolled downward, limp.

"Can I get up now?" Mink asked as Juré shuffled toward Nyam, near the camp Fire.

Exhausted, Juré only nodded, indicating weakly for Mink to rise with a gesture barely visible to his son's down-turned eyes.

"You look awful, Juré," Nyam said, concerned over his weariness. "You need to eat."

Nyam had lunch waiting for her husband as he came and sat beside the Fire. He reached out for the plate, eyelids drooping, but instead shook his head and without a word, slumped over into a deep sleep. Mink had never seen his dad, one of the nation's top Intelligence Operatives, so wiped out after a combo before. This had definitely been some heavy lifting. Having met only six Spirit users more powerful than his dad, he wondered if Juré had now surpassed them in skill.

Nyam, half the size of Juré and yet twenty times stronger, reclined him more comfortably in his seat. Though small, her Body was chiseled, balanced by a round and disarming face. Her light tan skin and feminine hips further reduced the intimidating appearance of her muscles. She looked up at Mink, face aglow with excitement.

"Well? How was it? What happened?" Nyam had been preoccupied with making lunch, and wouldn't have learned anything from Mink and Juré's telepathic conversation anyway.

"I can't move my eyes because the muscles are all torn up. That happened," Mink reported flatly, moving his head up and around to compensate for his damaged sight, trying to see more of the camp. The shadows of the chairs and cart showed that it was still barely past midday. Earlier than he thought.

"That's an easy fix. This food will do that," Nyam assured her son, all too familiar with healing serious injuries, and apparently well aware of the consequences of Juré's new effect. "What about the meditation? Did you settle on an Element?"

Mink evaded answering his mom's question, not wanting to admit defeat. He hoped she would realize the failure on her own, but admittedly he was known to be coy and tease his parents when there was good news to be shared. Instead, he asked, "Did your brother really let Dad do this to him?"

"Yes. What Element?" she persisted.

"Repeatedly?"

"Yes. And Aunt Lynn, Gutti, and I would have tried it if we could." Nyam became impatient. Being opposing Elements meant that Nyam and Juré couldn't cause any effect, good or bad, on each other. This was typical with couples as a means to avoid accidentally harming a mate.

"Well, it's probably the worst pain I've ever felt in my life and it didn't help."

Nyam must have thought some rather harsh words about the bad news with the way her brow creased and her head jerked. She shook her head and held up a plate of grains and fruit bits.

"Eat this. I've Imbued it to restore your eyes and give you more than enough strength for my testing."

Mink accepted the food, meaning to take as much time as he could to stall the next phase with her. His mother was never as gentle as his father. Body users weren't known for finesse. Nyam had been healing Mink for years of damage caused by every Elemental type. She had seen the worst of it and Mink didn't have so much as a blemish. In the more recent testing attempts, his mom became habitualized to causing severe damage.

"Thanks. I'm a little worn out still. You wanna just continue tomorrow? You know, relax for the rest of the day? Wait for dad to wake up?" Mink wanted to have his dad on hand to cancel out his mom's effects when she started giving a hundred and ten percent. Visions of all muscles ripped and bones broken invaded Mink's thoughts.

"Actually, we have to do it today," Nyam explained. "If neither plan works, we'll need the next couple of days to try our other methods."

Mink picked at his food. "So much for a vacation."

Nyam smiled, stretched, and looked around. Obviously her anticipation of their success trumped the severity of the methods needed to achieve it. "Speak for yourself. I love getting out of the city."

CHAPTER
3

A S MINK ate the Imbued stew of grain and fruit one spoon-
ful at a time, his excitement for the training fizzled. His
willingness to be on the family vacation lessened, too. Clearly,
Nyam's Body effect was canceling Juré's Spirit effect. His dad
had put the whammy on him after all. He looked at his food
and realized that he had regained full motion of his eyes. Anxious to negate the damage to his eyes and the brainwashing responsible for his agreeing to have any part of this madness, he
downed the rest of the food hardly chewing.

"Mind telling me what you have planned?" Mink managed to say between spoonfuls.

Nyam tied her long hair behind her head. "It's hard to
explain. But, I've been working really hard on finding a way
to test without giving you any pain. It sort of separates your
Spirit from your Body, but leaves your soul so it can still resonate with your Elemental affinity. It's probably easier for me to
show you."

Mink highly doubted his mother. She hadn't seemed too
concerned with his pain before. His emotional pain noticeably
broke her heart, lingering in her long after his father had healed

it. Yet she always made him feel like a sissy for succumbing to physical pain. "Look, Mom. You don't have to trick me or coerce me into going through with your testing. If you just tell me how much it's going to hurt, I'm more likely to cooperate."

Nyam laughed. Smiling, she reached for Mink's shoulder. "One thing I can promise you, Mink, is that you won't feel any pain." He wanted to trust her, but she was a little too excited.

He cleaned his plate and set it down beside him. Juré was still sound asleep.

"Can't we wait for dad?"

Nyam shook her head. "He slept for about six hours each time after he practiced that test before. We'll be done sooner than that."

Rubbing his face, Mink noticed he was completely healed. "Whatever. Let's get to it."

"Lay on your back then."

Mink obliged as Nyam exhaled a long breath and shook her hands, a move she believed helped her keep from laughing and get serious. She was an incorrigible nervous laugher, especially in dire situations. As if Mink didn't already have enough embarrassment to battle, he had to deal with his oddball mom. She'd probably be a really good Body user if she could reliably make it through a chant without breaking the rhythm and killing the power. When she did allow herself to laugh, she half-sounded like someone gasping for Air in a compost heap. She put on her game face and her voice dropped an octave as she chanted in the deep, strong rhythm of Body users,

> "*Body is under my control.*
> *I can change its shape with my mind.*
> *The Body is all I will —* "

Nyam stopped mid-chant. Her Body trembled and tears pooled in her eyes as she struggled to suppress the urge to laugh. "Dammit!" She exhaled a long breath and shook her hands again. "Sorry, I have to start over. Okay. Okay, okay,

okay. Sorry. I'm just really excited. I think this is going to work. It's really cool. I can't wait for you to see it." She exhaled another long breath and rolled her shoulders, beginning again,

> *"Body is under my control.*
> *I can change its shape with my mind.*
> *The Body is all I will need.*
> *Increase its density ten times.*
> *The Body is no more than flesh.*
> *Leave the Spirit behind to rest.*
> *The Body is like a statue.*
> *My power molds its destiny.*
> *The Body no longer has joints.*
> *All senses have been suspended.*
> *I cannot kill with this effect.*
> *This effect will not change its shape.*
> *Target's Spirit cannot be moved.*
> *The Fires of Symg empower.*
> *Curpo, give to me your blessings.*
> *Respond to me upon my touch."*

And with that, Nyam pushed her finger down hard into the center of Mink's chest. The firm, rocky ground beneath him compressed ten inches in the shape of his Body. Mink held his breath for a couple of seconds, waiting for the latent pain to strike. It never did. He felt nothing. Absolutely nothing. He could still see, but it wasn't with his eyes anymore. He sensed everything around him as if it were all in his peripheral vision.

His mother reached down and picked him up with just one hand on his shoulder. Many Body users kept an active chant on themselves to be more physically attractive, but Nyam kept one for strength. Most people wouldn't know that, though, as beautiful as she was. She stood Mink's Body upright and pressed him down in the dirt to his ankles. Not only had he been numbed, he was solid as a statue. Giddy with her success thus far, Nyam pranced to retrieve something from a bag by her chair. From what Mink could tell, she had altered a simple thirty two syllable Manipulation chant, Change Look, into an ultra-powerful one hundred and twenty eight syllable chant.

First, she gloved her hands with animal hide, and then pulled out a small stone case with eight thin rubber tubes embedded in slots. She was steady and careful on her way back to Mink. Setting the case down, she eased out the first tube. Aiming at her son's chest, she gave it a squeeze and released weaponized dust Imbued with a Lightning effect. Mink couldn't believe it. He thought his mother must have lost her mind as the dust blasted a melon-sized hole into him.

> *"I know how much Body I see.*
> *Quantified so upon my touch."*

Nyam implemented the Quantification effect for Body users, Constitution, by touching the hole in Mink's chest with a finger. She took out a pad of paper and made some notes, nodding studiously.

> *"A pure Body holds no illness.*
> *Its natural state upholding.*
> *No injury remains to harm.*
> *Make Body pure upon my touch."*

She placed her hand into Mink's gaping wound. By the time she removed it, his Body was restored. She made her way through the rest of the tubes. Each one used a different Element to put a crater in Mink, which Nyam would scrutinize before healing with Recovery, the Body users' Purification effect. For a taxi puller, she was quite the capable healer.

By the fourth tube, Nyam had become grim. Then, having run the whole gamut, she gave in to her emotions. She never took failure very well. Grabbing palm-sized rocks in each hand, she stormed away, punching her stone-packed fists into the ground until the rocks turned to dust. Since the Body Element augmented the Soil Element, Mink mused that trees might actually be able to grow up here now. How nice that would be for the area, he thought, momentarily forgetting that he was still stuck in a statue form while his Spirit lay in a shallow grave and his mother was raging.

Wiping angry tears from her face, Nyam walked back to the campsite. Mink watched her sit and stare at the Fire. One of the nice things about being a Body user was that it took a lot to make the user tired, and the slightest bit of Fire sped recovery. After her shadow had grown noticeably longer, she started picking up and extinguishing embers in her hands, rubbing them into the back of her neck. Her mood improved greatly after this and she rose quickly, dusting herself off.

"Now you," she said to his Body before toppling it over in the Mink-shaped impression still carved into the ground. She stood over the Body and chanted Unfeel to Dispel the effect in a deep, strong voice,

> *"May Curpo undo the effect.*
> *Take back the power which you gave."*

With that, she pressed her finger to Mink's forehead.

He sat up from his personal crater, rubbing his chest and belly. "Whoa, Mom. It doesn't hurt at all."

She extended a hand to help him up. "See? Told you so."

After Mink got back to his feet, he hugged his mom. "Sorry it didn't work."

"Me, too. I'm very sorry I couldn't find your Element, Mink." Nyam's mood soured again. "I could have sworn I was on to something."

"It was totally crazy. I mean, when you shot me with that dust, I thought I wasn't going to have a Body left."

"Well, it did more damage than I thought it would, but I had strengthened your Body several times over. I wonder now if I strengthened it too much..." Nyam lost herself in thought for a moment. "No. That's not it. They all did damage. One of them shouldn't have. And one of them should have strengthened you."

Mink could tell she was about to cry again. "It was an amazing effect anyway. You did really good at it. How much did you practice?"

"Sixteen times. With a double-blind study. Worked every time." Nyam shook her head and went to the sleeping Juré and poked him on the shoulder. "Juré? You awake yet?"

"Yeah," he said without opening his eyes. "Can I have a little more time, though?" Sleeping in the wind shortened the time he needed to recover. Only about four hours had passed according to Mink's best guess.

"We only have three or four hours before the sun sets. I'd like to start Plan B now."

"I thought yours was Plan B," Juré complained, rubbing his eyes.

"Not that Plan B. Our Plan B."

He stood and stretched. "I thought we were doing that tomorrow."

"We were, until both of our methods came up with no rotting clue to his Element. I can't wait. That means you can't either."

"Four hours isn't going to be enough time for that plan to work." Juré helped himself to the leftovers sitting by the Fire. "Better to get an early start tomorrow."

That evening, talk of Elements were set aside in favor of games with dice. Before long, Mink had nearly forgotten about the bizarre ways his parents had tested him that day. They played long into the moonlight and it wasn't until Mink settled for sleep that the fear of the following day swept over him.

CHAPTER
4

BREAKFAST HAD been scant, more carbs than meat and only enough food to remind Mink that he had eaten. The sun had yet to rise over the eastern horizon, but the sky lightened to a pleasant, deep teal that he much preferred to the plain aqua of daylight. The wind rushed up the slope of the ridge with enough of the previous night's chill that he fastened the hooks of his pocket jacket up to his chin. The cool Air refreshed Mink, who slept horribly thanks to yesterday's events and the threat of today.

Here he was, with his own parents ripping apart his eyes, blowing up his Body, and plotting who knew what and he didn't have the slightest idea what Element was his. He longed for the days when his parents tested him by training him on the basic chants of each Element. Nothing ever happened, but it was easier than this. It was beyond him to even decide which Element he would rather be. He disliked them all equally.

Nyam stoked the Fire until it produced some flames she could wring her hands in while Juré came and stood by Mink to take in the wind. It could have been his imagination, but

Mink swore more of his father's hair had blanched overnight. Swatches of gray now peppered the deep black of his hair.

"I'm getting old, Mink," Juré said, reading his son's gaze. "Gotta expect life to leave some marks of accomplishment."

"So, you're first up again?" Mink stretched and tried in vain to psyche himself up for a long day. Why couldn't they just test him while he slept?

"Your mom and I are going to work together on this one." Juré winked. "Lucky you."

He didn't like the sound of Plan B so far. To his knowledge, Mink's parents had never collaborated on Elemental work before. It would have been self-defeating since Body canceled Spirit. This piqued his curiosity more than anything. What could Plan B be, and why might it take two days?

"You're going to want this," Nyam said from behind Mink.

Turning, his mother offered him his weapon of choice, a paddle. It measured a couple feet long, two and a half feet at its widest point, and three inches at its thickest. Dreh, Mink's best friend and a Wood user, had made it for him after learning Imbuing. Mink knew how to use it very well offensively and defensively. The only benefit to not knowing his Element was being able to put more effort into his other studies to compensate. Mink took the paddle from her with no small amount of dread.

"We're going to invoke a defensive reflex in you," Juré explained.

"What does that mean?" Mink asked, not really wanting the answer.

"Life or death situation," Nyam deadpanned.

Mink's parents backed away from him, chanting at the same time in a way that made it very difficult for Mink to tell which effect they were planning on using. The one thing he understood was that they were going to Attack him.

"I pin the Spirit back with aim.
Through my focus on my target.
My power severs the Spirit.
With hit or miss, my attack stops.
Instant Spirit push through brainstem.
My attack cannot do me harm.
With all of Eternsa's blessings.
Remove Spirit when I say, 'Spear.'"
"I destroy by hitting with aim.
From my contact with my target.
My power creates breaking force.
With hit or miss, my attack stops.
Contact magnified hundred-fold.
My attack cannot do me harm.
With all the blessings from Curpo.
Break my enemy when I touch."

They were really going to use Attacks on him! In battle situations, Elementalists tended to ready their effect with a chant and not carry out the implementation until conditions ensured success. Body users had to touch the target while Spirit users only needed to say a word within sight of it.

It would be impossible for Mink to avoid Juré's sight, due to the flat of the land and lack of even a shrub or rock large enough to conceal him. Ah, another probable reason they chose to come here! If Nyam used the Quick Legs effect, and Mink had no reason to think she wouldn't since her daily job required it, avoiding her touch would depend on his paddle skills. Mink's innate strategic ability, which had been fine-tuned through years of Elementless training, told him one thing—he could only lose.

Mink held his paddle in front of him in a readied stance as his parents finished their chants. They separated, flanking him in a wide circle. Mink rushed to his father's side. There was a chance that he could get them to make some kind of sound be-

fore implementing their effect, nullifying their chant and forcing them to start over. That strategy would be more successful
with his mom than his dad.

In a blink, Nyam had zoomed behind Mink, putting him
on the defensive with a barrage of kicks and punches. He deftly
rolled forward, using his paddle to guard his blind side. Mink
waited for an opening and swung his paddle flat at his mom's
stomach. She evaded in a blur and disappeared from sight.

Mink kept an eye on his dad while he scanned left, right,
and behind for where his mother had gone. She was no where
in sight. That meant one of two things: either Nyam had run off
to charge up an effect, or Juré had used an effect to make Mink
unable to see her. That Juré continued to maintain a distance
silently gave Mink reason to expect the former. Besides, Nyam
had most likely grunted or otherwise negated her chant and
needed to redo it.

Nyam was a very capable fighter. She captained her high
school's Brawling Squad and, though she hadn't placed at the
national level, she had never failed to qualify. If Mink could
hold his own at all, it was purely because his mother had spent
the last eight years training him how to fight against constant
bullying. Therefore, he knew all her best moves.

Juré, on the other hand, was hopeless at hand-to-hand
combat and not much better with a weapon. Still, Mink was
more concerned with what his father was capable of. Not only
could Spirit users make it impossible to fight, but they also had
a fair number of instant kill effects. Mink just couldn't figure
out why Juré hadn't done much yet.

The sound of Nyam's approach woke Mink from the staring contest he was having with his father. Even though he managed to thrust the paddle into Nyam's shoulder, the force of her
momentum pushed him backwards. His feet slid several yards,
her extended finger threatening within a couple feet of his face.
Her wrist snapped inward, putting her within easy reach of

Mink's forearm. Flipping the paddle, he fanned Nyam's arm away from the outside.

Mink saw his counter-strike open in a split-second. The handle of his paddle was close to Nyam's rib. She must have seen it too, the way she jerked her arm in to protect herself. Instead of blocking the attack, she caught the handle with her elbow and inadvertently helped him jam it against her. The force of the blow elicited an "Oomph," followed by a roll of her eyes. In a blur, she ran off to start her chant over.

They continued their battle for three hours past lunch, yet Mink was the only one sucking wind. Juré, conserving energy, hadn't done much more than taunt his son. Nyam's lack of fatigue prompted Mink to believe she set up a secret Fire to revive herself, and not all of her disappearing acts were for chants. Hunger and exhaustion would soon get the better of Mink, and he wondered how he could make it through the rest of the day without a break.

"Any chance of a time-out?" Mink wheezed. Not surprisingly, neither parent said a word. There wasn't any reason for a stalemate considering how much his parents overpowered him. The purpose of this training was to identify his Element, but all it did so far was keep Mink away from food. He worked up some energy to move the fight closer to their campsite so he might find an opportunity to grab something to eat.

He made it about halfway before Nyam was on him, using Quick Legs to give the impression that she was Attacking him from two-sides at once. The hours of using the paddle as a fan, shield, and edged weapon had taken their toll on Mink's shoulders. It felt three times as heavy as it had in the morning, but he still managed to block his mom and make some forward progress.

Juré rushed into the fight. The sudden change in battle dynamics gave Mink an adrenaline rush and second wind. As soon as Juré arrived behind Nyam, she jumped in the Air, forcing Mink into a high guard. It was difficult for Mink to track Juré's movements while blocking Nyam's kicks over his head, but he did glimpse the flash of a weaponized dust tube extended toward him.

He spun on his back heel and swung the paddle to fan the dust away from him. Nyam and Juré quickly backed off to avoid the fanned dust. Much to Mink's dismay, his paddle caught a fair amount of the dust. The crackling and fizzing sound confirmed that the dust was Imbued with Lightning, canceling out Dreh's Wood effect. Nyam wasted no time punching Mink's paddle and pulverizing it into splinters and shards.

CHAPTER
5

MINK STOOD and stared in disbelief, weaponless, breath-less, hungry, his hair clinging to his skin with sweat and dirt. The electric cloud of dust floated and crackled between Mink and his parents, who showed no sign of slowing down their offensive. Conversely, Juré had stepped up his game. Without a paddle, Mink had no way of avoiding Nyam's touch, even if he were at full energy.

Desperate to protect himself, Mink wanted to make for the cliff-side of Rift Ridge and take his chances jumping down to a ledge for cover. What happened instead was his leg gave out when he stepped, dropping him to his knee. His eyes pleaded with his parents. He didn't think he could move anymore. The last of the weaponized dust settled into the ground and Nyam wound up a punch.

Juré seemed to have a difficult time looking Mink's way. Twice, he glanced over, but quickly dropped his gaze. Setting his jaw, Juré finally looked Mink in the eye and implemented by uttering, "Spear."

Instantly, a sharp pain shot through Mink's chest and ex-tended far behind his back as his Spirit was stretched out and pinned about twelve feet behind him. A completely unfamiliar buzzing sensation mixed with the pain. He recognized Juré's instant-kill effect on an intellectual level, but he couldn't rationalize that his father had actually used it. The last of Mink's Spirit was pulled out the back of his head. He died with the snapping feeling of the severance of Body and Spirit.

Death consciousness was nothing like when his mom turned his Body into a statue. Mink felt both as small as a speck of dirt and as large as Georra. Peace washed over him. He noticed the absence of any physical sensation, and felt no curiosity about anything, let alone his Element. His remaining consciousness focused on his parents with a dim familiarity. Time stopped.

But, there was something else—another presence. Mink's awareness expanded to include a personal vehicle on the cliff three miles up the ridge from where his Body lay. A person moved quickly toward the vehicle through tunnels inside the mountain. Tracing a line east from the vehicle through the ground and downward from the person approaching it, Mink's focus honed in on a very large crystal. It was huge, encapsulated by a geode as large as any of the buildings in the Capitol. Mink was overcome with the sense that he now knew many things that were once important to him. He began to resonate with a different dimension.

He snapped back into his Body to see his mom with an outstretched fist as he fell hard and fast on his rear, very much alive and sore. "Time! Time out!" Mink screamed, scooting away on his butt. "I rotting died!"

"Language, Mink," Nyam admonished.

"Did you not hear me? I died!"

Juré helped him to his feet. "Mink, your Element should kick in to try to save you now that it knows you can die. This is our next-to-last resort. Trust us. You won't suffer any permanent damage."

Nyam folded her arms. "We need to exhaust you and take your weapons away so that you'll only have your Element to rely on. You've probably gone so long without identifying with it that it's retreated deep inside you. We must draw it out. This is for your own good."

So that was their game. Wear him out, destroy his paddle, and then strike him simultaneously. One of them was bound to hit a fraction of a second earlier than the other. Long enough for Mink to experience death, but not so long that the second Attack couldn't cancel the first, bringing him back to life. Had Nyam been any later taking action, there would be no turning back.

Something had happened while Mink was dead, although not even a second had passed. Had he made any kind of connection with his Element? He racked his brain for any sense of it. Only a flash, whatever it was. Then, Mink remembered what he saw.

"Wait! After I died, I saw someone." Mink pointed in the general direction. "Three miles up the ridge. A Machinist. Some ore scout, or something. He found a huge crystal buried inside the ridge."

Nyam turned to Juré with an unquiet look. He returned her gaze with a combination of recognition and disbelief. They paused in prolonged silence. Finally, Nyam spoke to Juré, "What do you want to do? We're not prepared for this."

"We should investigate," he replied adamantly. "If it is what I think it is, we can't let the Machinists know about it."

Nyam had sprinted up to where Mink indicated within just a few seconds while the other two huffed to catch up. She crouched and peered over the edge. Backing up, she signaled for her boys to approach quietly. She became impatient and sat, flicking small stones across the plateau, while she waited for them to bridge the distance she had managed to cross in no time.

"Still there?" Juré asked in a hushed voice once they had arrived.

Nyam leaned over to check and nodded. "The vehicle is. I don't see the scout though. He may not have reached it yet."

Juré turned to Mink. "Is he alone?"

"As far as I could tell. And it was like I was seeing all over the place, even through things."

"Juré, you should report this. We can't do anything else about it."

Juré peered over the cliff and got a good look at the vehicle. He scooted back and looked west toward Freeland.

"I'll go inside his mind once he appears. Hopefully, I'll be able to find out what he knows and what he plans to do. Maybe he didn't see the crystal, just ore deposits."

"Well then," Nyam said. "You better get the chant ready. He could come out at any time."

CHAPTER
6

M INK GAZED with growing fascination upon the vehicle. A few hundred yards below, it clung vertically to the
cliffside by way of anchors at each wheel dug into the rock. He
imagined that operating such a contraption would be fun. Elementalists ridiculed the need to use machines, but without an
Element to use, he hardly felt superior. It wasn't unheard of for
Elementalists to abandon their abilities and defect to Freeland.
In fact, part of Juré's job was to identify and facilitate dissent-
ers. Still, Mink's unique perspective helped him see the beauty
of the vehicle and he felt like his life could be easier if machines
were allowed back home.

The scout was taking forever to emerge from inside Rift
Ridge. Of course he didn't know that people were waiting for
him and, had he known, he might not even come out. Waiting
was not one of Mink's strong suits. He got that from his mom.
It actually crossed his mind that he might be able to see how
close the Machinist was if his parents killed him again. He obviously needed a distraction.

Juré couldn't say anything until the scout emerged lest he
have to recite his chant over. By then, the risk of the Machinist

getting out of Juré's sight was too high. If his parents weren't so serious, Mink thought to entertain himself with trying to get his dad to make a sound and ruin his effect. Nyam entertained herself by throwing rocks at a tree a couple miles down the slope of the ridge. By the way the tree shook, Mink could tell when she landed a direct hit.

"Do you think he decided to camp inside for the night?" Mink asked.

"Shh!" Nyam warned. "We can't give away our position."

Mink's restlessness got the better of his tongue. "Hey, Dad," he whispered. "When you're in his head, see if you can make him drive his vehicle up here and let me take it for a spin."

At that, Juré became cross and almost uttered a sound. Instead, he gave Mink a knock on the head with his knuckle.

"Mink," Nyam whispered, face contorted into a scowl. "Don't ever say things like that! Machines are evil!"

"All right, all right. Sorry," Mink said. "Just bored with all this waiting."

"Well, get over it. You can borrow my music crystal."

"No thanks, Mom."

"It's your own fault for forgetting yours."

Mink didn't exactly forget his. He opted not to bring it to avoid one of his parents picking it up and lecturing him about his musical tastes. It'd been so hard for him to fit in with young adults his age, listening to music his parents approved of would only make things worse. He had to admit some of their music was pretty good though. Mink sat in silence, passing time by replaying his favorite songs in his head.

The scout finally swung out of the cave onto the vertical rock face of the cliff. As he shimmied along a ledge over to his vehicle, Juré set his eyes and said, "Scout."

Mink held his breath as he watched the scout open the machine's shiny door and climb in. Whenever Juré had entered Mink's consciousness, he always felt it. Or had he? The Machinist didn't seem to notice any change, let alone the people staring at him from the top of the cliff. The vehicle roared to life, released the anchors from beside it's wheels, and rolled down the steep incline in what looked to Mink like controlled falling.

"I'm in," Juré confirmed. "All his recent memories and thoughts are coming to me now. They're very scattered. Just like a lazy Machinist. No concentration. They had used some kind of imagery equipment from space to locate a potential mine here. He was just supposed to confirm the find."

"And did he?"

"Yes. He's very pleased with himself and thinking of ways to spend his bonus."

"What about the large crystal?" Mink asked. "Did he find that?"

Juré's shoulders slumped. "Yes. He found and tested it. The magnitude of the energy readings were off the charts. He's only trying to think of a name for it before reporting it. There is a very good chance it is a Tear of God."

Mink laughed aloud at the mention of the ancient Geor-ran myth. The Book of Origin mentioned God shedding a tear for each of her eight children. One was allegedly discovered and used to unite the Elementalists 16,000 years ago under the flag of Octernal, but no trace of its existence had ever been found. There was no way such a thing could be real, and Mink thought the suggestion that it would hold any divinity was preposterous.

"Juré," Nyam said in a grave tone. "Slow him down."

He nodded and began the Spirit user's Area of Effect chant,

> *"Deep sleep spreads like a contagion.*
> *All those nearby drop instantly.*
> *Their minds have no idea they sleep.*
> *Nearly comatose in dreamland.*
> *Those sleeping cannot be woken.*
> *Hewl's essence be the fuel I need.*

The wrath of Eternsa take form.
Dream when I say, 'Hibernation.'"

"Hibernation," Juré said.

Mink thought Hibernation was a good choice since it could also effect any Machinists who were hidden from his dad. All three of them watched the vehicle speed down to the base of the cliff wall where it sloped toward the flattened riverbank, not slowing at all. Had the vehicle perhaps blocked the scout from Juré's view at the moment of implementation? The serious nature of his parents creeped Mink out. Finally, the vehicle reached a copse along the river and halted. Nyam and Juré stared at it in silence, long enough to be sure the scout had finally fallen asleep.

"Okay. Now what do you want to do?" Juré asked Nyam.

"We have to confirm the find ourselves. If he's wrong, let him waste their time. On the other hand... we have to act fast."

"Then your work is done," Mink interjected dismissively. "There are no Tears of God, so let's move on."

"Could what you saw fit in the Cradle of the Citadel?" Nyam prodded.

"Yeah, I guess so. I haven't been there since I was eight."

"Then we can't take the risk. We have to evaluate it ourselves." Juré turned to Nyam. "I'd go with you, but I have to babysit the scout. No telling how long he'll sleep."

"But I need you with me to relay his memories of its location. I can't run around blind in there."

Mink rolled onto his back and stared at the few wispy clouds sneaking by in the outer layers of the atmosphere. This had already been a strange day and he suspected there would be a few surprises yet. At least his parents had busied themselves with something other than him for a change. He envied the clouds. So much better to be a distant passing observer of this world than its de facto whipping boy.

"Take Mink then. He saw it."

"Uh-uhn. No way," Mink protested from his prostrate position. "This is your guys' show. You wanna go look like idiots chasing a tale of the ancients, please, leave me out of it."

"Then tell me what you saw." Nyam stood up and started stretching out. "Is it a straight shot to the cavern, or are there a bunch of forks and dead ends?"

"I dunno. It wasn't exactly like seeing, y'know? There were other caverns and stuff. Could be a straight shot. How should I know? I didn't have enough time to trace a line through the maze. Dad's going to be much more useful than me here."

"Your dad has to stay here. I need a guide, someone who has seen inside there. Otherwise, I could be searching for days in the dark."

"I tell you what," Juré broke in. "If you agree to let me Silent Signal Fire you and help your mom, you can hold the glow crystal."

Mink chuckled at the childish bribe. "Oooh. The hard bargaining begins, I see."

"And I'll throw in that I won't tell anyone that we asked you to look for a Tear of God," Nyam offered.

Mink felt that his parents weren't going to leave him alone on the matter, but also that he was in the enviable position of making demands. "If you promise me that you'll leave the Element thing alone for the rest of the vacation, I'll go."

Juré reached into his right thigh pocket and handed over his glow crystal. Mink accepted it with both hands and mocked the excitement he used to show as a four-year old.

"Do you want to be harnessed? Or just hold on?" Nyam asked Mink regarding the way in which he preferred to be carried.

Mink looked down the cliff to the opening the scout came from. "Harness. Please."

Nyam sprinted back to the campsite at an incredible pace. Puffs of dust rose from her footsteps, which touched down at least seventy-five yards apart. It took her longer to untangle the harness from their cart than to run to camp and back. Mink marveled at how she could run so fast and yet still breathe normally. Then again, he was used to seeing her come home with labored breath after a full day of using Quick Legs to run her taxi business.

He helped her tighten the harness. It had been years since his mother had carried him this way. She rotated a hand behind her for him to use as a step. Mink was quite a bit larger than his mother, yet he looked like a big baby held by her formidable Body user strength. He climbed into the seat on her back and secured his arms and legs by tightening the straps. Mink paused long enough to second guess his role in all this before clipping the back guard in place.

"All set," Mink announced.

CHAPTER

7

MINK AND Juré had communicated through Silent Signal Fire often over time. On occasion, Mink would catch himself trying to talk to his dad telepathically when it wasn't active. The main advantage of this effect, over the Astral Id effect Juré had used on Mink the previous day, was that Juré could stay in his own Body, thus using a lot less energy. As long as he didn't Dispel the effect, it would remain active even over great distances and out of sight.

"Mind your step. No need to be reckless." Juré gave his wife a modest kiss and squeezed Mink on the shoulder.

"Don't worry about us," Nyam said. "Just sit tight and try not to doze off."

Mink hoped that someday he and Gyov might know each other as well as Juré and Nyam. He was impressed by how smoothly they worked together. He figured all he needed to do was discover his Element, preferably Air in this case so that he would oppose Gyov's Soil affinity. That, and remind her he existed. It was hard to say which was more likely at this point.

Without warning, Nyam jumped over the edge and turned to face the cliff. She and Mink free-fell much too long for Mink's

liking. She waited until they were a few yards above the opening
to the scout's cave before slamming a fist into the rock, bringing
their drop to an abrupt end that didn't agree with Mink's go-
nads. The discomfort was aggravated each time his mom drove
a fist or foot into the cliff face for a makeshift hold.

"Dad says to take it easy before you shake him off the
cliff," he lied.

Nyam did make smoother progress, but by then they were
only a few feet above the cave opening. She swung into the
tunnel. Mink held the glow crystal aloft and the light filled an
impressive amount of the tunnel's length. His mom rushed to
the edge of the light and stopped so fast that Mink struggled to
keep his grasp on the crystal.

"Try to keep the light out of my eyes, please," Nyam said.
"I need to see."

"Give me little warning on the stop-and-go and I'll still
have arms to hold it."

"See any other tunnels yet? Still a straight shot?"

Mink lifted the crystal high over his head. "I think it's
straight. I didn't exactly — " Mink got cut off by Nyam zipping
to the edge of the light once more. He looked back to the pin-
hole-sized opening of the cave. It resembled a lone star in a
sea of night. Holding the crystal directly above, he searched for
any paths they might have missed.

"Much better. Keep it just like that," Nyam said. "I can see
a bit further. That, or my eyes are adjusting, finally."

Before Mink could respond, they sprinted twice the distance they had already gone. There was a time when he loved
his mom's sprinting, but unfamiliar territory and dim light
were such killjoys. She veered a few times and then slowed to
a gradual stop.

"Better stop? More comfortable?"

"Yes. Thanks." Mink looked forward with raised crystal.
"I think I see a few tunnels ahead."

"Me, too. That's why I stopped. Any idea which way?"

"Hold on." Mink checked in with his dad. "Hey, Dad? Can you hear me?"

"Yes. Go ahead." Juré's voice sounded so clear that Mink looked over his shoulder.

"We're at the first junction, I think. Any memory?"

"He explored three tunnels there. The one on the right should lead to the stone."

The right tunnel felt like the way. "We agree to go right."

No sooner had Mink spoke than Nyam shot down the right tunnel. The floor sloped downward at a sharp angle and, judging by the jostling Mink felt, Nyam hadn't expected that. Once the floor leveled out again, she slowed to a stop.

"That was close, wasn't it?" she said, catching her breath.

"Mom. Just don't tell me these things."

"Fair enough. Sorry. So, looks like this is just an open cavern. See a way out?"

Mink scanned the walls for a crack, shadow, or any indication of a continued path. No obvious tunnels in sight, Mink worried that the way forward would be narrow and he would wind up scraped over several yards of sandstone.

"Just don't take off until I can confirm anything. It might be too narrow. But the direction to the crystal should be about twenty degrees to the left."

"What about that crevice right there?" Nyam pointed to a sliver of black running up the far wall about thirty degrees from center.

"Maybe. Lemme just check — "

Nyam reached the crevice in question with three very quick strides. It was wider than it looked from across the room. Wider than the two of them shoulder to shoulder and several yards tall, the crevice bent off to the left, not the right as Mink had hoped.

"I'll wait," Nyam said.

Mink thought to his dad, "We're in a very large room with no obvious exits. We found a crack that seems to be the only way forward. Any idea? From what I recall, we need to go right, but this goes left." No response followed. "Dad? You awake?"

"Sorry, buddy," Juré finally said. "I was just going through his memories for more information. Concerning your crack... snicker, snicker. Follow that until you go down to an underground lake, hug the bank around to the right and count five tunnels, take the fifth tunnel, and check back with me after you come upon a connecting room with two high exits and one low."

"Okay. I got it."

"And tell your mom that the scout is expected back in a couple days. A lot of people are awaiting the results of his find. Still, we've got a bit more time to be thorough and careful."

"No problem. Talk to you later." Mink spoke up to Nyam, "Dad wants me to tell you that a bunch of people are waiting for the scout, but not for a couple days."

"What did he say about this path?"

"He said to take it until—"

Nyam zoomed through the crevice at a breakneck speed. Mink could scarcely tell which side his Body was leaning with each turn. He would have protested if he had managed to catch his breath. Before he could, Nyam slid to a stop in knee-high Water.

"Kinda slippery here. You didn't mention anything about Water."

"You didn't exactly give me the chance. We're supposed to follow the bank to the right until the fifth tunnel."

"All right. I'm guessing we came out of that one." Nyam pointed and counted five openings and then sprinted through the fifth.

"Wait, wait! Mom! Hold up!" Mink screamed, bringing Nyam to a halt.

"What is it?"

"You're going really fast through here and there's not much room in places. I don't want you to take off my head, or something. It wouldn't be like the last time you killed me."

"Haven't you noticed? I've been breaking our way through to make plenty of room for you to fit."

"No. I didn't notice that. But, still, not so fast, please."

"Mink, we don't have time. We need to reach the crystal and make it back out before the scout wakes up. Not to mention possibly racing back home before the Machinists can act. If you don't have any more information from Dad, let's not stop, okay?"

"Whatever. Dad said to check back with him when we get to a connecting room with something like a couple high exits and one lower one."

It only took Nyam a few more seconds to reach that room. On the way, Mink found himself more concerned with his mom causing a cave-in. Since Soil mitigates Body, this wasn't the best environment for her to expend so much energy.

"Now which way?"

"I recognize this. We're close. It's the lower path."

As Nyam charged down the lower exit, Mink checked in with Juré. "We're moving on. I remember having a sense of this part. What info do you have going from here?"

"You'll keep going until you come out at the top of the crystal's chamber. Be careful, it's a long drop. Too high for your mom to jump."

Mink leaned close to his mother's ear. "We're going to reach a drop at the chamber ahead. Dad says it's too high."

He felt Nyam moving slower than she had been, and heard her getting winded. He hoped she had enough energy to get back out. True, she had pulled him, his dad, and all their camping gear for nearly a day and a half across the wilderness. But in that case, they had taken breaks, there were no rocks to break through, she didn't have dirt clinging to her sweat, and she hadn't run quite as fast. Mink never trusted his mom to know her limits.

CHAPTER
8

N YAM RAN slow enough now that Mink could see where they were headed, but no opening to a large cavern was in sight. Mink noticed a growing sense of pressure in the Air. Perhaps that was an indication that the crystal could be around any corner. He wondered if the resistance contributed to his mother's slower pace. She did almost seem to be struggling.

"What's that noise?" Juré asked from inside Mink's head.

"I dunno. There isn't any noise here," Mink thought in reply.

"It's too loud. I can barely hear you. Whatever it is, I'm getting a headache. I have to stop the Silent Signal Fire." With that, he was gone.

"Dad just left. Said something about a noise." As Mink reported this to his mom, his voice sounding muffled to him.

Nyam nodded, and without warning they were at the opening of the cavern. Mink braced himself for a fall to the death as Nyam dug her hands into the tunnel walls, braking them within a step's distance from the edge. A constant force met them like a dry wind, and yet the Air was still as it pressed against Mink's face. The glow crystal shone more brightly than

Mink thought possible, forcing him to hold it behind his head lest he be blinded. Bright as it was, the chamber's size prevented it from doing much good.

There was just enough light for Mink to see in person that which he had seen previously in death. The geode sat partially buried in the chamber floor and still almost reached the top. It's massive curved surface bore a stark contrast to the dull craggy rock of the cavernous chamber that housed it. If this wasn't a Tear of God, it would still be the most miraculous natural object in all of Georra.

Mink snapped out of his stupor. "It's too high!" he screamed, without so much as a sound escaping his throat. "We have to climb down! Dad said!"

Nyam looked back at Mink with an ear-to-ear grin and wild eyes. In the light of the glow crystal, she looked on the verge of a psychotic break. Whether she could hear Mink or not, it didn't matter. She wasn't going to listen to any advice.

Before Mink could unfasten the buckles to his harness, Nyam thrust herself into the room with him in tow. Mink couldn't tell if the faint sound of a sustained scream was his mother's shout of joy, his own official protest, or a mixture of both. All he knew was that the fall would kill him. Then he passed out.

The sudden stop shook Mink back to his senses. He should have been able to hear the floor of the cavern crack and crumble under his mom's feet, or her invigorated laugh, or even some kind of buzzing, if that's what it was. But, Mink heard nothing. The energy pressed against him with a constant push, unlike any sensation he had experienced before.

Nyam looked back at him and mouthed the words, "Can you feel that?"

Mink nodded for lack of any effective way to communicate verbally. Nyam approached the crystal with level, measured steps. It occurred to Mink that either she might not be able to run against this pressure, or that she wanted to take her time out of some sense of respect or savoring of the moment. Despite her steady approach, the crystal didn't seem any closer. That gave Mink a clearer sense of just how large it really was.

While he was dead, Mink had perceived the crystal to be as large as any of the buildings in the Capitol. But now he realized that was from a distance. It was in fact many times larger. His whole town might fit in it. What on Georra did either the Machinists or his people hope to do with anything like this? Just getting near it was more than Mink could handle.

He looked down at the ground and to his surprise, it moved under them at an incredible speed. Nyam was running as fast as before, perhaps faster. The absence of any objects passing nearby and the immensity of the cavern threw off Mink's perception of the pace. He began to wonder if the pressure he felt emanated from the crystal, or was simply the g-force of his mother's sprint. But, hadn't he sensed the pressure when they were standing still atop the cavern?

Soon, they could no longer see to the top of the geode, its own girth blocking the view. Mink got a better sense of how fast they were traveling as they passed under the upward curve. A rush of adrenaline went straight to his heart.

Mink closed his eyes for the rest of the approach, not that he could see much anyway. The crystal's outer shell stretched beyond their peripheral vision and got closer way too fast for comfort. He kept his eyes shut until he felt Nyam come to a full and decisive stop.

The pressure remained, so that settled that debate. It certainly came from the crystal. In front of where Nyam stood, Mink saw a deep gash in the side of the geode, possibly from a blast, exposing a man-sized portion of the crystal. The reflected light from the glow crystal shimmered and bounced around inside, swirling and breathing with color. The shell wasn't as thick as Mink expected, and he figured he could easily reach through and touch the crystal inside.

Nyam spoke, but Mink couldn't hear her voice at all. He guessed she was chanting.

Once her lips stopped moving, she reached out and touched the crystal. Tens of thousands of tiny needles and spikes bristled throughout Mink's Body. Then he was numb all over. Oddly enough, he felt better than he ever had. Stronger. More confident. He looked upon the site where Nyam had made contact, and smiled. Without understanding why, he felt overwhelming gratitude for the crystal, and tears ran down his face.

Mink looked at his mom and noticed that she had changed too. Her disposition had calmed and her typically soft, lean muscles were tighter and larger. Nyam let go of the crystal and looked back at Mink, completely nondescript. Then, without warning, she began her swift climb up the side of the geode. Using hands and feet to find shallow footholds in the shell's surface, she moved easily up along its steeply curved side, practically upside down.

Mink wanted to pass out, but instead he stared downward. The floor dimmed in the distance as they climbed. In no time, Nyam reached the widest point and ran swiftly up the top slope. Mink's view of the chamber floor was obstructed as the top of the geode quickly approached. He flashed back to the sensation he experienced when Nyam had touched the crystal. It was no doubt energy conducted through Nyam into him. He was convinced that this actually might be a Tear of God.

Once they reached the top, Nyam turned to look at Mink and began to speak. She formed her words slowly and deliberately, but Mink hadn't the slightest idea what she was going on about. Still, he knew his mother well enough to understand she was apologizing for something. Mink decided the pressure of the crystal's energy must be preventing his eardrums from vibrating.

Peering into the darkness, Mink tried in vain to locate the tunnel they had come in from. Whichever one it was, Mink hoped to God that Nyam wasn't about to jump for it from here. Perhaps she intended to propel her way across the stalactites scattered along the cave ceiling. Neither option comforted him.

Nyam stopped talking, reached behind her, and struck Mink on the shin. In a heartbeat, he went completely solid. Even his skin cramped. Everything hurt. She flicked him on the knee a couple of times and, satisfied, leaped straight up from the top of the geode. She landed a heavy punch into the chamber's ceiling, and small clumps of rock crashed into Mink's face, cascading off harmlessly.

Using both hands, Nyam dug upward through stone and dirt as Mink rode on her back. They were both impervious to being pummeled by the debris, and Mink had forgotten to agonize over the solidification of his Body. He had no idea how far below they were from the surface of Rift Ridge, but he knew the more his mom dug through the Soil, the weaker she would get. Mink panicked at the possibility that she might run out of strength before they broke through.

CHAPTER
9

S WEAT POURED off Nyam in rivulets of mud. Digging straight up took a toll on her. Every few seconds she needed to stop and catch her breath for half a minute. They had made enough distance from the geode that Mink's hearing had returned partially, but he felt too much pain from the Hard Body effect to care. He tolerated this pain once it occurred to him that, should his mother's strength give out, both of them would fall straight down the tunnel she had just dug.

In the light of the glow crystal, Mink recognized the sheen of metal ore beside them as they continued slowly upward. His mom was actually digging through raw metal! Fighting his immobility, Mink strained in vain to grab the protruding ribbons of ore to use as hand holds. If his mom would just loosen him up a bit, he could help take some of the load off.

Nyam toiled away for several more worrisome minutes. When at last a blinding shaft of light assaulted them, she wasted no time hooking an arm through the opening and pulling them both back up onto the ground of Rift Ridge. Fighting for breath, she crawled a few feet away from the hole with Mink still strapped to her back. She stood on her knees and grabbed her head to expand her chest while she drew deep breaths. Until she could control her breathing, she had no chance of making it through the Dispelling chant to free Mink from Hard Body.

He could hear perfectly well at this point, but would have rather not been an audience to his mother's gasping. Reflecting on what she had just accomplished, Mink welled with pride. He might have occasionally bore witness to his mother struggling, but he had never seen her fail. After a long, deep breath, Nyam managed to chant,

> *"May Curpo undo the effect.*
> *Take back the power which you gave."*

Nyam tapped Mink's shin. He felt lightheaded and warm as blood began circulating again and his Body returned to normal. "I hate when you do that one," he complained, flexing his arms and legs.

"Sorry about that. I didn't have much of a choice," Nyam spoke through deeper breaths. "We have to get back to your father now."

As Nyam carried them, Mink scanned the plateau and saw the cliff of the ridge more than a mile away. Following the cliff line south, Mink hoped to locate where his father waited. He couldn't see anyone. His mom ran quickly, but it certainly wasn't the incredible speed she was known for. She made a straight path to a specific point on the horizon. It took Mink a moment to recognize what he thought was a rock as his father.

"We're back," Nyam announced as they came upon Juré, who still looked over the cliff.

Juré took time to fully appreciate their muddy and exhausted condition as Nyam and Mink worked together to remove the harness. "Where did you come from?" He asked as he plucked a clod of mud out of Nyam's hair, amused. "What happened to you?"

Nyam gushed between gasps, "It's real! We found a Tear of God. Absolutely incredible. You should see the size of it. We would need about a dozen Body users to get it out of the ground, but that's all. The stone will give them all the strength they need to get it out." Nyam ran at the mouth, giddy from the rush of their discovery despite being nearly exhausted. "I dug a tunnel straight through to help the team locate and extract it. I touched it. You should! Direct contact makes you understand things... I can't explain what very well. After you break contact, the knowledge part doesn't last long. But the power, the strength you gain—I dug through about two miles of dirt! Two miles! I can't believe I did that!" Nyam beamed, catching her breath, and looked down at the copse where the scout slept. "How's your man doing?"

"Well, after I broke off the Silent Signal Fire with Mink, I maintained the Eavesdropping effect on the scout," Juré explained. "I learned from his memory that he has a direct communication to his superiors from inside the vehicle, so it won't take days for them to find out. He's just waiting until he finishes writing his speech, convinced that they're going to record the announcement for posterity. He is aware of being asleep in his vehicle now, so he won't be sticking around long."

Mink wasn't sure how he felt about his time in the cavern yet, and he didn't have any way of describing it. His mother's take helped him fill in some gaps, but he knew their experiences were very different. Even with improved strength, he couldn't imagine a hundred Body users moving the geode, let alone lifting it straight up two miles, then carrying it all the way back to the Cradle of the Citadel. Maybe his lack of an Element restricted his understanding. And, he reminded himself, he didn't actually make physical contact with the crystal.

Nyam spoke to Juré in a hushed tone, hesitant for Mink to hear. "We need to kill the scout."

"I agree," nodded Juré. "Too much risk."

"Hold up," Mink interjected. "You don't have to kill him. Dad, you can put him in a coma."

Juré shook his head. "I won't have enough strength for that until tomorrow, and by then he'll be long gone."

"Then what about making him feel like staying here for a couple more days without telling anybody?"

"His desire to become famous is too great. Even if I could convince him to finish his speech here, that wouldn't take long enough. We need to allow almost a week for us to get back with the news and have a team come out here. Trust me. We don't have another way of buying time to prevent the Machinists from claiming the Tear of God. We must secure it for our country."

Mink wondered about the scout's life. But the more he thought about it, the more convinced he was that he didn't want to know. He invented all kinds of reasons that made the scout out to be a horrible person. None of them gave Mink the feeling that he deserved to die.

Thinking back on his own brief death experience, he realized that the Machinist's consciousness was about to expand over the whole area, becoming aware of Mink in the same way Mink had become aware of him. He hoped that he would feel the same kind of peace that he had experienced. Perhaps with the universal knowledge he would gain, the scout would understand why he had to die, and even agree. Then he'd have one up on Mink.

Nyam put a consoling hand on Mink's shoulder. "I need to do this while I still have enough energy. It will be quick and painless. Why don't you go take your dad back to camp and stoke up the Fire?"

"Will you be okay on your own?" Juré asked his wife.

"Sure. The river will give me a chance to wash off this mud," Nyam replied shakily. Mink was relieved to see that Nyam was at least uncomfortable with her dark errand. Maybe she wouldn't kill the scout, just smash his vehicle to bits and blind him so he would be later returning to Freeland. Mink decided a quick death was better than spending days scared and starving in the wilderness, only to wind up dead anyway.

Nyam sighed heavily, then rushed over the edge of the cliff. Mink and Juré turned toward camp and walked in silence. Mink knew his father never killed unnecessarily. It wasn't in his nature. He hoped his mom was the same way. As much as the logic of killing the scout rang true in Mink's mind in the context of their plan, he kept trying to think of another way to accomplish the same goal.

"It's a putrid business," Juré said, breaking the silence. "I almost feel like I got to know the guy."

"Yeah?" Mink didn't want to encourage further conversation, but he felt like Juré needed some acknowledgment.

"I learned a lot from him about the current state of affairs in Freeland. If they get the Tear of God, they will make a weapon capable of wiping out Octernal. Any of us who survive will be their slaves. I tried to think of a way to break the news to your mom before she said it on her own. This really is for the best."

"I know, Dad. It's… whatever, right?" Unable to find the words to express his concern, Mink ended the futile conversation.

CHAPTER

10

NYAM RETURNED to the camp clean of any mud, but more haggard and weak than Mink had ever seen her. The Fire that Mink and Juré had prepared lapped up the Air with greedy intensity. Without a word, Nyam plunged her arms down under the logs. She let out a long, satisfied sigh and pulled out two fistfuls of embers, recovering quite quickly as she rubbed them on her arms and massaged them into her neck.

"I just need to get my strength and then I'll run back to the High Council and convince them to send a team." Nyam kicked off her shoes and sat with the soles of her feet in the flames.

"You can't leave us here," Juré protested.

"We don't have enough time. I'll get there much faster alone."

"Exactly. We don't have enough time. Even if you could be at the Capitol by morning, the soonest a team could make it here would be at least four days from now. And realistically, it would take you two days at peak condition. Assuming the Machinists send a search and rescue team in two days, they could still have an army here before our team. Mink and I won't be able to hold them off. I need you."

"They won't find the scout or his vehicle. That'll slow down their response, but I see your point." Nyam lost herself in thought, rolling a burning log between her hands.

Juré's words made grim sense to Mink. The Machinists' vehicles transported multiple people over long distances with great speed. Rift Ridge was closer to Freeland and, from Juré's description of their imaging, the Machinists had better maps. The more people they sent, the greater the chance that some of them would have an Elemental affinity for Body or Water, in which case Juré couldn't use any effects on them. Not favorable odds when Machinist weaponry could kill all Elemental types.

"I'll stay. We'll send Mink," Nyam resolved.

"What?!" Mink and Juré replied in unison.

"Nyam, it would take him five days to make it back. That puts us here by ourselves for sure when their reinforcements arrive. How long do you think we'll survive?"

"Mom, Dad's right. I slept half the way here. I'll get lost going back."

"I think I can put the Quick Legs effect on Mink," Nyam said, growing adamant. She gestured toward the Great Barrier Range. "If he just heads to that point on the eastern horizon and keeps going, he'll be in the Capitol early on the second morning." Mink swore he remembered thick forests on those mountains.

"Put Quick Legs on him?" Juré echoed. "That's a self effect, not a target effect."

"Mom, you're crazy. I can't handle that kind of speed. I'll wrap myself around a tree!"

"Listen, you two. If either of you have another idea about how to get Mink to my brother any quicker, I'd like to hear it," Nyam countered.

Mink racked his brain. For the last two years, he'd been taking independent studies in Strategy and Tactics, lately focusing on unwinnable situations. Real life was so much harder than the classroom. Finally, he said with a shrug, "Let them get here first and have all the ore they want. I don't think they'd be able to move the crystal anyway."

Juré rubbed his face and sighed. "We can't chance it, buddy. From what I learned through the scout's memories, they've exhausted almost all their resources. They're desperate. The scout had seen maps of large ore deposits throughout Octernal. They plan on expanding eastward. With force."

The three of them sat in silence. Eventually, Nyam rose and started the process of making dinner. Juré followed. Mink needed time to adjust to the gravity of the situation. Not acting would mean war, and the end of the Elementalists' way of life. All the same, if Nyam managed to somehow give him the Quick Legs effect, he doubted he'd be able to use it well enough to make it to the Capitol. If by some luck he made it back to the Capitol, having a team of Elementalists come to the aid of his parents in time seemed unlikely.

Hypothetically, if Mink succeeded, the Elementalists could conceivably reach the geode in time. But they would still need to somehow get the crystal to the surface and find a way to move it to Octernal. Assuming that was possible, if war was inevitable, they would need a Tear of God in the Cradle of the Citadel to fend off and outlast the Machinists, just like they did sixteen thousand years ago during the Water Age. In that case, let them have all the resources they needed from Rift Ridge.

"Tell me your plan, mom."

Nyam dished up a meal of stewed roots topped with shreds of seasoned roast meat. "First, I'll put the Regenerative Cells effect on you to help ensure you make it all the way. I'll follow that up with Tunnel Vision so you can focus over great distances and avoid obstacles. The tricky part will be the Quick Legs effect. I think I can change the wording of the chant to allow for adding the implementation."

"Turning a self effect into a target effect? If it works, you need to apply for a professorship." Juré took a plate of food, clearly impressed by his wife, but no less confused.

"I'll keep that in mind if we get back home. I do remember Professor Whodly theorizing that all effects were originally self effects and the advent of implementations created target effects."

"Must have been in your grad school days. I don't remember that."

"I had a sense of it when I touched the Tear of God. It felt like we are on the cusp of a new progression in Elemental use. Can you imagine being able to put Quick Legs on an Air User? Multi-Element combos? Anyway, I have to try. If it doesn't work, our chances are grim to the extreme."

Mink swallowed a mouthful of food. "I trust you, Mom. If you think I can handle it, I'll head back tonight."

"I need tonight to train you as best I can on speed control."

"Train me on the way. Once I know enough to handle the speed, you can come back to dad."

"That could work, Nyam," Juré broke in. "He won't reach the tree line until light, so he'll have time to adjust."

"We'll begin right after dinner then," Nyam said, digging into her own plate.

Mink had been on the receiving end of countless effects, but never one he could actually use. He liked the idea of running with super speed, the more he thought about it. He would finally know what it felt like to be an Elementalist. Between his mom and Dreh, he wasn't new to the experience of traveling at great speed, just not on his own legs.

"I'm going to record a report of the events for you to deliver, Mink," Juré said. "When you get back, don't tell anyone about this except the High Council. And only answer their questions with information that you can verify personally. Some of them may try to use this situation to their own advantage and will twist whatever you say to that end. Best to try not to say anything at all."

"I understand. I don't think I would even know what to say. I didn't really see or do much."

Nyam set her empty plate down and stood. "Just stick with that. You'll know what to say. I should start Regenerative Cells now."

Juré selected a crystal from his travel pouch and walked away from the Fire. "You do that and I'll record the report."

Nyam shook her hands and exhaled a long breath before starting her chant, a standard but advanced-level adaptation of the Materialization effect, Implant,

"I bring Body into this world.
My power makes it manifest.
Newly formed flowing from your cells.
You can change its shape to your form.
My Body completes partial ones.
By my intention be defined.
My creation pauses when whole.
No injury can be sustained.
Curpo guides the Body's power.
Create Body upon my touch."

She took Mink's face in both of her hands and held him for a second. He braced himself for something horrible, but it never came. As Nyam backed away, she was suddenly tired. Stretching her limbs, she picked up an ember and rubbed it briskly between her hands.

"That's a brutal one. I feel like you sucked the life out of me," she said softly.

"I don't feel any different."

Nyam approached Mink and pressed the ember against his forearm. He howled and tried to pull away. Nyam released him and he immediately examined his arm. He couldn't find any indication of a burn.

CHAPTER

11

"WHY DID it hurt?" Mink rubbed his fingers over where the burn should be.

"The pain will help your Body correct and protect itself at high speeds. You're going to fall, cut yourself on branches, and maybe even puncture your feet. The more you reflexively avoid getting hurt early on, the better you'll fair in the end."

So much for having fun with super speed. The burning had stopped as soon as Nyam pulled the ember away. Intense as it was, Mink knew he could handle it. Still, what excitement he had felt gave way to dread. This wouldn't be easy.

"I'm ready to do the Tunnel Vision effect now," Nyam said, tossing what was left of the ember back into the Fire.

> *"Focal point brought within arms' reach.*
> *Eyes can see over distances.*
> *The periphery is unchanged.*
> *What is focused on cannot blind.*
> *Light is the Fire which gives strength.*
> *Tunnel Vision upon my touch."*

Mink squinted, anticipating a poke in the eyes. Instead, Nyam slapped the back of his head. To Mink's relief, it didn't hurt. She peered closely into his eyes. He backed up as she leaned in, but quickly realized that his mom hadn't moved at all. It was his vision that had changed. Wagging his head, he became nauseous. He felt like he was looking through a telescope while maintaining normal peripheral vision.

"This is horrible, Mom. Is this how you see?"

"Not since before you were born. I have a more advanced vision enhancement. You move around and get used to it while I regain my strength for making Quick Legs a target effect."

Mink looked around for his dad. Juré motioned for Mink to come over to where he was. Mink noticed that his father appeared to slide closer and closer the faster he walked. Whatever he focused on looked like it was within arm's reach. Using his peripheral vision for balance, he was able to jog comfortably once he was halfway to Juré. It wasn't bad if he kept his head steady.

He felt quite proud of himself for stopping a casual distance from his dad. Juré's head looked comically large and Mink focused on the horizon instead to avoid laughing. Juré placed the crystal with the recorded message into a small leather pouch and tied it securely.

"I need you to take this first thing to your Uncle Durren. He'll know what to do with it." Juré handed the pouch to Mink, who tucked it safely inside his travel bag. "How are you feeling?"

"Fine, I guess," Mink said, staring off down the river at a fish. "It's all kinda hard to get used to, but I'll deal."

Juré clapped Mink's back. "You're all right. I want you to know I'm very proud of you for doing this."

Mink shrugged. "I have to, right? It's cool though. I get to do something huge for our country and I don't even have an Element."

"Yet," Juré corrected. "You don't know your Element, yet."

Mink smiled but he didn't mean it. "I'm going to jog around and try to get a better handle on this vision."

"Okay. Don't look at the sun."

Mink couldn't help but glance at the sun, which instantly zoomed into his eyes with its blinding light. Juré chuckled at the success of his reverse psychology. As Mink jogged toward the edge of the cliff, he was careful to make slow, sweeping movements with his eyes and head. The green negative image of the sun burned into his retinas, blocking the focal point and helping him avoid the motion sickness he had been experiencing.

As the latent image of the sun subsided, he became dizzy. It seemed like a good idea at first to avoid looking in the distance and turn his gaze to his feet. The ensuing somersault that flipped him on his back proved otherwise. Thankfully, the fall didn't hurt for long. Mink closed his eyes and lay on his back for a quick breather.

He sat up and checked his distance from the cliff. He wasn't close enough to risk falling, but figured it was just the right distance to look for Freeland. He rose and shielded his eyes from the sun, peering across rocky hills to where the sky met the ground. Tunnel Vision had another aspect he hadn't expected. If he concentrated on a smaller area within his focus, he could zoom in even more on that spot. In this way, Mink discovered the outer wall of Freeland. He noticed a tower built into the wall and focused on the windows at the top. Now seeing into the room, he marveled at the array of lights, buttons, and screens that filled it. A Machinist passed his field of vision, but when he tried to track him, his zoom was reset to an enlarged view of the hazy horizon.

Thrilled with the feeling that he was spying on the enemy, Mink turned and tried too hard to act casual. He moseyed toward the campsite to see that color had returned to Nyam's grinning face. Although she appeared to be right in front of him, it would take at least fifteen seconds to reach her. He ran back, now accustomed to his new eyesight. In fact, it felt like he was taking a long time to get anywhere. If Nyam proved successful in targeting Mink with Quick Legs, that would soon change.

"I think I got the hang of this now," Mink boasted.

"Good," Nyam stood up from her chair by the Fire. "Just in time to tackle the next challenge."

"I have got to see if this works." Juré took a seat by the Fire, fidgety with excitement.

Nyam chanted.

> *"Target's Body makes longer strides.*
> *The faster my feet — "*

Juré ran his fingers through his hair while Nyam shook her hands and exhaled a long breath. Out of habit, Nyam had started chanting the original version of Quick Legs. Mink let his disappointment out in a groan. He almost regretted it when he noticed the sobering effect his tone had on Nyam, but if it helped her get through the chant, it was probably worth it.

Nyam began again,

> *"Target's Body makes longer strides.*
> *The faster your feet, the longer.*
> *The toes push off with great power.*
> *The front leg lands with momentum.*
> *No extra effort required.*
> *Stopping by not taking a step.*
> *Target's muscles' Fire Strengthens.*
> *Move great distances when I touch."*

They all held their breath in anticipation. Nyam pressed her palms against both of Mink's hips simultaneously.

"Now don't move an inch," Nyam instructed. "I have some things to tell you first. We're going to start off just walking." Nyam folded her arms, pacing. She tried to act serious and authoritative, but Mink could tell she was beside herself with joy at getting to teach an Elemental use to her son. "Each stride is now going to take you about six to ten feet. You'll feel like you're falling backward because your center of gravity will still be far behind you. Always keep your gaze at least two steps ahead.

"If you feel that your foot missed the ground, that means you are falling on your back. Protect your head by tucking your chin to your chest. As soon as you feel your back hit the ground, do a sit up and roll forward until you're on your hands and knees. Always, always, always get up with your head pointing where you want to go. Are you getting all this?" Mink had been paying attention. So what if he'd rather watch a beetle struggling to traverse cracks in the dirt instead of his mom's embarrassing teacher impersonation?

Mink shoved a lock of hair out of his eyes. "Yeah. I think so. How do I just walk normal?"

"Moving slowly with Quick Legs takes years of practice. The slowest you'll be able to go will be twelve to twenty feet per second." The determination on Nyam's face could only mean that she felt beyond a doubt that she had successfully put Quick Legs on someone other than herself.

Mink looked down at his brown lace boots. He tried to imagine what it would be like to run so fast. He didn't see how his boots could handle it. "This is going to be so embarrassing."

"After you meet up with Uncle Durren, just have a Body user Dispel it, or get a Spirit or Soil user to cancel it. You won't be the only person going through the Capitol building using Quick Legs, I assure you." A soft smile appeared on Nyam's face as she lost herself in thought, presumably reminding herself of how momentous this occassion was.

"Yeah, it's just... Never mind. I'll feel stupid." Mink flexed his knees, as it was becoming difficult to resist moving his feet. He didn't dare shift his weight to his toes.

"Okay. I'll go beside you and work with you until you're up to a good run. We need to make our way to that tree."

Nyam pointed down below to a specific location along the Great Barrier Range on the eastern horizon. Mink had no idea how he was supposed to find any kind of point on that wavy green line. "See the one tall tree with all its branches growing to the north?"

Mink followed his mom's line of sight. It took several seconds for the range line to even come into view. Amazingly, he could make out details as to which trees had needle like leaves, long, flat, and funnel shaped leaves, and which ones were broad leafed. He scanned the trees along the tops of the mountains. The sun was low enough behind Mink and his mother to bathe the green of the mountain in a purplish hue. He noticed a pergnut tree that fit his mother's description, and focused on it. As his vision zoomed in, the tree appeared to be standing right in front of him. He noticed a broad yellow cut of sailcloth tied around its trunk. The knot of the sash, tails brushing the ground below, now looked like it was close enough for Mink to untie.

"The one with the yellow belt wrapped around it?" Mink asked.

"Yes. Very good. We're going to walk toward that tree."

Juré had been maintaining a distance, but now came up to Mink and gave him a hug. "Be careful, buddy. I know you can do it."

"Thanks. Love ya, Dad." Mink finger-combed his hair back, settling his nerves for the big step he was about to take.

Juré moved out of Mink's way. "I love you, too. God's grace be your keep."

Mink drew in a deep breath. "Moment of truth, people. Let's see if it worked."

When he stepped forward, his foot touched the ground so quickly it threw him off. His second step happened automatically, but never touched the ground. He slammed down hard in the dirt and skidded on his side for a couple feet with no lasting damage.

His mother stepped up to meet him. "Remember. Tuck in your chin, do a sit up, and roll forward."

Mink tried to get up. As he moved one leg out, he slid on his back eight feet and then rolled. The random jabs, burns, and scrapes were punishment enough despite the brevity of their pain. "I know! I know. Get up from my stomach, head pointed at the tree. Got it." Mink rolled to the proper position and pushed up, carefully setting one foot, then the other, underneath him. "No problem."

Nyam came beside him. "Just keep focused ahead of you. Don't try to control your legs. You don't think about them when you usually walk, do you? Just walk."

Mink set his gaze upon the pergnut tree, and had taken six steps before his first one truly registered. The mere effort of walking sent him sprinting down the slight grade that headed into the basin of the wilderness. This speed gave him an appreciation for how much the slope actually dipped. He kept going straight in the direction of the tree, feeling the moment his center of gravity caught up with his momentum. His movements grew more natural. Eventually, it no longer felt like he was going quite so fast.

"You found your rhythm," Nyam grinned, effortlessly walking backward in front of him. "When you're ready, try walking a little faster."

Mink leaned forward and put just a bit more effort into stepping. This speed blew wind in his face. He guessed he was walking about twenty miles an hour. He felt encouraged. Without prompting from Nyam, Mink began to jog.

"Be careful not to overdo it," Nyam warned, matching his stride. "Small increments are going to be more productive than large ones."

Mink could tell the jog speed was much faster. Reeds of grass whipped against his legs as he advanced down to the greener elevations of the wilderness. He didn't have a clue how fast he was going now, and his biggest adjustment was being able to breathe in the rushing Air. The only way for him not to trip or lose his balance was to stop thinking about his steps at all.

"I'll go ahead of you a bit. Try to stop right in front of me," Nyam said as she sprinted off, making Mink feel like he was standing still.

Nyam stopped directly in his path. By his best estimate, it would take five seconds to reach her. He slowed his jog down to a walk and stopped by face-planting on the ground and plowing through the grass. He slid ten feet to a stop about thirty yards from his mother's feet.

"That's one way," he heard Nyam yell. "But try to keep at least one foot forward next time."

Mink pressed himself up and walked a few steps to meet his mom.

"I guess you haven't exactly told me everything yet." Mink brushed himself off.

"Well. Some things are better learned through experience."

From her thigh pocket Nyam grabbed a flat wrap, a single square of ruddy leather folded into an envelope. Her eyes shifted over Mink's shoulder and he turned to look out of curiosity. If it weren't for the thin wisp of smoke rising from their camp Fire, he probably wouldn't have been able to locate where they had just come from. He followed the smoke down as his eyes zoomed in on it. The campsite couldn't be seen at all from where they were now, on the slope leading up to the plateau of Rift Ridge.

"You can't see your dad, can you?"

"Nope. I guess he's by where the smoke is."

"That's fine. Just double-checking. He'd kill me if he knew I was giving this to you."

Mink whipped his head around and lost his balance. He almost stuck a foot out to catch himself, but thought better of it just in time. Teetering, he tried to make sense of Nyam's flatwrap.

"Your father doesn't even like me using this. But, given the circumstances, I don't think you'll get to Protallus City in time without it."

CHAPTER
12

MINK WATCHED Nyam unfold the flatwrap. Her hands appeared ridiculously large in his focus. The distortion coupled with the dimming light eliminated any hope of recognizing the flatwrap's contents. "What is it?"

"A couple of boost bars." Nyam's voice took a conspiratory hush in spite of their total isolation.

"Boost bars? As in, banned boost bars?" Mink raised the question too loud for her comfort. "That'll make my heart explode. I can't handle that kind of energy."

"With the Regenerative Cells effect, you can," Nyam asserted. "You'll find out tonight that this speed takes its toll on you. You've got about thirty-six hours of running to do. Have you ever run thirty-six hours in a row before?"

"No. Of course not."

"That will kill you," she confessed. "Unless you take these and eat some when you feel like you're about to collapse. But, promise me you won't eat any after my effects are Dispelled."

"Mom. I don't want to eat them anyway. That won't be a problem."

Nyam closed the flatwrap and handed it over to Mink. He tucked it away in one of the easily reached interior pockets of his jacket. He had yet to fully consider just how long his journey would be. He took for granted that whatever his mom did would make it possible. Now, the gravity of her tone and the falling dusk reminded him that time was of the essence.

"Is that all the training I'm going to get then?"

Nyam gave Mink her special unsettling smile. "Why, Mink, this is where your training begins. I just thought it'd be kind to teach you how to walk first."

Mink was afraid she'd say something like that. "Shall we?" he said reluctantly.

"Now, find that target tree again, and be sure you can find it from anywhere."

"What do you mean?"

"Tag! You're it." Nyam's playfulness helped to lighten the mood. She ran off as soon as she touched Mink's shoulders, but slow enough that he could see where she was.

"Okay then." Mink took off after her.

She musn't have been going very fast because Mink caught up to his mom traveling at a slow jog. He reached out for her shoulder, but before he could make contact, she darted off to the right up a grassy hill, leaving swirling green blades in her wake. Mink changed direction in a wide arc and found it very hard to speed up while running uphill. Before he could overtake Nyam, she veered off to the left and down into a shrub-filled valley.

Going downhill was insane. Mink tried his best to check his speed by walking. He lost sight of Nyam during the descent and had to scan the valley below to find her. Once he reached level ground, he resumed a quick jog. He shot across the plain adjacent to the valley so comfortably that he sped up to a run, headed straight toward his mom, who was now hurdling shrubs.

Thinking himself close enough, Mink jumped down at her. Both of them jolted with surprise at how quickly he had caught up. Still, he failed to tag her before she lept over the bank to the south toward some gray rocky outcroppings. Mink followed instinctively until she began taking long strides from the top of one distant rock to another. His lack of confidence in stopping superceded that of his ability to choose his footing carefully atop the rocks. He had no choice but to press on, the hard, sharp surfaces of the rocks promising danger.

Mink held his breath and concentrated as each foot passed over the jagged stone tops. It would be difficult enough to run around their bases on the ground without Quick Legs, let alone try to find his way over them at this speed. Falling in-between could only result in pain Mink would rather avoid. He understood perfectly well what his mom had said earlier about reflexively avoiding pain. She mocked him with dancing leaps from left to right, egging him on to quicken his pace. The process reminded him of a childhood game he used to play where certain steps were safe and others were traps.

Beyond the rocks stretched miles of grassy foothills spotted with random trees and flowering shrubs. Nyam zig-zagged ahead of Mink. He picked up his pace after passing the last of the rocks, trailing her movements. He managed to switch direction with considerable speed after a few wipeouts. Suddenly, he realized that it would be better to anticipate her location, rather than wasting energy trying to catch up. Her pattern proved to be rather basic, and Mink picked where he might intercept her.

Diverging from the chase, he sprinted ahead to his chosen spot. With a welcome sense of predicability, Nyam came straight to Mink and he touched her shoulder as they crossed paths. After tagging her, he turned his hips to the side and slid on his feet for several yards before coming to his first standing stop.

"Tag," he said, grinning ear-to-ear.

His mom smiled too, and stepped up to him in a second.

"Well done. You aren't ready to start using this effect until you can think and run at the same time. You just finished three months of Quick Legs training faster than I had hoped."

Mink felt exhilirated by his first experience using an advanced effect, and could scarcely believe that he had already become accustomed to it in less than an hour. "Does this mean I'm some kind of genius?" He asked, face flushed with exertion and pride.

"It means you're on the same level in that effect as most ten-year old Body users. Congratulations." Nyam curbed Mink's ego, but was obviously pleased with her son. "How's your breathing?"

It didn't even occur to him until she asked, but he wasn't winded at all. He barely had any sweat on his forehead. "Wow. Great."

"Find your tree."

Mink took no time locating and pointing it out. Dusk still hadn't quite given way to twilight. The amount of ground that Mink had covered in so little time really messed with his internal clock.

"Remember to only go as far as you can see when you reach the forest. Use your new vision to pick your direction, and stay two steps ahead. Once you see the Capitol from the range, pick another landmark in that direction to locate when the city isn't in view. When you come to the roads, you'll know the way, and the running will seem very easy then."

"Thanks, mom." Mink hugged her.

"Thank you, Mink. I hope you know how huge this thing is that you're doing. I'll head back to your dad now. Stay safe. God's grace be your keep." Nyam kissed Mink's forehead and sprinted off to the west. He tried to keep an eye on her, but every time he found his focus, she moved out of range again.

Twilight was upon them, and his mom hadn't gone through this much effort just to have him stand around. He pivoted carefully on his heels and aimed himself at the chosen destination of the tree.

The darker night grew, the harder it was for Mink to select his footing. The gentle rises and falls of the foothills did make for easier passage than the terrain at higher elevations. He navigated the shadows of the landscape, wondering when one of Georra's seven moons would clear the horizon to illuminate his way. He remembered seeing at least three of them last night when he got up to relieve himself. It could be hours until their light would aid his travel.

CHAPTER

13

B Y THE time two moons had crested beyond Mink's right to the north, he was breathing hard and caught his eyes closing too long when they blinked. He was unmistakably fighting off sleep at very high speed. He worked up the nerve to try some boost bar, wanting to see what effect would come from only one small bite.

It tasted like rot. He almost stopped running to retch, but it went down smooth enough and almost instantly shook him awake. One more slightly larger bite of the foul, crunchy bar and he was hyper enough to sprint with reckless abandon. He doubted he could free fall faster. He might actually be able to beat a Lightning user in a race. Maybe even that rotting Blin.

His yellow-festooned tree on the horizon beckoned, daring for him to increase his speed. He decided to see how fast he could go. The Regenerative Cells effect would kick in if he couldn't handle it, even if he did accidentally bounce for a quarter mile or so. He broke through to a speed where it felt like he was standing still, watching the environment fly by. He checked his hubris with the reminder that hundreds of thousands of Elementalists were probably capable of traveling faster. Still, he knew he'd have no problem maintaining this speed for the rest of the night.

In the quiet, dark hours of the morning, Mink reached the forest. Or, rather, struck his first tree. It came out of nowhere. Mink hardly had time to take inventory of his injuries as he careened off the first tree and into a couple of others like a hotshot ball. He rose carefully, shook off the pain, and laughed at himself. Judging from the position of the moons and absence of dawn over the range, he had a few hours left of this night. Still amped from his sampling of the boost bar, Mink decided to press on more carefully through the forest.

Jumping up the final slope to the tree took less effort than running, and helped him control his path. At last, he reached his tree guide and patted it appreciatively, taking in its unique nature. The limbs, upon closer inspection, were deliberately bent to one side, probably by a Wood user's Manipulation effect. Judging by its sun-faded and tattered look, the yellow sailcloth had been tied around it years ago. This tree had obviously been dedicated to use as a landmark for travelers in the wilderness. Having reached his first checkpoint ahead of schedule, the approaching morning opened up with possibility.

As Mink looked out toward Octernal from atop the Great Barrier Range, he saw the tree served for travelers on both sides. Pockets of cities spread out over his country before him. Beyond them, close to the horizon and still quite far from Mink, Protallus City lay shrouded in the early morning mist and deep purples of dawn. Even with a sense of how fast he could run, it was difficult to understand how he was going to reach the Capitol in time.

Mink allowed himself another bite of boost bar and hurried on, eager to leave the mountain and have the space to sprint again. Halfway down the mountainside, he thought one more bite would probably increase his focus on the trees. Several miles of forest still lay at the base of the mountain until he could reach the first clearing. It took the better part of the sunrise to make it through the forest.

He wasted no time getting into a sprint once he reached the low grasses that stretched beyond him toward the first towns. At this rate, he figured he'd be in the Capitol that night. The sleepy border towns were slow, pastoral places. Squat barn domes made of octagonal panels were hunched amid flower pastures. Quaint single-level mudhouses cooled under grass thatch roofs. A stark contrast to the looming stone ramparts of the border wall that once held back oceans.

By the time Mink reached Riverpark, there was a good chance Gyov would be awake. Even if just in passing, it would be so great to get her attention! To have her see him actually using an effect, that alone would make the trip worth taking. It looked like things were finally starting to go his way.

It wasn't long before he reached the hard-packed Soil of the main road connecting his city with the outer towns. Cities of Wood, stone, and glass heralded Mink's return to civilization. Traffic got heavier the farther in he went. Wood users on their Wooden sleds, Body users either pulling carts or running solo, and Lightning users with Flash Feet cracking by on bolts of Lightning went about their daily commute. One putrid-faced Body user passed, shooting Mink a look that made him wonder if it was obvious that he wasn't really a Body user. Or maybe he was going too slow for the guy's liking? Mink decided he just always gave people that look.

He took the exit toward home, trying to figure out what time it was and, therefore, the best place to find Gyov. His heart beat faster than his feet. He couldn't wait to see the look on her face. Her face! He could be standing a normal distance from her and her face would seem like it was right up next to his. Nose-to-nose almost. He was worried he might be slowing down a bit, so he took another bite of the boost bar.

If the sun was any indication, it was probably around two of the second clock by now. Today was Grachnitok, the start of the weekend, so there wouldn't be any school. Gyov could be one of two places: leaving home, or already at the lake park. It could get crowded at the lake park on a morning like this, and he would rather not attract much attention. Best to swing by her house first and try to catch her before she left.

He had to slow down a bit through the neighborhoods in order to keep track of where he was, which annoyed him. He felt like he was losing precious time. Yard after yard, house after house passed by without him really recognizing any of it. Frustrated, he shot off to a main road so he could take his usual path to school. Then, from school to Dreh's house, which is how he had found out where Gyov lived in the first place.

He recognized the school grounds with a feeling of eureka mixed with dread. The eight-foot tall solid Wood fence blocked off, or in, as Mink perceived it, the sixty-four acre school property. Dead center of the trimmed-grass plaza sat the single-level octagonal stone building where Mink had spent most of his waking hours. He hated that he would still have to take one more class with five-year olds at the innermost elementary area, enduring yet another year of mockery for it. All grade levels studied in the same building, the grades separated into concentric circles. The nearer the students' classes were to the outer walls, the closer they came to freedom.

The entrance Mink had run through faced the Spirit wall of the school, just beyond the white flower garden the students used for meditations. The exit he needed would be around the right side of the school across from the Fire wall. All of the trees grew to the left beyond the Wood wall, which made his trip through the Air and Lightning sections of the yard a breeze.

As he approached the flickering Eternal Flames and Body users' training equipment beyond, a loud crack and bright light slammed him down with tremendous force. The pain only lasted a second, and he wasn't damaged at all in spite of bouncing and sliding for a quarter mile. Mink lay on the ground in a daze, wondering if he had passed too close to a generator the Lightning students used for practice. He had been running for so many hours now, it felt weird to be on his back and motionless.

"Blankey?" came Blin's voice, the only sound Mink hated worse than his infamous nickname. "Who would have thought it was you tearing off like that?" Blin looked down at Mink and stood on his chest. "Come here, everyone! It's Blankey! He was using Quick Legs! I think he found his Element."

Blin was probably thinking real hard about what he could do to Mink that would be as painful as it was embarassing. Only this time, Mink didn't have Dreh around to cancel Blin's effects. He did still have the Regenerative Cells effect. At least until it, and the Quick Legs effect, were canceled. If Blin was here, that meant Thoy would be close. And Thoy was a Spirit user.

"Unless," Blin sneered in a low voice, "mommy's the one who did this to you."

CHAPTER
14

MINK STRUGGLED enough to satisfy Blin's ego, but hesitated to break free. As a twisted benefit to a decade of bullying, Mink knew him better than Blin probably knew himself. Blin wanted to be strong, not fast. Lightning wasn't the best Element for demonstrating strength.

Blin spent an unhealthy amount of time dedicated to working out and picking on the only one on Georra who didn't have an Element. To further overcompensate, he kept up an impressive training regimen in his Elemental use. Blin had a light olive skin tone, fair by even feminine standards. Everything about him, from his over-spiked macho hair to his six-buckle boots and matching jacket, screamed insecurity. Nyam's Tunnel Vision effect brought all of these details uncomfortably close.

Mink didn't have time to be a punching bag today. All that boost bar had made him very antsy, too. Diverting from his course had turned out to be a huge mistake. Only a matter of time before Thoy would cancel Nyam's effects and leave Mink not only helpless at the hands of Blin, but also incapable of completing his task of informing the High Council.

Twisting onto his side, Mink tried to stand up in the direction of Blin's weight bearing leg. Quick Legs sent both of them into a tumble over some yards of grass. There was no telling how much of a toll the fall took on Blin, but thanks to Regenerative Cells, Mink only got dirty. Concerned that the Soil might weaken his mother's effects, he set his mind to avoiding going to the ground anymore.

Mink rolled to his belly and stood up properly. He scanned the Lightning wall of the school beyond the glow of the Lightning Imbued stone pillars, to find Thoy with his unmistakable bowl-cut and big glasses, hobbling closer. He was followed by Boun, a long-haired Fire user, and some other guy wearing clothes two sizes too big. Thoy was overwieght and slow, but he only needed his sight to perform effects. Mink saw with Tunnel Vision that Thoy was chanting, although he was too far away to hear what effect he intended to use.

The shock of being rolled wore off of Blin and he sprang to his feet, running straight for Mink as he chanted in the speed-talking manner of a Lightning user,

> "I move on a bolt of Lightning.
> It carries my feet in a flash.
> My legs control the direction.
> The Lightning goes where they so choose.
> Contained, nothing electrified.
> My foot touches to end the bolt.
> All Lightning adds to my speed.
> Hasten my movement when I point."

Mink couldn't take the chance that Thoy's chant would target him and cancel Nyam's effects. He had to interrupt the chant before Blin could stop him with Flash Feet. He sprinted straight for Thoy, who gave out a yelp. The thundercrack of Blin's Flash Feet came to Mink's right just a step before he would have reached Thoy. Quickly changing direction to his left, back to the open Air section of the yard, Mink felt the wind of Blin's arm narrowly missing a punch.

Thoy's chant was interrupted this time, but he would surely start over and now Mink was forced to run away from him. Blin zig-zagged enough from Mink's left and right to disorient his sense of which side the thundercrack was coming from. Given that Blin had seven years of Flash Feet training and Mink was essentially self-taught for fourteen hours following his mother's crash course, he was woefully outclassed. He hadn't tried reversing direction before, but this was the perfect time to try.

The thundercrack pattern was random, but never less than two on the left. Keeping up with Blin using Tunnel Vision would send Mink into cartwheels, so he had to rely on his hearing. Immediately after the first thundercrack to his left, Mink set the side of his foot in front of him and spun his hips to step behind. The g-force wrung his organs queasily, but they recovered before he made his next step. He caught a glimpse of Blin's shocked expression as he darted by on his way to Thoy, who stood about fifty yards from the Enervated pillars. Mink knew he could reach him in three seconds.

Thoy was chanting again, flanked by Boun and his friend. Blin didn't have any trouble adjusting to Mink's new direction, and Mink wished for a moment that his mom had thought to chase him as part of his training. Evading proved to be more difficult than chasing. Thoy stepped behind the other two for protection as he chanted, recognizing that Mink was headed back his way. Time was about as short as Blin's temper.

Clearly the faster runner, Blin criss-crossed in front of Mink while hitting, kicking, and generally herding him off his path to Thoy. Mink avoided Blin by keeping up his speed and randomly altering his stride and direction. After a couple of long seconds, Mink was finally a sprint-stride away from Thoy. If he zoomed past Thoy by just a few inches, he could be sure to interrupt his chant.

Mink aimed for the side Boun stood on, since Boun being a Fire user could only strengthen the effects put on Mink. He had no idea about the new bully's Elemental affinity. Whether Boun flinched, or Mink's aim was off, or both, didn't matter. Mink slammed hard into Boun before knocking Thoy flat. Sliding on his face and shoulders for several feet before he was able to get his legs down, Mink heard Thoy scream over the thundercrack of Blin's approaching Flash Feet.

"I have bad knees, you rotting puppet!" Thoy rolled on the ground, howling. It would be a while before he could chant again.

Blin shot every which way in such a small area that he was able to surround Mink with a disorienting and deafening roll of thunder. Every time he tried to stand, Blin knocked him down. Looking over while he was on his back, Mink watched Thoy's friend tend to him. This must've made him an Air user, which meant he couldn't heal injuries very well, just aid in strength, energy, and pain management. Mink must have hit Thoy pretty hard to cause that much whimpering.

Mink kept trying to stand, but not because he thought he could. He knew keeping Blin on this task would buy him a little more time to think. The stomps and kicks didn't hurt long. Meanwhile, he kept an eye on Thoy to avoid being disoriented by the thundercracks. Boun and the other guy couldn't Attack Mink for fear they might Attack Blin, too. Their Elements drew power from Blin's, so anything they did would hurt Blin many times more than Mink could hope to achieve.

Blin didn't have to worry about hitting the other two, because his Element would only give them more strength and power. However, his Attacks would hurt Thoy. Mink needed to find a way to get to Dreh. If he was close enough to Thoy, he'd have time to catch his bearings and make a break in the direction of Dreh's neighborhood through the fence opposite the

Fire wall of the school. The Eternal Flames would light the way, if Mink could find them.

After Blin struck Mink from Thoy's direction, Mink used Quick Legs to scoot and roll on his side toward Thoy. He took advantage of the resulting bounce to set his feet under him. Stepping toward Thoy, Mink stopped hard against Blin. He had become slower from all the knocks to the ground after all. Blin stopped him from falling backward by grabbing his neck with one hand. Then he chanted,

> *"I bring Lightning into this world.*
> *My power makes it manifest.*
> *Newly formed flowing from my palms.*
> *I can mold its shape with my hand.*
> *My Lightning provides energy.*
> *By my intention be defined.*
> *My creation ends with a fist.*
> *Create Lightning upon my point."*

Mink listened helplessly and struggled to breathe as Blin chanted Charge, the Lightning Materialization effect. Blin poked the finger of his free hand right against Mink's chest. Lightning rushed into Mink's Body from both of Blin's hands. Even as any damage caused healed immediately, the constant flow of electricity was unbearable. Boun and the Air user each took one of Mink's hands, drawing greedily from the excess Lightning, and adding to their strength.

CHAPTER
15

M INK WRITHED in agony. Blin bent him backwards, trying to get him on the ground. Muscles stiffened by the
electrocution and constant state of healing held Mink in an
awkward arch. Boun and the Air user stretched out his arms
and helped push him down. The pain was all Mink could
think about.

In a desperate attempt to free himself, Mink kicked Blin
off of him, momentarily forgetting all about the Quick Legs effect. Both of them shot through the Air in opposite directions.
It happened so fast, Mink thought it was something one of the
bullies had done. Blessedly pain free, he looked back down. All
eyes were on Blin.

Tracing their line of sight, Mink found Blin flying feet
first in a lower, farther arc than his own. Mink flew back-
first in more of a seated position, higher but a shorter distance. He wasn't concerned about his own landing because of
the Regenerative Cells effect, but he felt compelled to judge
where Blin may land. He watched as Blin, apparently oblivious, headed straight for the school's training equipment in
the Body section. Tunnel Vision gave Mink a new perspec-

tive on the Wood climbing equipment and balance challeng-
es students used to improve their strength. The cagey forms
with their protrusions and climbing bars became a matrix of
bone-breaking dangers.

Blin broke through several bars and handles before his momentum slowed. Then he flipped and spun over several more.
As Mink made his own rough landing, he was certain Blin had
at least a couple of broken bones. He almost felt remorse, but
more so he knew Blin had done it to himself. Mink rose to his
feet and saw Blin's companions rush to help him, seemingly
unconcerned with Mink at this point.

This was the distraction he needed to get off the schoolyard. Next, he had to find the way out of Thoy's sight and over
to Dreh's house. There was a drainage ditch that bordered the
school's property on the side of Dreh's neighborhood. The small
Wood bridge that crossed over it just beyond the fence would be
his best bet. The fence could also help conceal him from Thoy if
he made it in time. He traced a line from the Eternal Flames in
the yard to the exterior wall of the school grounds.

As soon as he spotted the bridge, Mink focused on it and
ran as fast as he could. His speed paled in comparison to what
he had achieved prior to his altercation with Blin, so he figured more boost bar was in order. That's when he discovered
his mom's flatwrap was missing. It must've fallen out during
the fight!

Mink stopped and frantically scanned the schoolyard area
with his telescopic eyes. They had covered so much ground
over the the Lightning, Air, and Spirit sections, it could be anywhere. His heart pounded. His mom would kill him for sure if
he lost it. And who knows what would happen to her if someone else found it and was able to trace it back.

Panicked, Mink caught view of Thoy looking at him and
chanting. Vowing to find the flatwrap later, Mink dashed for
the Wood bridge. It seemed to take forever, but he managed

to reach it with effects intact. Cutting a hard right turn, Mink ducked low and close to the fence. He checked each street sign ahead of him, found the one that led to Dreh's, and made a break for it in a dead sprint.

Less than halfway to his turn, his vision stretched out in front of him, returning to normal. He tumbled hard into the drainage ditch, legs giving out. The pain from the fall lingered now. As he stood back up, he looked in the direction of the schoolyard. The Air user had climbed high into view with Air Walk, presumably using Featherweight to carry Thoy within a clear view of Mink. His mother's effects were gone.

The next effect Thoy might implement could only go very wrong for Mink. He couldn't afford to wait for the right street to appear. He took off at his old, painfully slow pace down the closest street. He had hardly passed two of the typical two-story octagonal houses before he was sucking wind. After all that running he had done since yesterday afternoon, now his legs were threatening to leave him here.

If God would only let him live through this, he promised never to run again. He made for a side street to his right, hoping for more cover from Thoy. It took forever. He couldn't believe he was ever this slow. Looking over his shoulder, Mink couldn't see Thoy. It wouldn't be long before Thoy had an effect chanted out and ready to implement as soon as Mink came into sight. The houses stood high and close enough together to provide some protection, but there weren't any guarantees.

Dreh's house should be four blocks away from here. Two blocks later, Mink realized he was passing Gyov's house. Of all the rot! He kept reassuring himself that she had already left for the lake. But just in case, he acted like he was running for exercise, rather than for his life. Still, he wouldn't expect Gyov to be impressed with his wheezy, heavy-footed jog.

One last turn to the right, and Dreh's house was finally ahead of Mink. He risked one more look over his shoulder to find no one in pursuit. For some reason, it creeped him out that he couldn't see anyone on the ground or in the sky. He calmed himself by assuming they were tending to Blin, but he still scanned the area as he ran.

He reached Dreh's porch, alternately clutching his chest and knees. Mink took long, deep breaths to regain his composure. The door opened before he could knock. Dreh repositioned his Wood-rimmed glasses to better appreciate Mink's condition. There wasn't anything wrong with his vision, but he insisted on wearing his first pair of Materialized glasses as a fashion statement. Dreh's chestnut hair matched his skin tone so closely that Mink almost thought he had gone and shaved his head. He did a double-take and saw it was just slicked back. Jacketless in a soft orange shirt, Dreh leaned against the open doorway.

"Gyov called and said you might be coming over," Dreh teased.

Mink collapsed on the porch, panting and leaving a sweaty impression on the Wood. "Don't care," he managed to say. "I... don't care. I'm not dead."

"Just kidding, champ. I saw you run down the street from my room. I thought you were at Rift Ridge. Back early?"

"Long story, Dreh," Mink gasped. He managed to sit up, hugging his knees and getting better control of his breathing. "Can't tell you."

"Please. Come in. Unless you want me to go jogging with you."

Dreh's house often held the aroma of some kind of thick stew, but the smell hit Mink's greedy lungs stronger than usual. He started feeling lightheaded just a few steps inside.

"I'm going to be sick," Mink half-joked. "You safehousing Reeks here?"

Dreh led Mink up the stairs. "Yeah. I thought you could use a girlfriend."

Mink doubled over and threw up well-digested boost bar on the stairs. Dreh started laughing first, but Mink joined as soon as he was able.

"I'll clean this up," Mink offered. "Just grab me a cloth or something."

Mink sat beside his vomit and concentrated on recovery while Dreh ascended quickly to fetch a small towel.

"Now you're going to have to tell me what you're doing here," he said before he disappeared.

Mink knew he wasn't allowed to tell Dreh anything about the crystal, the Machinist, or why he was back from his trip early. He had to clear his head and focus on what might be okay to divulge. If there were any way to reach his uncle in Protallus City in time, Dreh was his best bet. He had to give him some information to be willing to travel that far. He was roused from his thoughts by a towel falling on his head.

Dreh sat a few steps above the mess. As Mink cleaned, he told Dreh close to every detail about the trip, up to the point where he experienced death. Not knowing how to be vague with regard to the events that followed, Mink skipped to the part where his mom put effects on him so that he could deliver a message to his uncle. Dreh listened with great amusement until Mink began explaining how she put the Quick Legs effect on him, at which point Dreh got up and climbed the stairs.

"Mink," Dreh grumbled, shaking his head. "I was believing all that rot, too. You don't even know how to lie."

'M NOT lying, Dreh. Serious. My mom figured out a way to put Quick Legs on me. How do you think I got back so fast? I left Rift Ridge before sunset yesterday!"

Dreh shot Mink a harsh look from the top of the stairs. "I watched you run up here. Your Quick Legs rot. I could run faster uneffected."

"You haven't let me finish, man. I was on my way to Protallus City when Blin and crew jumped me. Thoy canceled the effects my mom did."

"If you were going to Protallus City, why'd you go where Blin could find you?"

Mink felt embarrassed to tell Dreh the truth about his detour to see Gyov, even if he knew about Mink's crush. He didn't want to betray his friend's trust by lying to him, but it felt like the only option. There were more important things about Mink's mission that he had to lie about anyway.

"I thought I'd have time to grab a music crystal and another paddle and junk from home to take with me. I got kinda lost trying to find my way with the Quick Legs and Tunnel Vision. So, I wound up at the school. That's when Blin jumped me."

Dreh offered to take the towel, but Mink ascended the stairs instead and walked down the hall to throw it in the hamper. Dreh's silence drove Mink to weigh the consequences of sharing something confidential to win his trust.

"You're telling the truth? Your mom was able to put Quick Legs on you?"

"On my honor, may the Reeks take me."

"Okay, okay, no need for all that. I believe you. Still, that's amazing. Is that so... what? You going to work for her taxi business now?"

"I dunno. She'll do what she does, you know that. She did it because she and pops need to stay at the campsite and I have to take a message crystal to my Uncle Durren."

"That sounds like serious business. What's going on out there? Your dad see something?"

They entered Dreh's room. It was hard to believe that he spent almost all his time in here, he kept it so neat and orderly. All of his crystals were arranged in a case on the wall with glass doors. Books sat, alphabetized by author and chronological by title, on a set of bookcases that Dreh had Materialized himself. Mink looked out the window and satisfied himself that no one had followed him.

"Man, please, trust me. I can't tell you any of the details. But, now I need you to take me to the Capitol."

"Nope. No can do," Dreh said.

"Why not?" Mink asked.

"I didn't think you would be back for days, so my social calendar is filled. I've got places to go and people to see and none of it is at the Capitol."

"What? What do you have to do tonight? We'd be back by tomorrow night. I promise."

"Sorry. The details of my evening are classified." Dreh spoke in a way that Mink understood to be a bargain. Quid pro quo. Mink might have to violate some confidentiality in order to complete his mission. The last time he told Dreh classified information, his dad found out before Mink even got back home, so he was anxious not to make the same mistake with this.

"Look, Dreh. This is for my dad. I don't even know what it's all about. I just know that I have to get to my Uncle Durren by morning. My parents are still out there to take on the Machinists by themselves if war breaks out before the Capitol can respond. You'd be doing everyone a huge favor. Not just me."

Dreh thought about it while jostling around an egg-shaped animal skin thornball. His fingers deftly avoided the thorns lining the stitches, which were laced with a specific neurotoxin inhibiting speech. This was his way of pretending to think after he had already made up his mind.

"Did you scratch yourself, man?" Mink prodded. "It's not like you to be this quiet."

"Promise me this," Dreh began.

"Maybe."

"Let me finish, Mink. Promise me that if I take you to the Capitol, you'll come with me to a party tomorrow night after we get back."

Mink hated parties. At some point in the festivities, he inevitably became a target for effect after effect. Other students delighted in showing off their skills by picking on him. Mink could count on one hand the number of people his own age who didn't exploit his lack of an Element. He no longer even had birthday parties for himself.

"That's not fair, man. I have to get to Protallus City for national security. Not an option. If you have to resort to petty blackmail, I'm wasting my time."

"I only ask for one teensy-weensy favor." Dreh skillfully tossed and spun the thornball in the Air. He knew he had won.

"I need you and your sled. That's my fastest option now. You're extorting me."

"You didn't say the magic word," Dreh taunted.

"Fine. I'll go." Mink already started thinking of a way to get out of the party. Maybe Uncle Durren could detain him for questioning or something.

"Okay. Wanna swing by your house and get your stuff?"

"Nah. There isn't enough time. Besides, Blin's friends might be waiting for me there."

"Not Blin?" Dreh clarified.

Mink didn't want to admit to himself, let alone Dreh, what he had done to Blin. He almost hoped Blin made it out okay. However, if he were alive, their next meeting would be night-marish. Mink needed Dreh's protection. Staying by his friend's side made the most sense, even if that meant placating him and going to some stupid party.

"No. Blin won't be there," Mink said without elaborating.

"Let's get going then." Dreh sprang into motion.

Dreh put on his jacket and stuffed the pockets with a few essentials before they went back downstairs. Mink had reaccli-mated to his natural sight and gait, but would've liked to keep the Regenerative Cells for all the soreness he felt going down the stairs. It occurred to him that Pulti could easily heal his legs, but there just wasn't any time to spare.

"Yathi!" Dreh yelled from the middle of the house.

"What?" his sister's voice sounded muffled by a couple of walls at least.

"Tell mom when she gets back that I went to the Capitol!"

"Why?"

"Because I won't be here to tell her myself!"

"Why are you going?"

"I'm starting a petition to lower the legal working age to twelve! You better start thinking about what—"

"Fine! Whatever!" Yathi cut him off. A prolonged silence followed. "Is Mink with you?"

"No! He's at Rift Ridge!" Dreh lifted a finger to his lips. Mink didn't betray Dreh's ruse, but signaled that it was past time to go.

"Then who were you talking to?"

"Myself!"

"Did you throw up on something?"

"Are you going to tell mom, or not?"

"I already said I would!"

They hurried to the garage where Dreh's sled was parked. The way he had painted it red, black, and silver, made the sled appear to be assembled from several parts. On the contrary, Mink had watched Dreh make it from one solid piece of Materialized Wood. It had two seats in tandem, high-backed with grips for each occupant, and a sloping nose in front that resembled a beak. The four runners underneath were sleek, road-only style lengths of Wood, specifically tuned for speed.

"By the way," Dreh said, mounting the driver's seat. "You're buying the food."

Dreh passed Mink a helmet which he securely fastened, tucking in his hair. Dreh made final preparations for depature, using one hand for his helmet and the other to pull a couple of thumbless gloves out of a compartment between the handlebars. Mink mounted the seat while Dreh pulled on the gloves. Then Dreh chanted the Sledding effect for Wood users' Movement,

> "I ride upon a sled of Wood.
> The sled and my power are one.
> My thumbs steer and control the speed.
> The runners under the sled glide.
> Thumbs up, forward. Thumbs left and right.
> My sled won't move without my thumbs.
> I feed off Soil and Water.
> My sled and I move when I reach."

As soon as Dreh grabbed the handlebars in front of him, his thumbs sank into them, becoming Wood themselves.

CHAPTER
17

D REH EASED the sled out of the garage, down the drive-
way, and accelerated along the residential roads. Either
he had been ticketed in the past couple of days, or was trying
to catch Mink off guard before zipping off. The neighborhood
roads were made of natural Soil which contained rocks, shells,
and glass that could damage the runners. Materialized Soil was
expensive due to its purity and higher density, which made it
almost exclusively used on the main roads. There was an au-
dible difference between the pops and cracks of natural Soil
roads and the shushing sound of the highways.

Mink braced himself as they approached the on-ramp for
the main road, lest Dreh inject a large amount of his energy
into the sled in an oft-attempted move to throw him. A Body
user's medic cart rushed by with a sense of urgency. The Body
user pulled the cart with such speed that, by the time Mink
turned back to look, it had already disappeared in the direction of the school. The sled lurched forward, almost spilling
Mink onto the road. Dreh threw his head back and laughed.
Mink settled back in, grabbed the handles more tightly, and
then laughed himself.

Compared to his Quick Legs experience, Mink decided it really was much nicer to be the passenger. He was able to lean back and take in the sights passively. Dreh moved to the left a couple of lanes, then doubled the speed. The sled hugged down close to the road.

"Did you do something different to your sled?" Mink wasn't sure if he could be understood in the muffling wind.

He could barely make out Dreh's voice through his helmet, leaning forward a bit to make sure he heard him right. "I think I finally found the right amount of mud for the runners. I'm getting a big boost to the effect without any extra weight to slow it down."

"What kind of mud are you using?"

"Top of the line stuff. Both natural Elements Purified with apostrophication."

"That's awesome. Your dad paying for that?"

Dreh snorted. "Ya think? The only drawback is the mud dries out after four hours. We'll need to stop regularly for application, but the extra speed should more than make up for it."

Mink was impressed by Dreh's ingenuity and resourcefulness. Mud made the perfect enhancement for Wood effects. A mixture of Soil and Water, both augmenting Elements for Wood. True, the boost lessened as the mud dried, but as the only Element augmented by two others, it held a huge advantage for the user.

"Is this the top speed then?"

Dreh shot a sly look over his shoulder by way of an answer, then pressed the sled to a frightning speed. There was no way Mink could have traveled this fast with Quick Legs and he doubted even his mom could have kept up. After a few seconds of showing off, Dreh backed the speed down to a cruising pace. Mink was glad he had come to Dreh.

"I'll buy you all the mud you need if it gets us to Protallus City before breakfast."

"Thanks, champ. You're the best!"

Mink leaned back into his seat and watched the towns come and go along their route to the Capitol. Octernal shone with particular beauty to him today, though he didn't usually consider himself a patriotic person. Yes, his dad worked for the government and his uncle was an elected official. Although it was hardly the first time Mink had been a courrier of sensitive information, now he was more or less going to be in the government's employ. It connected him in ways that he had yet to experience.

Elementalists went about their day, commuting, contributing, and generally enjoying their lives. Everything seemed peaceful and happy. That any peril should loom over this land felt wrong and out of place. Securely stowed in his thigh pocket, a satchel held a singular crystal encoded with a classified message revealing the probable existence of a Tear of God. With it came the promise of a new era of enlightenment and progress, as long as the Machinists didn't get it first.

Given this time to decompress and reflect, Mink felt immensely honored to be the one to deliver the crystal. For the first time in a long time, he sensed that he belonged among his people. Considering that a few billion Elementalists lived throughout this vast country, how could he be the only one without an Element? It didn't seem fair. It was certainly a ridiculous fate to be the one to discover the supposed Tear of God.

Mink delighted in the fact that he now got to share the journey with his best friend. The comraderie and levity made for a much improved state than sprinting on his own in a boost bar induced fervor. Mink traveled this route to the Capitol very regularly, but rarely without his family. It gave him reason to feel grown up and mometarily forget that he still had a couple of classes with five and six-year olds.

Around four-thirty of the second clock, just before midday, they crossed the border of Floth into the Rhocke Prefecture, Mink's favorite leg of the journey. None of the Flothian architecture back home related to Water, despite Floth being the God of Water. The road maps of Floth resembled rivers and streams from an arial view, but the buildings were traditional octagonal shapes. The more interesting ones looked like eight-sided crystal clusters, jaunting angles radiating from a common base, and panels polished to glint in the sun.

The typical Flothian shades of green dividing sprawls of suburbia transitioned to the vibrant Rhockeine hills of the spice farms. Each ranch went to great lengths to impress passers-by, or rather potential customers, by painting landscapes with brightly colored leaves and flowers that danced in the breeze. Every season became a new work of art, particularly during the blooming season of Roysive.

They decided to stop for a late lunch and mud application in Albus, the principle city of Rhocke. Nyam almost never stopped until she reached the Protallus Prefecture town where she grew up, so an authentic Rhockeine meal was a rare treat. Dreh pulled into a Wood Spa and got a recommendation for a local favorite eatery. They walked out their leg cramps, musing over the anti-corner architecture of the city. Every building, including the city's towers, had been rounded to avoid any flat surfaces or edges. As such, this area paid greater homage to Water with flowing lines and wave-like entrances. Yet, Mink couldn't decide if it was the look he yearned for in Floth.

"You sure you got this?" Dreh checked once they reached the restaurant.

"Absolutely. It's what my dad would want."

"Ah. Nice to know I'm getting some of my tax dollars back."

The lunch was exquisite. Mink could never find anything so richly fragrant and deliciously sour back home. Heavy with portions of reptilian meat and steamed vegetable stalks, neither of them could finish their portions, but they kept trying. Once the waitress offered dessert, they gladly exchanged their plates for a crispy, warm cake made with sautéed fruit peelings and topped with cultured heavy cream. They left with full bellies for about the price of a drink in Floth.

Conversely, Mink underestimated how expensive the superior quality mud would be, and it more than made up for the cheap food. Natural Water was hard to come by on Georra and became more costly closer to farmland. As they headed back onto the main road, Mink hoped his dad would understand about financing this trip. Mink was supposed to be on his own with no need for mud. There wasn't much he could do about that now.

Mink was slightly disappointed that the mud application they got in Albus lasted all the way through the Atriarb Prefecture. All of the Atriarban cities had been built away from national roads. From a distance they looked like pale forests. It had been nearly eight years since Mink had seen them up close. Most of the buildings were made to look like fat trees. All they really got to see up close of Atriarb were the backs of the industrial districts. Mink daydreamed about living in an Atriarban house where he got to crawl through a branch to go to his room, and look out through a matrix of leaf-shaped shade panels.

Dinner was obviously going to be somewhere in the Protallus Prefecture. Mink hoped that it wasn't the same place he always ate with his mom. If the mud would just hold out a few extra hours, they could dine on herb and cheese laden root vegetables and braised meats while looking out at ancient castle cities, deep in the heart of the country.

CHAPTER
18

THROUGHOUT THE night, Mink and Dreh became increasingly goofy. Their stops grew longer and they fought off sleep with kwona, a caffeinated drink made from roasted and ground seeds. This also made their stops more frequent. The light of the moons and castle cities outshone most of the stars, but the dense banding of the rest of the galaxy couldn't be dampened.

The light of dawn on the citadels and castle cities only lasted for about an hour, but long enough to give Mink a sense of the ancient times when Octernal was still several divided countries. Times when most of Georra was under water and cities were islands. The last time a Tear of God sat in the Cradle.

They arrived within the borders of Protallus City very much a couple of youth on a road trip. Dreh showed the wear and tear of pulling an all-nighter at top speed. They had made seven mud stops, now finally arriving at the Main Cameral building. Mink thought it boded well that their destination should be the eighth stop, the Elementalists' holy number.

"I can't believe we made it," he said, delirious from lack of sleep.

"Thanks, champ. I feel the love."

They both laughed as Mink stretched his way off of the sled. "Oh," he exhaled and arched his back. "I do not want to be here."

"Duty calls, young man," Dreh mocked.

"Yeah, yeah. Whatever. You gonna be all right for a few hours?"

"Champion, I'll be snoring in a mud bath at the spa."

"What am I supposed to do after I'm done?"

Dreh pulled a smooth, flat piece of Wood out of his pocket. "When you're ready for me, break this. I'll meet you right here."

Mink took the piece of Wood hesitantly. "How is this supposed to work? Some kind of an effect?"

"Fine. Don't use it and just wait here until I get back."

Mink put the Wood in his arm pocket. "Have a good nap."

"Good luck with your secret mission."

Dreh sped off, leaving Mink to complete the most nerve-wracking leg of his journey alone. He felt increasingly dirty and worn with each polished stone step he climbed. Would security recognize him as nephew to one of the most powerful men in the country? Or would they assume he was a homeless vagrant in search of a boiler room to sleep in? The whole concept of delivering the news of a Tear of God and protecting the future of his country felt so much larger than he could manage. His simple task of passing off the message crystal would be easier if he could just put all the grown-up stuff out of his mind.

Mink was humbled by the marble colonnade and gilded reliefs that loomed over the crystal doors leading into the Main Cameral building. There was no way on Georra a person such as himself, devoid of an Element, had the right to step through these doors which his parents had held open for him dozens of times.

He decided that if security turned him away, he would find a secure place to leave the crystal at Uncle Durren's house.

No alarm sounded when he entered. Mink stood in line without being escorted out, or asked to step aside. The stone and glasswork of the interior recalled the craftmanship of Elementalists thirty-six thousand years ago, when the Capitol was relocated to Protallus City from the ancient island of Stonecliff. They certainly didn't make them like this anymore. What would the ancestors say about a descendant without an Element? Would he even have been allowed to live, let alone roam their royal halls?

Mink knew he had seen the guard at the gate several times before but could not recall his name. He simply gave Mink a big smile and handed him a visitor badge with blue clearance. Mink half expected it to be yanked back, meant for someone else.

"Good morning, Mink," the guard spoke with a warm familiarity. "Would you like me to find your uncle for you?"

Surprised and relieved, Mink wished he could return the simple courtesy of calling him by his name. "No thanks, man. I'll just see if he's in his office and wait for him there."

"If that's what you want." The guard leaned close, whispering, "You belong here, Mink. Don't let this place get to you." So he was a Spirit user. Useful for a guard, Mink supposed. It was kind of him to attempt to placate insecurities he had gleaned from Mink's mind. With that, he straightened and waved the next person up.

Mink slid the pass over his jacket's outer chest pocket and heard behind him, as he walked toward the hall to the left, "It's Gumy, by the way. Don't worry, I've never told you." He wondered how Gumy managed to achieve Eavesdropping without being heard. Looking back at the clear crystal front door, Mink figured he chanted it while visitors climbed the steps outside.

The hall was a hub of activity. People garbed in clothes made from a variety of silks and skins of vibrant colors walked and talked with purpose. It was frowned upon to wear anything that bespoke of the wearer's Elemental affinity, which suited Mink fine considering he wouldn't have anything to wear. However, he felt that dressing according to status could be even more discriminatory. He couldn't help but assume he knew all about these Octernalians from their overpriced suits and robes. He checked himself, lest another Spirit user Eavesdrop on his thoughts and mistake them for dissent. Instead, he focused on navigating the halls to Uncle Durren's office, preparing to explain the purpose of his visit.

Once Mink located the proper wing, he knew exactly which door was his uncle's. He entered the office and was greeted immediately by Huosh, Durren's frazzled assistant. After a string of apologies and many beverage choices, Mink finally determined from him that his uncle hadn't come in yet.

"That's fine, really, Huosh. I'll just wait for him here."

"Are you sure? If I had known, I would have added it to his schedule yesterday and then he would have been here by now. I really should get you something while you wait. A Gleem? Are you drinking kwona yet?"

Mink figured that taking something would be the end of it. "A Gleem would be fine. Thanks."

Huosh wasted no time producing a cold bottle of Gleem from the small fridge under a stack of binders. "I'm sorry, but I don't have any clean glasses."

"Bottle's fine. I prefer it from the bottle."

"That's a relief. It's a shame your parents couldn't be here. Are they well?"

Mink just realized he had no idea how is parents were. He had last seen them almost two days ago. "They're awesome," he covered. "Busy. As usual."

"Oh," the assistant cooed, scuttling about with daily tasks.

Mink opened the bottle, thanked Huosh again, and drew a big swig of the flat, syrupy drink that his dad swore would ruin his teeth. It tasted vaguely of berries and spices, but the acidic aftertaste required a fresh application of drink to the tongue.

The heavy front door swung open and his Uncle Durren hurried in, bedecked in dark purple silks. He did a double-take halfway across the room. "Mink?"

"My father sent me." Mink stood and took another nervous pull from the bottle.

"Great! Let's talk in my office." Durren stretched out an arm and led Mink through a private door.

CHAPTER
19

DURREN'S JET black hair smoothed around his head and face in a very stately manner. Mink envied his uncle's naturally brown skin and coal eyes, very masculine features which hadn't failed to attract voters nine times running. Now those coal eyes peered at Mink with a twinkle that complimented his sparkling teeth.

"So, tell me," his uncle said, sitting behind his massive Wood and crystal desk. "How did the tests go? What Element is it? Water? I've always said you were a Water user."

Mink sank in his chair and relived the failure. "We still don't know."

Durren sat back with a furrowed brow. "Is this a joke? Those methods your parents developed proved flawless."

"To be fair, we were interrupted on the second day."

"Interrupted? How?"

Mink took out the pouch containting the crystal into which Juré recorded his report, and handed it to Durren. "For your hands only."

Durren opened the pouch and dropped the crystal into his palm. He propped his feet up on his desk as he held the crystal firmly, absorbing the resonance of Juré's report. Mink sat quietly, taking regular sips of his Gleem. The office was wallpapered with maps marked in ways that Mink couldn't decipher. He recognized a few of the areas as his own city and prefecture. If there was any order to the binders, books, and crystals filling the shelves, Mink gave up trying to figure it out. After a while, Durren set the crystal on his desk and thoughtfully ran a finger along one of its facets.

At last, he addressed Mink. "We must present this to the Main Cameral's High Council by way of proxy. Thurbst is the best choice. You have to make like he was the intended recipient of the report. He's one of the good guys. You'll like him."

Mink was a little perturbed that his delivery was getting more complicated, but he knew never to second guess his uncle. "Sure. Okay."

"We need to talk about this, but let's do it in Thurbst's office."

Durren's mood turned sullen in a way that brought dread to Mink. They both rose and Mink waited at the door. Durren opened it, cupping the back of Mink's head with his hand.

"I'm very proud of you, Mink."

"Thanks, Uncle Durren." Mink wasn't sure what his uncle was talking about, but he didn't ask for clarification, because he wasn't ready for it. On the way out to the hall, Mink saluted Housh with the nearly empty bottle.

Thurbt's office ended up being in another wing of the building. From what little Mink knew, that indicated he represented a distant area of the country, perhaps one Mink had yet to visit. When he and Durren arrived, Mink was surprised to see that the reception area looked exactly like his uncle's, save for the assistant.

Thurbst leaned out of his private office and waved Mink and Durren in, shaking their hands as they passed him. Thurbst also wore his hair in the smooth way of a statesman. However, his plump features and marble-pattern suit made him less appealing in Mink's opinion. Once he noticed that Thurbst also used powder to darken and dry his oily complexion, he lumped him in with all the politicians who tried too hard and did too little.

"Thurbst, I'd appreciate the honor of introducing you to my sister-nephew, Mink." From the way Durren spoke, referencing the matriarchal title, Mink figured Thurbst was from somewhere up in the plainslands' prefectures of the north.

"Mink, be my friend and call me 'Thurbst.'" His thick accent, heavy on consonants, confirmed he was from the far north. Mink glanced at the maps on the wall. Millshur Prefecture. Yikes. Conservative to the point of fundamentalism.

Hoping he remembered his manners correctly, Mink extended his hand and said, "Thurbst, my friend, the honor is mine."

Thurbst bowed and shook Mink's hand warmly with both of his own. Mink patted the handshake with his free hand, as was the custom. He started to think that Thurbst should just take the rotten crystal, but stopped for fear that he might be a Spirit user.

"So, Durren. What's eating at you to prompt such an early visit?"

"My sister-nephew brought a report from his father, who is an Intelligence Operative, and I think you should be the recipient and presenter of this information."

"Why me?" Thurbst asked, intrigued.

Durren handed over the crystal. Thurbst held it and leaned his forehead in, indicating to the other two that he was concentrating on the frequency embedded in the crystal. He occassionally cocked his head from one side to the other. Eventually, Thurbst started to cry. Now Mink did want to know what his father said in the report. Thurbst wiped his eyes and stared at Mink quizzically. Mink returned his gaze for a couple seconds, but it became too uncomfortable and he had to look away. Finally, Thurbst tucked the crystal into his own leather pouch.

"Mink, my friend, you have honored your country more than it can repay you."

Durren clapped Mink on the shoulder. "I take great pride in my sister-nephew. Will you be the presenter, Thurbst, my friend?"

"Yes, sir. It will be my great honor."

"What do you think the split will be when it comes to the vote?" Durren asked.

"There aren't enough isolationists to prevent a three-fourths in favor of taking some form of action. The struggle I see is keeping emotions in check so the majority action won't be an all-out war."

"I know what you mean. Please do the honor of making my sister-nephew available for questioning after you present. It could help our cause for maintaining the peace."

Mink straightened nervously. He was prepared to answer a few questions from his uncle, but not in front of the High Council. Maybe he wouldn't have to go to that party with Dreh after all.

"Certainly, my friend. It'll take more to ensure peaceful action when a Tear of God is at stake. We must make a few bargains and trump up the scenario of war being brought to our borders. A war on Rift Ridge would be too costly on all levels. Priority one is to get the Tear of God across our borders and away from the Machinists. Then we can be fortified here and impervious to their attacks, as we were in the early years of our country."

"Please excuse the interruption, huthph Thurbst," Mink stammered, using the Smranksth word for friend to emphasize his respect. "Won't all of that bargaining take too much time? Wouldn't the Advocates see to do the right thing?"

Thurbst laughed longer and louder than Mink felt was necessary. He leaned close to Mink and whispered conspiratorially, "This is politics, my huthph boy. Right and wrong don't have anything to do with it."

CHAPTER
20

THURBST AND Durren prattled on about their chamber strategy as Mink did his best to keep up. He found that Advocates' offices held little to no lasting interest for regular people. When visiting with his family, Mink had always thought to bring along something to do. Without, he became painfully aware of how tedious and frustrating dealing with the politics of his country could be.

At last, the two statesmen left the private office, ushering him along. In the hall, they engaged in small talk about their families while Mink people-watched from a couple of paces behind. A courier zoomed by with the characteristic cracking sound of Flash Feet and Mink remembered Blin with a shudder.

Security was tight around the Main Cameral's High Council deliberation chamber. Eight guards stood silently, only nodding to the group as they approached. Mink knew each of them must represent a different Element, and figured they had some crazy effect or another chanted and ready to go as soon as they gave the implementation. All being dressed alike, it was impossible to guess each guard's affinity.

Inside the chamber, the Advocates' seats were arranged stadium style with four rows of sixteen seats. The few Advocates who had gathered were busying themselves at their seats and didn't seem to notice Mink's entrance. In front of the Advocates' seating, a Wooden dais held a glass podium and eight high-back chairs. Behind the eight chairs, the Octernal flag hung, depicting a red eight-pointed Star of Order against a blue background.

Durren directed Mink up to the dais. Mink found four slots for holding crystals, each a different size, carved into the top of the glass podium. The Wood of the dais had grains, proving that it was natural Wood and not Materialized. Very fancy.

"Mink, please have a seat over there," Durren said, indicating one of the eight seats behind the podium. They were also natural Wood and possibly thousands of years old. Mink had never sat in a chair worth more than his house before. "Thurbst is going to call you up at some point to answer some questions. Only answer what you are absolutely certain about and can verify."

"That won't be a whole lot, but we'll see." Mink shuffled off to the closest chair and plopped down.

Durren took his seat in the upper tier in the column of seats for the Floth Prefecture. Ready to call in the other Advocates for assembly, Thurbst went to the podium on the dais. He removed a crystal from a cloth pouch and placed it in the recess on the top left of the podium, where it began to flash red, signaling Advocates throughout the Main Cameral building to come to the chamber. Turning briefly back to face Mink, Thurbst winked and then put his game face on.

In no time at all, every Advocate had entered the chamber and taken their seat. Mink expected to have plenty of time to work up a maybe-next-time excuse for the party. His presence sitting on the dais did not go unnoticed, but it didn't cause as much of stir as he had feared. Mink knew Advocates from the same prefecture sat in the same column of seats, two elected and two appointed. He made a game of trying to guess which prefecture each one represented. Thurbst stood statuesque at the podium, waiting quietly until all eyes were on him, and all voices silent.

"My fellow countrymen, I ask you here to work with me on addressing what will be the most significant turning point of our time." Thurbst held aloft Juré's crystal. "A classified message from one of our intelligence operatives in Floth, Juré Jolle, has been brought to me by his son, my friend Mink Jolle." Thurbst gestured grandly toward Mink. To the mild amusement of several members, Mink waved to the Advocates.

"In just a moment, I will ask all of you to honor me by listening to Juré's report. But first, I will ask all of you to empty your thoughts of the prefectures you represent and the agendas you have waiting for you back in your offices. Please, listen with unburdened mind and heart, thinking only of the country we serve. The direction this country's history will take is in your hands." Thurbst followed his preface by ceremoniously placing the crystal in the slot at the top right of the podium.

All of the Advocates, even Durren, placed their hands on the crystals that sat on the table in front of their seats. The room fell quieter than a thornball factory. Mink watched as some became emotional. At certain points, all members turned to one prefecture or another. No one said a word. Just before they released their crystals, they looked at Mink. The room then buzzed with chatter as the Advocates started discussing the message with their neighbors.

Thurbst raised his hands and stood at the podium until all focused silently on him again. "We must make ready for war!" shouted an elderly stateswoman from the left of the room. Conflicting reactions to the declaration filled the room simultaneously. Mink looked to Durren who reassured Mink with a patting motion of his hand.

"That's a move for action of war from Briph Prefecture." Thurbst presented, settling the room once more. "Do the other Advocates from Briph support this action?" One stood and voiced his favor, but the other two remained sitting. "The action has been quashed." A long silence followed. Thurbst took the initiative, saying, "First we must secure the Tear of God for Octernal. Do the other Advocates from Millshur support this action?"

All three of the other Advocates from Millshur stood and gave their favor. "We have an action on the floor for securing the Tear of God. Does the assembly support this action?" Mink counted ten Advocates who remained seated. He wondered what reason they could have for not wanting to secure it, but guessed he might never know.

"Fifty-four for and ten against. We have decided on action for securing the Tear of God for Octernal. We will now hear suggestions for actions by which to secure it."

"This is a Tear of God we speak of," trumpeted a statesman from the middle section. "We must send all of our army to bring it here. We cannot risk losing it."

"There is a motion for action of sending the army from Atriarb. What say the other Advocates from Atriarb?"

The stateswoman sitting behind the one who presented the action stood and declared, "I have an objection to the motion. Sending the army will be seen as an act of war."

"Do the other Advocates support the objection?" asked Thurbst. None stood or spoke, and the stateswoman sat. "Do the other Advocates support the motion for action?" The other two Advocates from Atriarb stood and gave their support of the action. "The motion for sending the army goes to the floor. How does this assembly support the action?"

A small number of Advocates stood and gave their support, including the stateswoman from Briph. It was clear to Mink that there wasn't enough support.

"The motion for sending the army has been quashed. Is there another motion?"

After a long stretch of silence, Durren stood. "I move that we send a smaller team, just large enough to extract the Tear of God and bring it here."

"What say the other Advocates from Floth on the action of sending a smaller team?"

"I object to the action," said Maino, who Mink recognized as one of the two Advocates appointed by the Prefect in Floth. "It puts successful transport of the Tear of God at risk, as well as jeapordizing the lives of the entire team, should the enemy catch up with them."

"Do the other Advocates support the objection?"

Brop stood and supported the objection. Mink remembered that Brop was related to Pulti somehow and had met him once many years ago at a picnic. He never really liked him and figured he wasn't going to start now.

"The motion has been quashed. Are there any other motions for action in securing the Tear of God?"

The ensuing silence became crushing. Then the elderly stateswoman from Briph stood again.

"If there are no new actions, I would like to state my case for preparing for war."

Thurbst inquired of the assembly, "Are there any new actions to move?" Silence was the reply.

"Advocate Plisthb, please state your case," Mink detected a tone of animosity in Thurbst's voice.

"As we all know from the report," Plisthb began. "Machinists have been collecting data on sites where ore can be found on our land. They are running out of their own resources and plan to expand their borders, with force if necessary. How long do you think the ore in the wilderness will satisfy them? The largest lode in Octernal extends into my Prefecture of Briph. I have the safety and lives of my constituents to consider. I do not propose that we initiate war. I say that war is already upon us!" Plisthb remained standing, seeming to expect approval.

"The lode you refer to is mostly located in my Prefecture of Millshur, Advocate Plisthb," Thurbst countered. "Millshur has more to risk than Briph and yet I do not advocate war."

"Whether or not you care for your constituents, I must leave for them to—"

Thurbst cut Plisthb off in Smranksth. "Nyskth Arphk Phobst!" Mink didn't recognize the words, but they couldn't have been kind. Plisthb sat down in a huff. Exhaling a long breath, Thurbst addressed the assembly. "War is not upon us. And if we bring war to our borders by sending an army, then we only have ourselves to blame.

"With the Tear of God secured inside our borders, we can ensure all of our constituents' safety for thousands of years. Within a matter of days the Machinists may take the Tear of God for themselves. I think Durren's action of sending a smaller team is the wisest option. A smaller group can move faster."

Thurbst continued his speech. "We know more now about the Machinists' surveillance capabilities from Juré's report. We must not send a message of aggression. Before we act, we should have as much information as possible. Juré's son, my friend Mink, has agreed to be available for your questions. Let us all have a clearer picture before we discuss further actions. Mink, please help us with your answers." Thurbst stepped aside and indicated where Mink should stand.

CHAPTER

21

MINK'S LEGS felt heavy as he approached the podium. Thurbst left the dais and took his seat in the Millshur column. In front of the assembly, Mink found it difficult to concentrate. He felt unsure of anything he knew. The sixty-four people that ran his country all turned their attention to him.

Then something happened that caught Mink completely off-guard. Every member of the High Council stood and applauded him. He felt both reassured and embarrassed. As they took their seats, he persuaded himself that they greeted all guest speakers this way.

"Thank you." Mink bowed his head in gratitude.

The senior Advocate from the top row in the far right column stood and introduced herself. "Mink, I am Dyarna of the Eternsa Prefecture." Mink had passed through Eternsa a few times, but his mother had pulled them so fast he never got a feel for it. "May I assume that your being here means that your mother succeeded in placing the Quick Legs effect on you?"

"Yes. She did."

Another round of applause filled the room.

"You were able to use it well, it seems. This is extraordinary. Were your parents all right when you left them?"

"Yes, ma'am. They were."

"Did you see any Machinists while you were with them?"

"Just an ore scout and his vehicle."

"You saw the scout?" Dyarna asked, surprised.

"Yes."

"Did you watch him die?"

"No. My father and I returned to camp before that." Mink felt anxious about this line of questioning. On one hand, his mother's success in turning a self effect into a target effect could earn her praise and recognition. On the other hand, Mink worried that killing the scout might get her in trouble. For the life of him, Mink couldn't remember why the scout had to die.

"I have no more questions and will pass the witness," Dyarna sat.

The senior Advocate beside her stood. "Mink, I am Shmecu, Advocate from the Hewl Prefecture." Mink noticed she had a light Pashmeetan accent, like Gyov. The zee sound over the 'th' was a dead giveaway. He relaxed a bit at the thought of her. "Did your mother tell you how she disposed of the scout's Body or vehicle?"

Mink racked his brain. If Nyam had told him or his father, Mink couldn't remember. Not the kind of thing that someone just forgets, so Mink opted to respond, "She never said. I'm sorry." Having a Spirit user for a dad, he learned to be evasive.

"Do you have any information about the scout that you can share with us, other than his appearance?" Shmecu's tone was so coddling that Mink got the feeling she was laying a trap. He remembered Juré, Durren, and Thurbst cautioning him to only answer with information that was personally verifiable. Even though his dad did share some details, Mink wouldn't know if they were the truth, or even if he remembered them correctly. Did he actually know anything at all about the scout?

"I only saw him briefly as he came out of the mine entrance and got into his vehicle. After my dad made him sleep and my mom and I went into the caverns, I never saw him or his vehicle again."

"Did either your mom or dad tell you anything about the scout?" Shmecu pressed.

Mink had to risk the lie. "No. They didn't talk about him."

"Your dad reported that he used Silent Signal Fire on you while you were in the caverns, and thusly communicated information to you and your mother. Is that true?"

"Oh. True." Sweat beaded on Mink's forehead and he resisted the urge to wipe it.

"And what information did he communicate?"

"Directions. He was telling us where to go so we wouldn't get lost."

Shmecu became quiet and pursed her lips. "I have no further questions and pass the witness."

Mink got dizzy and realized he was holding his breath. As the next Advocate stood, he consciously breathed deep and slow.

"Mink, I am Senior Advocate Hashem, from the Gynsgade Prefecture, and I only have one question." Mink tended to find the Pashmeetan accent to sound haughty coming from males, but something about Hashem made Mink like him instantly. "Are you certain that what you saw is, in fact, a Tear of God?"

Suddenly, Mink remembered that Hashem was one of the ten Advocates who had remained sitting during the vote to claim the geode. He worried that Hashem's stance would leave his parents alone and without rescue. Mink wanted to say that he did indeed identify the enormous crystal as the Tear of God, but how would he know? It was really his mother who was convinced, having touched it.

"Yes, sir. My mom and I verified it."

"How did you verify it?"

"We went up to where the ore scout had broken off a section of the geode. My mom touched the crystal." Mink did not like the sound of the gasps that followed.

"How many Tears of God have you seen before?" Hashem challenged Mink rhetorically.

"None."

"I have no further questions and pass the witness."

Mink couldn't let it rest. "It's larger than this building. It gave my mother enough power to—"

Hashem stood quickly and yelled back at Mink. "No one has asked you a question! If you cannot keep quiet, you will be arrested for contempt!" Whatever respect Mink had held for Hashem hardened to resentment.

Mink's nervousness and embarrasment were replaced by anger. His Uncle Durren would be next to question him, and Mink hoped to God that he would help get the story back on track. Durren stood with a calm that led Mink to doubt whether his uncle had been paying attention at all.

CHAPTER

22

"MINK, I am Durren, Advocate from Floth. You are my nephew and we are well acquainted, correct?"

"Yes." Mink was glad that only a few from the assembly seemed surprised by this information.

"My sister was the one who took you through the caverns, identified the Tear of God, and killed the scout by herself. She effected you with Quick Legs, Tunnel Vision, and Regenerative Cells, and then sent you back to Advocate Thurbst with the confidential message from your father, Juré, who is an intelligence operative. Is this information also correct?"

"Yes," Mink replied, and then added with aplomb, "All of it."

"What were the three of you doing out at Rift Ridge?"

Mink trusted that his uncle wouldn't ask a question that would endanger himself or his parents. "I still haven't discovered my Elemental affinity, so they were testing me with some advanced methods they developed."

The murmur that circulated around the chamber satisfied Mink. The looks he had been getting were increasingly dubious and hostile, but now there was a palpable atmosphere of awe and respect.

His uncle continued. "As we also know from the report, your father first saw the scout while using the Mental Vacation effect in search of you." The leading look Durren sent Mink telegraphed don't-screw-this-up. "Then he brought you and your mother to the spot above where he found the vehicle was parked. Do I have that right?"

"Yes."

"Had you finished your training?"

"No."

"You stated earlier that your father is able to communicate with you through Silent Signal Fire, correct?"

"Yes."

"Had he put other effects on you prior to that?"

Mink laughed. "Many, many times. Ever since I was very young." The rest of the room chuckled.

"So," Durren continued. "I guess you're not a Body user."

"That would be impossible, yes."

"Okay. And yet, you were able to make it here from Rift Ridge in less than three days using an intermediate level Body effect? Are you sure it was Quick Legs?"

"Very sure. My mom has carted me around with Quick Legs my whole life. I'm familiar with the effect."

"But how many times have you used Quick Legs before?"

"None." Mink was confused. His mom had quite possibly just made history as the first known person to change a self effect into a target effect. He couldn't have used Quick Legs before. Stupid question.

"And yet, you are positive, beyond a shadow of a doubt, that it was Quick Legs?"

Brop shot up from his seat. "Objection. Asked and answered!"

"You are right, Advocate Brop. I have asked the question before and he has answered it. I will withdraw the question." With that, Brop sat back down.

"When did your mother put Quick Legs on you? Before or after touching the alleged Tear of God?"

"After, sir." Mink began to see where Durren was going and he liked it.

"How long after making contact with the stone? Minutes? Hours?"

"A few hours. First, she had to dig her way up through two miles of dirt, rock, and ore. We met up with my father, they deliberated over what to do about the scout, and she went off to kill him while my dad and I returned to our camp. She met up with us later. That's when she put the effects on me and trained me on how to use Quick Legs."

"She dug through two miles of dirt?"

"Yes. Straight up from the geode."

"Are you telling us that a Body user was able to dig up through two miles of Soil and then, after first completing other tasks, she found a way to put a self effect on someone with no discernable Elemental affinity?"

"That's right."

"Well. How do you account for that?"

The majority of the assembly hung on every word. "After we got up close to the geode, my mom reached through a crack that was already there. While she was touching it, she grew visibly more and more powerful and… wise, you know? Like as soon as she touched it, she knew exactly what she had to do and how to do it."

"Please describe the stone for us."

"It's huge. I would say all of the Main Cameral building could fit inside of it easy. Maybe with some other buildings. And it's round."

"What did you sense from the geode?"

"Before we got there, I started feeling a steady pressure pushing on me. That's about when my dad complained of some loud noise and broke off the Silent Signal Fire. The closer we got, the more intense the pressure, but I never heard a noise. It was like all the sound got muted. Then, when my mom touched the crystal, I felt pins and needles inside, like they were growing out of my bones."

"Did you touch the crystal yourself?"

"No."

"And yet you felt its effects through your mother?"

"Yeah. It was intense."

"So, what is it, Mink?"

"As best I can tell, it's a Tear of God. I don't know what else it could be."

"Earlier, you said that you knew you were using the Quick Legs effect, even though you're not a Body user and you've never used it before. Now you're saying that you know the geode is a Tear of God, even though you've never seen one before. Do I have that straight?"

"Yes." Mink felt empowered. He loved his uncle.

"And now your parents are standing guard at the Tear of God, waiting for us to send people to remove it and bring it here. Is that right?"

"They have been for two days. Yes."

"I have no further questions and will pass the witness." Durren sat down and sent a small, quiet salute to Mink.

Mink swelled with pride. He could feel the collective attitude of the High Council turn favorably toward him. Indeed, the rest of the questioning went much more smoothly. It simplified Mink's perspective that he had not listened to his father's report. Durren had easily walked Mink through just about everything he could verify, and dodged the subjects that Mink would rather avoid. Somehow, enough sympathy was gained from his uncle's questioning that even Plisthb treated Mink with respect for the remainder of the proceedings.

Once each prefecture was satisfied, Thurbst called for a two-hour recess. It was time for the sixty-four person assembly to work some closed-door deals to best serve the country, and by extension, Mink's parents. He was glad enough for it. The Gleem ballooned his bladder to epic proportions and, as he shuffled his way to the bathroom, Mink made a note to correct his dad that Gleem posed more of a danger to his kidneys than his teeth.

After relieving himself in an ancient bathroom tiled in stone and crystal, Mink hunted his Uncle Durren down in the chambers of Dyarna. Durren excused himself and led Mink back into the hall. As casual and relaxed as his uncle was, Mink couldn't help but notice that Dyarna seemed giddy with the expectation of whatever Durren was promising in exchange for support. Afterall, Durren had quite the reputation for finding ways that everyone could get what they want without compromising his own needs.

"I'm very sorry about this, Mink. But... I will need you to disappear for a while. There's no telling how long this process will take and I'm sure you appreciate how quickly we need to wrap it up."

"I'd rather wait here. Maybe in your office?" Mink felt like things were going so smoothly and he hoped his uncle didn't have a different read on the situation. "I'm sure I can help a little more. Speed things up."

Durren shook his head and spoke more quietly to Mink. "As of now, everyone thinks you've already given all the information you have. We danced on the edge of some potentially compromising lies. It had to go that way to match Juré's report. If anyone prods further, especially a Spirit user, it could bring into question all of the information in the report. Your dad knew what he had to say and what he couldn't. I backed his play.

"You would do best to head back home and act as casual as possible under the circumstances. Any suspicion you raise will invite an Eavesdropping effect. This isn't like the intelligence you've been trusted with in the past. You need to be more protective. The only way to keep a secret is to never let anyone know you have one."

Mink processed all that his uncle just told him. It made sense on one level, but Mink didn't want to wait in an empty house without knowing what the government intended to do to rescue his parents. "Is there somewhere better than going all the way back home?"

"I'll send you word there as soon as a decision has been made," Durren promised, giving Mink as much assurance as he could. "The quicker you can get away from the capitol, the easier it will be to get the three-quarters majority we need. We simply can't risk the exposure to anyone's spies."

"I trust you." Mink's grasp of strategy told him it was the right thing to do. On the other hand, his heart told him he could do more for his parents here than at home. "Just let me know what the decision is as soon as you can."

"I promise." Durren gave Mink a parting hug. "God's grace be your keep."

"And my parents' rescue," Mink added as he released his uncle and walked away, heavy with thought.

Mink made for the exit of the building. He returned his visitor badge, thanking Gumy by name. The friendly guard gave him a salute and sent Mink off with regards to deliver to his parents. Descending the front steps and standing at the road, Mink pulled the piece of Wood out of his pocket, looked it over, and then broke it in half. Dreh Sledded up to the curb within seconds.

"How does this effect work?" Mink asked, handing the pieces over and fastening his helmet.

"First, I Materialize the Wood. Then I use it for months to rub my thumb on when I'm bored. Then I come up with the idea to hand it over to you and watch from a distance as you break it like a puppet. Then I drive up."

"Ah." Mink settled into the back seat. "Make fun of the guy with no Element. I get it. That's a good one."

Dreh pulled away and started down the road. "The mud bath was excellent. Thanks for asking."

"Sorry that took so long. Maybe we'll make the next party."

"It's all good." Dreh wove fast through traffic. "We'll just be the final decorations."

They were headed out of Protallus City before Mink knew it. He looked back over his shoulder toward the Main Cameral building. He hoped it wouldn't take the High Council too long to send people out to help his parents. For the moment, he was glad Dreh was forcing him to go to this party. Being alone at home would give him too much time to feel their absence. He reminded himself that they were both capable users and had the Tear of God amping up their power.

CHAPTER

23

MINK AWOKE at night on the back of Dreh's sled feeling more tired than before. He had no sense of the time, or where he was. A network of branches was wrapped around his Body, and held him to his seat. Four moons shone brightly enough to give a twilight glow to the neighborhood's surroundings. They must have just stopped because Dreh still had his helmet on and thumbs in the handles. They were parked in front of a house in an area Mink didn't recognize. Dreh pulled his thumbs out and slowly removed his helmet.

"Whew! Feeling it. Mud bath's wearing off." Dreh dismounted and stretched.

"I can't reach my helmet." Mink struggled against his Wooden harness.

"Sorry. I saw you dozing." Dreh started chanting in the low, soft rhythm of Wood users.

"Atriarb undoes the effect.
Take back the power which you gave."

The branches disappeared so fast that Mink almost fell off the sled.

"I'm so wiped out. What time is it, anyway?" Mink removed his helmet and rubbed the grit from his burning, swollen eyes.

"Time to party. Sleep deprivation kickstarts your buzz."

Mink suddenly remembered the promise, and couldn't believe Dreh was still making him go through with it in their current condition. "You rot, man. I'm just gonna crash on your sled."

"Come on now." Dreh hoisted Mink up off the sled and walked him to the house like an injured soldier. "Just thirty minutes and then we'll go."

"Where are we?"

"It's my cousin Pirk's birthday. This is my uncle Cralto's house."

"Ever notice how you never talk about the same cousin twice? Your family's too big, man." Mink could never remember if Dreh was the fifth oldest or fifth youngest in his family. When they were in Elementary school together, one or two of Dreh's siblings were already enrolled in universities.

As they approached the house, Pulti came out. Mink couldn't tell if it was the moonlight or makeup, but her skin looked lighter. Her shoulder-length brown hair had been twisted into corkscrews and highlighted. Mink couldn't ever remember seeing Pulti so dolled up before. She wore a tight-fitting jacket and a shadowy skirt that flared out as she walked.

Maybe she always looked like this at parties, he wouldn't know. It was quite a change from her usual low-key look. He made a mental note of pointing this out to Dreh.

"Took you long enough, Dreh. I've been bored for hours." Pulti carried two bottles of nutty and was in the process of extending one to Dreh when she stooped and squinted at Mink draped over his friend. "Well send a pie to my family! Is that really Mink? Are you really Mink?"

"Hey, Pulti. Am I glad to see you! I could use a little Recovery effect." Mink separated himself from Dreh and gave her a hug.

"Sorry, Mink. I'm a bit too tipsy to do a proper chant right now," she confessed. "Besides. Sleep deprivation kickstarts your buzz." Pulti and Dreh even thought alike. Mink knew they would be perfect together. "Aren't you out of the country, playing Animalist or something with your parents?"

"Dad stuff. I had to cut the camping trip short."

Dreh took over. "What's going on inside? Did we miss anything?"

The trio made their way to the house. It was all one level but huge, with a large central octagon flanked by two smaller ones. "It's just getting started. All the lame and tame is over with. Pirk loves the shoes you made her, by the way. I want a pair for my birthday, hint, hint. What took you so long? Something wrong with your sled?"

"Never! My sled is strong, woman. Nah, we left Protallus City late this morning. I cut a couple hours off my time by only making two stops."

"How did you wind up all the way out there?"

"Long story." Mink left it at that. Under the glow crystal by the door, he got a much better view of Pulti. He wanted to compliment her, or at least let her know he noticed the change, but he was too tired to think of anything to say. Seeing her all done up struck Mink with a disturbing realization. "Oh no! Of all the rot."

"What's wrong?" Pulti asked, startled.

"I've been wearing the same clothes for four days now! I can't go into the party like this! Do you have any idea what I've been through?"

Dreh and Pulti just about fell over laughing. Pulti had to set her bottle on the porch so she wouldn't spill. Mink laughed a little, but he was really upset about being in a crowd of strangers with dirt, snags, sweat, and Blin's scorch marks all over him.

"You look fine, Mink." Pulti straightened, but she still had the giggles. She smoothed his hair and tucked it behind his ears, all the while with a goofy grin. "Don't worry about it."

"I'm sorry, champ." Dreh managed to stop laughing. "I thought about getting you some clothes while I was waiting for you, but I forgot. It's my fault."

"I'm not going to know anyone in there anyway. They'll probably assume I'm another one of your rotting cousins. Thirty minutes, then I'm going back to sleep."

Dreh opened the door. Pulti and Mink followed him inside. The entryway to the house was empty except for a couple broad-leafed plants rooted down in wide dirt plots recessed into the floor. A Soil user's residence, most likely. The sounds of live music, talking, and laughter came from the back of the house. Mink hoped there would be dark nutty left somewhere as they made their way toward the noise. Lest someone Eavesdrop on his thoughts, Mink had to make special effort not to think too much about his parents, or the quest would be compromised. Dreh really shouldn't have brought him here, but explaining why would be self-defeating. Better not to think about it at all.

The parlor was standing room only, with every surface in use. There were a good many of Pirk's older adult relatives, but mostly the place was filled with young adults their age and younger. Mink barely recognized anyone, only able to take them in as one collective. The noise lessened as they walked through. This was usually when people started zinging him with random effects. Random was probably the wrong word, since the real effect they were after was laughter.

This was no small family birthday party. A set of open doors revealed that most of the party was taking place in the backyard. If this was a good night, Mink could make it through the room and outside, avoiding any pranks. Pulti must have sensed his uneasiness, judging by the way she took his arm and pulled him along.

"Let's go, Mink. We're not little kids anymore. No one's going to try anything." Then she leaned close to Mink's face and her tone reminded him of his mother's. "If they do, I'll pound them."

CHAPTER
24

MINK HAD just crossed the threshold to the backyard when a loud crack and brilliant flash of light startled him. He didn't feel anything. To the left, he saw Dreh with an outstretched hand between him and a quickly approaching Blin. Whatever effect Blin tried, Dreh would cancel it.

When Blin got closer, Mink checked for any tell-tale signs of extensive damage that he might have caused yesterday, such as Materialized Body. Only Blin's hands and face were visable. Half of his left hand looked dullish, wrinkle free, and darker than his normal skin tone. Mink could hardly believe that Materialized skin was actually darker than Blin's natural tone.

"Uh, what's he doing here?" Mink questioned.

"Boun and Pirk are friends," Dreh said dryly. "They go to the same school now. Boun must've brought him."

"You wanna finish what you started, Blankey? Come on!" Blin howled, closing the distance fast.

Pulti gave Mink a wide-eyed quizzical look, but he couldn't pull his attention away from Blin's left hand long enough to return her gaze.

"This isn't the place or time, Blin." Dreh tried reasoning with him, which Mink figured was more for show in front of the crowd.

"Then you pick it, Twiggy. I'll go through you if I have to."

Being opposing Elemental types, Blin and Dreh could not use effects against each other. Still, they'd had multiple physical fights, the majority of which Blin had won. Dreh started chanting in the Wood user's low and soft rhythm.

> *"Power of Wood is mine to give.*
> *Durability is my gift.*
> *The living can withstand impact.*
> *The devices resist damage.*
> *The objects cannot be broken.*
> *The Wood does not make it Wooden.*
> *I may use Wood from Atriarb.*
> *Imbue Wood as soon as I reach."*

Dreh turned back toward Mink and reached out his hand, placing on him the Wood users' Imbuing effect, Turgidity. At once Mink's Body felt tight and creaky, but nothing he couldn't handle. This was Dreh's favorite effect to use on Mink for protection. If anyone physically attacked him, it wouldn't hurt. And if Blin tried to use an Attack effect on him, it would only cancel the Turgidity, which Dreh would re-effect before Blin could make a second Attack.

Boun had worked his way behind Dreh, speaking out a raspy sounding Fire user's chant, but Pulti was on him instantly. Mink hadn't heard her utter a chant, and even remembered her saying she was incapable. She had been quiet, so neither Mink nor Boun could be sure. Pulti reached a finger out to touch Boun, who broke off his chant to concentrate on dodging. Body users like Pulti could hurt Fire users like Boun worse than anyone, and he wasn't about to take any chances. Nutty spilling from the bottle she still held, Pulti pursued Boun with her outstretched hand, acting like she was about to implement an effect Mink doubted she ever began.

Pirk emerged from the crowd and into view with a furious energy. Now Mink remembered having seen her at Dreh's house before, but had figured she was a sister. She stomped her foot in the way of a Soil user's implementation. Everyone recoiled, expecting some form of Soil effect, but nothing happened. She defnitely had her guests' attention. Surprising that a little girl robed in silks and crowned with flowers could instantly command so much authority.

"Boun! Control your friend or take him home." Pirk's ultimatum seemed to carry some serious weight with Boun.

He walked up behind Blin and snapped his fingers, a Fire user's implementation. Blin flinched, yet no effect followed. "Let's cool it." Boun put a hand on Blin's shoulder. Mink rolled his eyes at the trite play on words referring to a Fire user's Elemental use taking the heat out of things. Elementalists often psyched people out with chantless implementations. Mink was rotten sure he could never pull it off.

"This is your warning, Blankey. I will find you when your boyfriend's not around, and hurt you so bad your mommy won't be able to fix it."

Mink couldn't let the crowd see him cower under Blin's threats. "I don't need Dreh, or an Element against you, Sparkle."

The nickname that Mink had spontaneously thought up circulated through the crowd in hushed voices. Blin shook his head and pretended it didn't bother him. Mink really had felt bad about hurting Blin enough yesterday to cause half of his hand to be replaced, and yet relished having his public retaliation fizzled out. Mink knew that Blin had only brought it on himself, but looking into his eyes, he knew payback would not be pleasant.

Thoy appeared, weaving his way to Blin's side. They whispered amongst themselves, shooting Mink looks that conveyed a combination of disappointment, frustration, and pity. Being a Spirit user like Mink's dad, Thoy had most likely maintained a distance while keeping Mink in his sight, using the Eavesdropping effect on him. Mink caught himself worrying for a split second that his parents' mission might have been found out, and promptly supressed the thought with concern over Blin's attitude. Then Boun and Thoy turned Blin away and the three of them walked off across the backyard.

"Come on," Dreh led Mink in the opposite direction. "It's over. Now it's time to show you a little game I just came up with."

Pirk hurried up to Dreh, tackling him. "Dreh! Thank you so much for the shoes! Look, look, look." Pirk showed off the woven Wood wrapping her feet against a thick cork sole. The way Dreh had strapped the Wood over the feet allowed for full movement while staying securely on. "I've decided to forgive you for being so late."

"Well, lucky me. You remember Mink, right?"

"Yeah. I've seen you before," Pirk said squarely to Mink's face. "What was that all about?"

Dreh answered for Mink, but Pirk kept her gaze locked on him. "Those guys always pick on Mink because he doesn't know his Element yet."

"Sparkle," Pirk giggled, breaking her attempt at intimidating Mink and seemingly unsurprised about his lack of Element.

Pulti hip-checked Mink. "You handled yourself really well."

"What, by standing there?" Mink laughed at himself. Without Dreh and Pulti, he wouldn't have been standing long. Then again, if not for Dreh, he wouldn't even be at the party.

"I'm going to go talk to Boun. Nothing like that will happen again tonight." Pirk started off and then turned around with arms raised, her enthusiasm undampened by the night's interruption. "It's my party!"

Dreh, Pulti, and Mink drifted over to the unpopulated, darker side of the yard along the fence. Glow crystal lanterns were hung from lines of rope, their light not reaching quite this far accross the yard, perhaps as a means of corralling guests closer to the house. Just Mink's rotten luck that Thoy was attending the party, and with reason to use Eavesdropping on him. It would therefore be more important to repress thoughts of his parents, but these times of being bullied were when he tended to think of them the most. As the embarrassment of having been the center of attention subsided, Mink wondered how Dreh and Pulti dealt with such things. They appeared to be completely unfazed by the confrontation.

"How's that treating you?" Dreh tapped his fingers against Mink's Turgid chest.

"Better than electrocution. Takes some extra effort to move but, you know, I'm used to it. I appreciate you being excited about showing me your little game, but I could really use a dark nutty."

"I'll go," Pulti offered. "I need more anyway. Those rotheads are a real buzzkill."

Dreh and Mink watched Pulti rush off.

Mink turned to face Dreh. "I think she's working up some liquid courage for you, man."

Dreh grabbed the back of his neck. "Mink, I love you. But you are one clueless little puppet sometimes."

CHAPTER

25

M INK STOOD dumbly, irritated that Dreh would be so cold and dismissive. It didn't seem right for him to discredit the idea of being with Pulti when she was looking so hot. Even though Mink only promised to be there thirty minutes, if he could get Dreh and Pulti to dance together, it may be worth staying later. He watched Dreh crouch down and rub some dirt on his hands.

The party had lost interest in them and resumed normal chatter and festivities. Dreh remained low to the ground as he chanted the Materialization effect, Construct,

> *"I bring the Wood into this world.*
> *My power makes it manifest.*
> *Newly formed flowing from my palms.*
> *I can change its shape with my hand.*
> *My Wood builds improvements to life.*
> *By my intention be defined.*
> *My creation ends with a fist.*
> *I create Wood upon my reach."*

The Wood growing from both of Dreh's hands fused together seemlessly along the ground, contouring into the shape of a leg. He slowed down, allowing the Wood to fill in the space for the torso, and carefully shaped his Materialized figure up to the head. After the head was formed, Dreh scooped the Wood down the neck to add shoulders and arms. The arms brought him back down to the hips so he could make the other leg without having to stop.

At the feet, Dreh sculpted a solid, flat base and stepped on it to bring the figure to a standing position while sweeping his hands up the back. He brought his hands over the shoulders, down the front to the feet, back up over the shoulders, continuing to spread the Wood over the figure in this way to cover it with a cloak. On the last pass, after the cloak had been finished, Dreh brought his hands over the back of the head, cupped them around the face, and then made fists with both of his hands, ending the effect.

Especially in the low light, the dark Wood color Dreh used gave the cloaked figure an unsettling resemblence to a Reek. The likeness was a little rough but still enough to send a shiver down Mink's spine. Nothing was more perverse or revolting than the Reeks, who worshipped death and controlled corpses commonly called puppets.

"What do you plan to do with that thing?" Mink asked as Dreh backed up and took a knee, admiring his handiwork.

"Whew. That took more energy than I expected. I must still be worn out from driving all day." Dreh grabbed some dirt and rubbed it virgorously into his hands. "A target game," he explained, standing. "Kill the Reek."

Pulti arrived with a few bottles of nutty in her hands. "Guys! Feel these! Pirk made Boun freeze them. Oh, they're gonna be so good." She extended a bottle to Mink and gave a start, finally noticing the dummy Dreh had made. "The rotting mess is that?"

Mink almost dropped the bottle as soon as he grabbed it. It was so cold it burned. He rubbed the frost off the label. Rusgert, the same kind he always had with his dad. He yanked the cork out, took several gulps, and then felt Dreh's hand gently lowering his bottle.

"Easy, champ. This game's for you," Dreh explained. "Don't lose your head yet."

Mink toasted Pulti.

"You're welcome," Pulti beamed.

"So, tell me about it, man. I'm curious."

Rather than directly addressing Mink, Dreh yelled to the crowd, "Can I please have everyone's attention?" The partygoers looked Dreh's way but continued their conversations. A couple of guests noticed the cloaked figure and gasped, pointing it out to their neighbors. A wave of curiosity spread throughout the crowd, piquing interest in Mink's corner of the yard.

Satisfied with the attention he was getting, Dreh went on, "Allow me, kind sirs and noblewomen, to present to you part of this evening's entertainment! The soon-to-be-popular party game of 'Kill the Reek!'" Dreh's showmanship impressed Mink about as much as his skill with Wood. "You heard right. Everyone gets a chance to fatally strike the Reek!"

A bolt of Lightning streaked across the yard with an echoing boom and struck the dummy's right shoulder, leaving short-lived flames on the cloak.

"I win," Blin shouted from a distance. "Fast kill."

"No. Fast miss. You have to hit the neck where the cloak opens, Sparkle. Now let me finish explaining. No effects! Assuming that no one else brought weapons to the party, we will use these." Dreh pulled out a flatwrap from his jacket pocket and opened it, showing off a set of three spikes.

The way they glinted in the light, Mink could tell the spikes weren't made out of stone, glass, or crystal. "Are those metal?" he asked in a hushed voice.

Dreh nodded with a devious smile.

"Where did you get them?"

"Family heirlooms, champ. Let me finish." Dreh read-dressed the crowd. "With these spikes, you have three chances to strike the neck of the Reek without using effects. Everyone who hits the neck will win a Wooden object of their choice, created by yours truly. If all three spikes strike the neck, I'll even Imbue the object for free! Step right up, don't be shy!"

"How many puppets does the Reek have?" a voice from the crowd asked, followed by laughter.

"Just one. Sparkle," Dreh pointed at Blin. "So you know it's hunting for more. Kill or be killed, people." The crowd roared.

Mink stole a look over at Blin, who didn't appear to relish his new role as party whipping boy, but he was dealing with it better than Mink would've thought. In no time at all, a line had formed before Dreh, who made Mink wait at the tail end. It was soon decided that anyone who missed the neck all three times would become the Reek's puppet for the rest of the party. The line moved more quickly than Mink expected, considering how carefully most people were aiming. Many attempts missed the dummy completely, which required a time-out while someone fetched a spike from the dark. A dozen or so people managed to hit the neck once. One person, twice. But, no one had hit the neck three times.

Mink drank his Rusgert, realizing Dreh's plan behind the game. Almost everyone at the party was useless without their Element. Mink had worked extra hard on his weapon training, as it was all he had to defend himself. He could hit the neck even if he were drunk. Sober, all three attempts would land a bulls-eye. He wouldn't get another drink until after he showed everyone how it was done. For now, he and Pulti amused themselves by taking a sip every time the Reek gained a new puppet. He was running out of nutty.

At last Mink's turn came up. The crowd degraded to chaos as the puppets went around harassing people in good humor. No one paid much attention when Dreh handed the spikes to

Mink, for which he was grateful. Just because he knew he could hit the neck with all three, didn't mean he wanted an audience while he did it. In his periphery, Mink caught a few people pointing and snickering as "Blankey" took up the weapons.

"Do something flashy," Dreh advised under his breath. "Remember that old Machinist knife we found in Ontillustad a few months ago? You couldn't miss. That's why I brought these. Closest things I had."

Mink turned the spikes over in his hand. They had simple round handles. Two blades bisected each other to form a plus-sign. As Mink got used to them, he did notice that the balance between the blade and handle was very close to the Machinist knife Dreh referred to. How was he supposed to be flashy, though? When they were playing with the knife, he didn't have the Turgidity effect. He wouldn't be able to make his regular throwing motion. He'd have to put his whole Body into it.

"You got this, champ," Dreh encouraged, stepping to the side.

Mink drew more attention as he backed away from the Reek, doubling the distance everyone else had used. Maybe it was the Rusgert talking, but Mink was going to prove that his Elemental lack hadn't made him incapable. Satisfied with his position, he jumped up and spun around, letting the first spike fly before his foot landed. He kicked his other foot around to add to the momentum of his spin and loosed the second spike while nearly sitting as he turned.

With his back to the Reek dummy, Mink now jumped with both legs into a backflip. When he sent the third spike flying, he was completely upside down. Landing in a push-up position looking away from the target, Mink relied on the applause to verify that all three spikes had found their mark. More than that, it just felt right. He stood up, slow and cool.

Pulti shot straight to Mink's side. "That was amazing!" She squeeled, and hung off of his neck. "Don't forget who taught you how to backflip," she reminded him coyly, her breath thick with nutty. She smiled at him without talking, glassy-eyed and blushing.

"Thanks," Mink said. "I'm actually glad I—"

A bolt of Lightning cracked across the yard and struck the spikes on the dummy in a shower of sparks. Startled, Mink broke away from Pulti. The head and upper torso of the Reek were completely gone.

"Looks like I killed the Reek, huh?" Blin boasted. "Didn't miss that time."

"Those are antiques, Sparkle!" Dreh took his riding gloves out of his pocket and put them on. He picked up the spikes and inspected them. "You're lucky you didn't damage these." Unfolding his flatwrap, Dreh put them away. He nodded to the crowd, "Thanks for playing, everyone. Game's over."

Mink looked over at Blin, who appeared pleased with himself despite having several looks of disapproval cast in his direction. A group formed around Mink, pouring on congratulations and assaulting him with questions. As Pulti began to edge away with her empty bottle, Mink pulled her close again. He wasn't about to face the onslaught alone.

CHAPTER
26

WHILE MINK was busy gladhanding the last of the crowd congratulating him on his marksmanship, four Wood users built a stage at the very back of the yard, complete with a wall behind it to amplify acoustics. When they had it finished, Pirk jumped onto the stage to thank everyone for coming to her fifteenth birthday. Now Mink understood why the party was so huge. The fifteenth year of age was a very big deal to Elementalists, beginning the first ten-year phase of adulthood. He had taken Pirk to be twelve or thirteen. Before leaving the stage, she introduced a band comprised of her classmates.

Mink had celebrated his fifteenth about a year and a half ago. At the time, his humble gathering with Dreh and Pulti was perfect. He had stayed up all night with just the people who cared about him the most. There wasn't a crowd, no big mess to clean up, no need to buy extra food. But now that Mink was part of a full-on fifteenth birthday party and actually enjoying himself, he wished he could have had a bigger celebration.

As the band took the stage and the attention away from Mink, they looked very much like wannabe musicians trying too hard to be professionals. But Mink was impressed as soon as they started playing. He urged Dreh and Pulti to follow him closer to the stage. This might be a good chance to start hooking them up, if the band would just play a song they could dance to.

The trio wove their way through the crowd, Mink receiving the occassional pat on the back for his skill with the spikes, but the notoriety was fading fast. Not that Mink minded a whole lot. For the first time he could remember, he was at a party without having effects put on him in jest. Pulti went to gather some more nutties.

Mink felt compelled to work his way right up to the stage, and even started dancing. The whole area surrounding the stage was alive with partygoers stomping, spinning, shaking, and singing. Pulti came back with a Wooden bucket of frosty bottles which she proudly set at Dreh and Mink's feet. Mink grabbed one, uncorked it, and took it in greedily. Dreh and Pulti hopped and twisted close by.

A few dozen Air users got above the crowd and danced with their Sky Step effect over everyone's heads. Mink laughed at the sight of them. He felt in love with the world. Catching sight of Blin, he even gave him a smile and a nod. Blin returned half a smile before turning his back to Mink.

"I'm really glad you brought me here," Mink confessed to Dreh, putting an arm around his buddy's shoulders.

"I thought you would be. I guess it's a good thing you came back early."

This sobered Mink a bit. He had temporarily forgotten about his parents being out at Rift Ridge. Worry crept into his mind, but he flushed it out with nutty. The group did an excellent cover of one of his favorite songs and he lost himself in it to further escape the things he couldn't control.

Pulti latched onto Mink's arm. "Dance with me."

Mink noticed that standing was a tad difficult for her, let alone dancing. Still, if she was in the mood to dance with someone, this might be his best shot at playing matchmaker. He waved Dreh closer.

"Pulti needs a dancing partner. I've got something to do right now. Can you dance with her?"

Dreh frowned at Mink. "What on Georra have you got to do that's more important?"

"Watch." Mink gave Dreh a wink and a smile.

He pried Pulti from his arm and presented her to Dreh. She made a grand theatrical gesture and laughed. Mink thought to himself, so far, so good. He turned to the stage and leaned up to the singer.

"Are you taking requests?" Mink asked at the end of the song.

"Depends. What've you got in mind?"

"As the Falling Rain."

The singer asked around to the six other band members. Four of them thought they could do it, but the singer returned to Mink saying, "I don't know it that well. Sorry. You got another one?"

"Back me up?" Mink pressed.

"What?"

"Could you back me up? I can play the runhammer and lead on vocals."

The singer laughed and extended a hand to Mink. "Sure, sharpshooter. I could use a break."

That's exactly the break Mink could use, too. The singer took some Water and addressed the crowd. "By now, you all know this guy," he indicated Mink, who was already putting the strap of the runhammer over his head. "He's going to join us for a tune and you might want to get those spikes ready in case he rots."

Mink positioned the runhammer diagonally across his Body and slipped the tips of his fingers into the hammer keys. He checked the glide over the strings and it ran comfortably from shoulder to hip. This one was quality, made from natural Wood, unlike his beat-up, second-hand Materialized Wood instrument at home. As he checked the tune, the slits carved into the base resonated with delicious sound.

Mink played the intro and the rest was automatic. It was a song he knew very well. He didn't have the best singing voice, but hoped his runhammer skills would make up for it.

> *"I found you in a chain.*
> *They said you were insane.*
> *Danger was your name.*
> *Your soul I felt I could tame.*
> *All you needed was a day*
> *Without a game to play.*
> *You showered me in pain.*
> *As the falling rain."*

As he sang, Mink watched Dreh and Pulti dance. The chemistry seemed off, but he hoped it was improving. He turned his attention to the crowd which, thankfully, was helping him sing the song.

> *"As the falling rain.*
> *As the falling rain.*
> *You played your part and filled my heart*
> *Until I spilled with love unfulfilled.*
> *As the falling rain."*

Then, down in front, to the left of the stage, Mink saw her. Gyov watched him and swayed to the song. She wasn't dancing with anyone and that made Mink glad. Her long brown hair swung around her head and shoulders. She wore a billowy dress, cut to her figure, and just a shoulder jacket on top. Mink kept singing, but now he sang only to her. Her deep brown eyes stayed on him. She smiled.

> *"There was something in your tone.*
> *You said you shouldn't be alone.*

You led me to your home.
Sat me inside a dome.
I could tell it wasn't wise,
But I was trapped inside your eyes.
When your nature I was shown,
You cut me to the bone..."

CHAPTER
27

MINK AWOKE with a pounding headache and no idea what time it was. He recognized his room, but wasn't sure if he had laid down in his bed, or was put there. Dreh probably brought him home, but the fact that he couldn't remember made him worry about what else had happened. Pulling memories off the nails in his head proved impossible.

His room, conversely to Dreh's, showed no discernable trace of attention to cleanliness. He considered it to be a certain arrangement of organized chaos. Everything Mink owned, he could see and identify. Even in his impaired state, he quickly selected and put on a clean undershirt, pair of undershorts, socks, pocket pants, and a long-sleeved jacket.

Having dressed, he felt more awake, but still unwell. This level of dehydration required either a Water user or a trip to the kitchen. Scooting out of his room, Mink spied his runhammer propped on the wall by the door. His serenade of the previous evening came back to him in a rush of embarrassment, and his head pulsed with pain. What on Georra had persuaded him to be so bold?

"Mom? Dad?" Mink called out into the ether, still disoriented as he exited his room.

Only after making his way downstairs did he recall that his parents were still out at Rift Ridge. His heart sank, burdened by not having any way to know how they were doing. He wanted to tell them that he had made it, that plans for their rescue were already underway, and how all the Advocates had been impressed by his delivery of the news. He also wanted his mom to make this hangover go away. His dad would just tell him to drink kwona. Mink had never made it himself and decided against that idea, since it involved grinding roasted seeds to a proper grain, and measuring specific ratios of grounds to infuse with boiling Water.

The kitchen had an eerie calm and cleanliness to it. Mink sipped Water and spent the better part of an hour rummaging repeatedly through the cabinets. Nothing appealed, but he couldn't risk overlooking the perfect remedy. He eyed the fruit on the counter as he drained his glass. It looked really good, but he figured the acids would aggravate his already compromised stomach.

It was time to descend to the basement and check out cold storage. Nyam had converted most of the basement into a well-organized warehouse storing family heirlooms, decorations for their eight seasonal holidays, linens, household tools, and dry goods. There was a large gap in the order of things where their camping equipment should be. The cold storage room sat all the way back in the far corner, as far as possible from the kitchen, which Mink never could quite understand.

The glow crystals in the ceiling hurt his eyes, so he concentrated on the stone floor in front of him. He thought back again to being on stage at the party, performing for a couple hundred people just to get Dreh and Pulti to dance together. With a start, he remembered seeing Gyov in the audience. The thought of it crumpled Mink to the floor. He liked having the cool stone pressed against his forehead. If only it could erase the past, or at least his memory of it.

"Stupid. Stupid. Stupid." Mink wanted to stay in the basement for the rest of his life. Perhaps his father could be reassigned to a different prefecture. He could change schools. Dreh and Pulti would have to come with him. They were his only protection in this cruel world.

Picking himself up off the floor, Mink continued to the far corner. Until he cleared his head, he wouldn't be able to come up with a decent strategy for damage control. He unlatched the thick Wood door to cold storage and it swung open stiffly. The blast of cold Air gave Mink instant relief. How long could he manage to live in here? The first things he saw were neatly arranged rows of nutty bottles, which he immediately swore off until next time.

He took a quick inventory of the rest of the provisions, realizing as his toes chilled that he wasn't wearing shoes. Meat and drinks abounded in the small, frigid room, with only one little section reserved for sweets and jars of Nyam's culinary experiments. Mink pulled out a few thick slices of smoke-cured bushtusk and exited with a dance-like shuffle to keep his feet from freezing.

Back in the kitchen, he set the slabs on the stove's hot rocks to warm while he selected some dipping sauces from a cupboard. So what if he had made a fool out of himself on stage? Everyone else was likely having too much fun to care, and he had received such applause for being the big winner of Dreh's spike game. Transferring the meat onto a plate, Mink even laughed about how bold he had been at the first party he'd actually attended in years.

Sitting at the table, it further occurred to him that later today Dreh would make him an Imbued paddle with a cutting edge and Air grooves to enhance the fanning. He sipped more Water and ate with improved mood, even letting himself believe that Gyov was among those who had clapped for him. She did smile and wave from the stage audience, too. His performance couldn't have been that bad.

Mink's mind turned to his parents' welfare. He had just met with the High Council the previous day, so help should arrive to them within a day or two. It would take his mom less time than that to pull their cart home, with his dad in tow. So, best case scenario, Mink had three days to himself. Technically, he had been excused from school through the rest of the week. However, he could go tomorrow morning to start making up his hours.

Just as he was deliberating over where he should spend the day with Dreh and Pulti, someone knocked on the door. He opened it, half-expecting them to have made his decision for him. Instead, he stared right at the face and trademark shaved head of his childhood thornball hero, Tolrin Makunam!

Tolrin had been captain of the Floth Riptides for a twelve year stretch. He led them to a total of eight national championships, including a five-in-a-row run. Employing an arsenal of reactionary defensive strategies, Tolrin still held the league record for the fewest goals allowed in a season. What surprised Mink the most was that despite his massive frame, Tolrin stood three inches shorter than himself.

"Mink Jolle?" Tolrin inquired. The excitement of being asked for by name left Mink mute. "Are you Mink, or not?"

"That's yes. Yes, sir. I'm me. Mink. I am Mink." Oh, man.

"Wonderful. You have been selected by the High Council to guide my unit to the location of the Tear of God." Tolrin spoke in matter-of-fact rote.

It took Mink a while to remember the reports he had heard of Tolrin enlisting in the army after retiring from thornball. The circumstances of this visit turned out to be neither as random nor pleasant as Mink might have hoped. And yet, Tolrin Makunam was at his house!

"What do you need me to do? Tell you where on the Great Plateau it is? Rift Ridge?" Mink's questions jumbled out. "I'm not sure if I can draw a map very well."

"No. You are assigned to the Guide Cell under my command. You will report directly to Corporal Alré and walk the Team back to the site the way you came."

"I'm sorry, I don't think I understand. I'm not exactly army material."

"I couldn't agree more. But, I have my orders. And now, so do you. Welcome to the service."

"What? Someone enlisted me? Is there an appeal or something?" Mink's voice squeaked.

"The High Council of the Main Cameral, in their infinite wisdom, decided that the most efficient way for my Support Unit to guide the Tear of God Extraction Unit to the site is to have you lead us there. Your Uncle Durren signed the order himself. So, you are reporting to Corporal Alré in one hour, or I will have to use Mental Change and Inspiration on you. Knowing who your father is, I trust you understand how that will work."

Mink gathered from Tolrin's tone that he wasn't exactly pleased with the arrangement either. Tolrin, being a Spirit user like Juré, could've chosen to chant either effect before Mink had even opened the door, speaking Mink's name as the implementation upon first sight. That would have prevented the whole argument. Maybe he wanted to give Mink the chance to decide for himself. Regardless, at least now he could see his parents sooner than expected.

CHAPTER

28

WOULD YOU like to come in while I gather my things?" Mink offered.

"I thought you'd never ask." Tolrin stepped inside just far enough for Mink to close the door. He looked around impassively.

Mink wondered what Tolrin's house must be like. The government paid Intelligence Operatives like Juré very well so they wouldn't be tempted by bribes. Nyam's taxi business had expanded to include cross-country routes with a network of stations. Having only one child, their money went a long way.

"My dad and I used to watch all your—"

"Less chat. More pack."

"Yeah, sorry," Mink mumbled from the top of the stairs and then rushed into his room.

He grabbed a weekend pack from the corner and started shoving clothes into it from the clean pile. He rubbed his thumb over a cluster of milky yellow six-sided crystals about the size and shape of his own fingers. Mink found which ones he wanted to help keep himself entertained, and placed them in the bag. The runhammer begged to come along this time, but Mink refrained. He gathered a notepad and a pencil in hopes of getting an autograph, as well as his wallet, toiletries, and a book that would allow him the comfort of being antisocial among an army full of strangers without seeming so. His pack was nearly full.

Mink couldn't wait to tell Dreh and Pulti that Tolrin Makunam had come to his house... Dreh! He was supposed to get a new paddle today. Mink closed up his pack, slung it over his shoulder, and ran out of the room. As he hurried down the stairs, he noticed that Tolrin hadn't budged an inch. Thornball players weren't allowed to move their feet at all when they were holding the ball. For a second, Mink imagined Tolrin hid one in his hands behind his back, about to toss him a pass.

"I just remembered my friend Dreh is making a paddle for me. I really should have it for the trip. Can we go pick it up?"

"No. Our Team should have moved out hours ago, but we've been detained rounding up a bunch of highly-skilled youth. We are late."

Rounding up a bunch of youth? Mink wondered if they were all going out to Rift Ridge, but why? The army had thousands of master-level users. Mink didn't figure Tolrin would be exactly forthcoming with the information. "Okay, but you'll want my friend, too. Dreh Hoy. He's a very good Wood user and—"

"I know about Dreh Hoy. We have all the Wood users we need. Are you ready? Or should I start making myself a meal?"

"Good to go." Mink adjusted the pack's strap higher on his shoulder and opened the door for Tolrin. Now at least he knew they were hand-selecting people and had specific numbers in mind for each Elemental type. He almost asked about Pulti, but as he stepped outside, the daylight split through his eyes like a tapping rod. Blinking away the lingering pain of his hangover, he reflexively turned to go back inside, only to be stopped by the firm grasp of Tolrin's hand on his arm.

Mink could barely keep track of where he was going. His head ached again and queasiness gripped his throat. Judging from the length of the shadows, the time of day was either three or seven of the second clock. Mink followed Tolrin down the stone walkway to a group of seven people waiting by the street, keeping his head down and avoiding eye contact.

"Sergeant Makunam," a female voice spoke to Mink's right. "Strike Cell reports two more to go. All other Support Unit Cells reporting complete."

"Does the Strike Cell have an ETA, Tréa?"

Tréa fell into a silence with which Mink was familiar. She must be communicating through Silent Signal Fire to get details from the Strike Cell. "Corporal Counkrat reports that they are following a lead on the whereabouts of both campers and should have them within the hour."

"Good enough. Tell all Corporals to rendezvous at the first checkpoint in three hours. Blin, I want you to inform Lieutenant Jannri that the Support Unit will await the Extraction Unit at the first checkpoint within three hours. Can you remember that?"

Blin?! Mink could hardly bring himself to raise his eyes from the ground, catching just a glimpse of the two-toned left hand. He certainly recognized the voice. "Yes, sir! Three hours. Checkpoint one. Sir!" With that, the cracking sound of Blin's Flash Feet faded into the distance.

"Let's see how he manages to screw this one up," Tolrin grumbled once Blin was long gone. "Nylki, be ready to run damage control. Now, let's go deliver Mink to Corporal Alré."

Tréa's reference to the youth being gathered as campers remained a mystery. Mink was just as puzzled that Blin served as some sort of messenger, and had been doing so long enough for Tolrin to have formed an opinion on his reliability. He wanted answers, but for now he'd have to keep his mouth shut and get his head back in order.

The delivery of Mink to Corporal Alré entailed traveling with Tolrin's Cell via a Body user's taxi cart all the way to checkpoint one. Four of the six people in Tolrin's Relay Cell were Soil or Spirit users, neither of which had effects to help them move quickly. The other two were Lightning users, Blin and Nylki. Flash Feet was faster than Quick Legs, but only when traveling solo.

The first checkpoint was located in Byndiwash, a town in the northwest corner of Floth, bordering the Gynsgade and Eternsa Prefectures. Byndiwash relied on its location for commerce, being little more than a convenient travel stop. It didn't offer much in the way of local flare, and overpromoted what it did have: the world's largest Water wheel, which Mink had never found particularly impressive. A larger one could easily be built, but with the scarcity of natural Water in Octernal, what would be the point? Water users Materialized all the Water the country needed.

Nonetheless, Byndiwash was an inconspicous spot for a large group to gather. By the time Tolrin's Cell reached the sprawling community park which dwarfed the famous Water wheel, Mink couldn't tell how many of the masses were part of their Team. Hundreds of Octernalian travelers huddled in scattered groups and chatted about their next stop.

The two hours it took to get to Byndiwash felt like days, with conversation limited to Tolrin relaying orders, and Tréa reporting after pregnant pauses in Silent Signal Fire communications. So far, the time Mink had spent with his hero only lessened the awe he once felt. For all of his intensity on the octagonal field, Tolrin now seemed dull and distant. With any luck, Corporal Alré's Cell would be more entertaining.

Tolrin led the group to a pavilion shaded by several very large and very old broad-leafed trees. Under the pavilion's vaulted roof, ten long tables could sit sixteen people each, arranged in two lines of five. A banner reading "Welcome to the Wilderness Youth Camp Experience" hung boldly above the entrance. Several small groups Mink's age or older hung around the tables.

Indicating for Mink to wait where he was, Tolrin marched right up to a trim, hardened woman whose short hair showed just enough gray to grant her an air of authority. She seemed very tall, even as she stood some distance away from Tolrin. Mink noticed from afar that the right side of her head and arm had been Materialized. Seeing a soldier with wounds during peacetime unsettled Mink. He hoped the injuries weren't battle related. After a few words, Tolrin waved Mink over to them.

CHAPTER
29

M INK JOLLE, this is Corporal Banni Alré. She heads up my Guide Cell. You will assist her in directing our path and otherwise do as she says, is that clear?" Tolrin actually seemed excited for the first time that day.

"Yes, sir," Mink replied carefully.

"Fantastic. In about an hour, we'll be setting out. Get to know your Cell before then. You move with them at all times. Once we exit through the western border into the wilderness, we will brief the whole Team together. You'll be called upon to speak on a few specific points. Location of the Tear of God, its approximate size, and the nature of the surrounding area. Do not add any information and do not answer anyone's questions but mine. Understood?"

"I understand," Mink said, weary of being told to share his story at the same time as keep quiet about the details.

Tolrin gave him a slap on the shoulder. "You'll do fine." He saluted Alré as he turned back toward his Cell. "All yours, Corporal."

Alré gave Mink a dubious smile and extended her hand. "So. You're the boy with no Element."

"Yes, ma'am," Mink replied, dryly.

"And you've been assigned to me. Great." Her voice relayed sarcasm in the deep, scratchy quality of a long-time Fire user. Mink tried to get a read from her flat brown eyes, but they were expressionless and cold. "Come sit and meet the rest of the campers in our Cell."

Alré led Mink to a table seating three people a little older than himself. He recognized the Penbik twins immediately. Both were genius Wood users who remained legends at Mink's school in spite of having graduated six years ago. They skipped two grades, and their Materialization exam produced an office building that still stood out as one of the more beautiful structures in Riverpark. They went so far out of their way to distinguish themselves from one another that most people would scarcely realize they were identical, let alone related. Tralé wore his auburn hair back in a ponytail. Mouké kept his short hair unkempt and bleached, darkening his chestnut tan by comparison.

A girl sat across from them. Her straight black hair hung heavily down most of her slouched back. Her pale skin made her appear both feminine and slightly ill. She looked up at Mink as he took his seat on the bench, and he noticed that her sea green eyes held tenderness and compassion. Mink had never seen eye color so light before.

"Now we have all of the Guide Cell together," Alré announced, scanning the group. "Tralé, Mouké, Sapo, and Mink: you are my campers. Our job is to blaze a trail for the rest of the Team to follow. Tralé, you will take Mink on your scooter. Mouké, you will take me on yours. Sapo, you will Slip Skate in-between. Keep that formation whenever we travel.

"The Scout Cell will be right behind us, with two Soil users to help flatten the road we make, as well as to maintain Tralé and Mouké's energy when necessary. Sapo, as a Water user, will also assist in keeping up their strength, but her main function will be to immobolize any hostile groups we encounter long enough for the Strike Cell to respond.

"We are under cover of a camping trip." Alré spoke on, finally alluding to the function of the youth group. "Sapo, wait until I give the order before targeting anyone who might pose a threat. It's my job to command our Cell and communicate with Sergeant Makunam. Mink's job is to point us in the right direction. Now, please introduce yourselves and tell us something about what you do. Starting with you, Sapo."

Sapo stood, towering over Alré at a height of at least seven feet tall. She waved to the group with elongated hands and fingers that could grab Mink's head like a piece of fruit. Her lips hardly moved when she spoke, and her voice was so quiet that Mink thought at first she was talking to herself.

"Hi, I'm Sapo. I'm nineteen years old. I work as an irrigator at the Sekmet Ranch. It's fun, I guess. They're nice people and I like what I do. It feels important. When I'm not working, I like to paint. That's about it." Sapo sat down and stared self-consciously off in the distance.

"Sapo's being modest." Alré reached up to put a hand on Sapo's shoulder. "She is ranked as the second best Water user under twenty-five and is the highest paid irrigator in Floth, doing the work of ten people."

Sapo flushed and looked down, letting her hair hide her face. Mink opted to go ahead with his introduction and help her recover from her embarrassment. He stood.

"I'm Mink Jolle. I haven't found my Elemental affinity yet."

Tralé threw a look at Mouké while pointing at Mink. "It's him!" Mouké just smiled back and elbowed his brother. Sapo looked away from Mink and was either giggling or about to sneeze, he couldn't be sure.

Undaunted, he continued, "But, I am the only person to ever attend Riverpark High that got an 'A+' on Mr. Gusky's Reactionary Strategies Exam." Tralé and Mouké took note and became noticibly more curious. "I'm at a post-graduate weapons proficiency. I don't really know what kind of job I'll get, but I was thinking about—"

"Mink's getting a little carried away," Alré interrupted and abruptly spoke for him. "The only reason he's here is because he has been to our destination site. Moving on to Tralé."

Mink dropped to his seat while Tralé rose and nodded. "Tralé Penbik. Twenty-one. I design and make buses for Grenk. I've won the Cross Octernal Invitational twice and I plan on racing again this year. Glad to meet everyone."

Tralé had barely sat before Mouké stood. "I'm his brother Mouké. I'm an architect until I finish up my doctorate. Then I'll try to teach at the University level. I don't race so that Tralé can win. I'm engaged and will marry in a few months. For now, I'm just working and studying." Mouké sat.

Mink felt completely out of place. No mental achievement or level of ability with weapons mattered in the company of these young Elemental geniuses. Friendless among strangers, now all he wanted to do was keep his head down, point the group in the right direction, and be reunited with his parents as soon as possible.

"Now." Alré sat between Mink and Sapo. "I'm sure you have lots of questions." She searched the group expectantly.

Mink had nothing but questions. Still, he couldn't bring himself to speak up. With any luck, someone else would ask the same ones. But no one wanted to go first. Were they all accepting of this arrangement? Did they come willingly?

Mouké finally broke the silence. "How long are we supposed to be gone?"

"Six to seven days."

Tralé let out a frustrated sigh. "This 'camping trip.' What's it to you? A training exercise? Recruitment?"

"Of course I can't speak for the rest of the army, but personally, it's the worst babysitting gig I can imagine," Alré retorted with restentment as she examined a paper set before her.

"Ah. Refreshing perspective," Tralé quipped before clamming up.

Sapo spoke next. "Are we leaving soon? I want to go."

Alré maintained her raspy, matter-of-fact tone. "Very soon."

CHAPTER

30

ACTUALLY, THEY sat for nearly an hour with nothing more to do than watch the pavilion fill up. Mink had reached into his bag for a music crystal, but was thwarted by a no-rooting order from Alré. The solitary interesting moment was when Blin showed up with someone Mink took to be Lieutenant Jannri. Tolrin did not look happy with Blin, but Blin puffed up with pride. That morsel of entertainment fizzled and everyone eventually took seats at one table or another. Mink resigned himself to passing the time by shifting different muscles of his legs and butt.

Finally, Alré stood and looked off in Tréa's direction, nodding. "It's time to go. Tralé, Mouké, are your scooters prepped?"

"Waiting right over there." Tralé gestured to where they were parked in the shade of a thick-trunked tree whose branches had been bent by a Wood user, up and over the roof. One was black with silver tribal swirls, and on the other, new-growth green modestly accented a warm white base. Both of them had a four-foot board for the driver to stand on, which curled up at one end like a wave cresting just above waist level.

Alré marched her Cell to the scooters, Tralé claiming the black one and Mouké heading for the white. Tralé's scooter had deep Air grooves and a squat, racing look while Mouké's was more the smooth, broad cruiser.

"Aht-tat-tat. Secure your packs on the wagon first," Alré corrected before they got settled.

Mink followed the others to a huge Wooden wagon, which was parked at the edge of the trees since it couldn't fit beneath them. It was a natural dark hue absent of any seams or joints, a strong indication that it had been Materialized all at once by a highly skilled user. Six large runners supported its bulk, but the flatbed was low enough that Mink could easily reach over the side rails to place his pack. A broad-shouldered woman climbed into the bubble-shaped cabin, wearing riding gloves that inversely exposed four of her fingers for Unification, and covered the thumbs. This wagon was easily the size of two buses side by side, and yet she was going to drive it herself, hauling everyone's gear!

Mink turned back toward the scooters, recollecting Tolrin's comment that the army had all the Wood users it needed. Mink felt sorry that Dreh had missed out on this mission for not being on the same level as the Wood users he had seen so far. Dreh had been at the top of his class since fourth grade and still didn't make the cut. Being without an Element of his own, Mink lived vicariously through Dreh's acheivements, and took his friend's absence personally.

He caught up with the Cell as Tralé and Mouké stepped onto their scooters. They stood in a sideways driving position with backs turned to one another. Tralé gloved his left hand, and Mouké his right. Mink wondered how they planned to steer single-handedly. Then he noticed that their pinkies, as well as their thumbs, were exposed for Unification with the scooter, allowing for balanced pressure to steer. These two were on a whole new level of control.

Tralé pointed Mink to one end of his scooter, where ledges on the board's edge were located at the base of the upperward curved portion. "Put your feet on those. And hold on here." Mink looked up to the top of the wave-like crest where a couple of scoops served as handles. "Let me know if you need adjustments," he added.

Mink mounted the scooter, hugging the outside of the upward curve. To his great surprise, it supported him very well under and inside of his thighs, as if he were on a seat. Yet, wasn't he supposed to be facing the other way? The scooter's design made him believe he was a hood ornament.

"It's perfect. Only, how will I see where we're going?"

Tralé thumbed to the open side of the board opposite Mink. "That's the front," he informed in a patronizing tone.

Mink nodded dumbly, then looked over at Alré, positioning herself on the other twin's scooter. Mouké had removed his glove and was busy Manipulating the curved portion to accomodate Alré's elongated form. Sapo spoke her Slip Skate chant in the elided manner of a Water user,

> "My feet slide on a Water flow.
> Gracefully, I glide where I want.
> My hips control the direction.
> The Water under foot remains.
> The side of my foot slows me down.
> I feel no friction to slow me.
> My Water enhanced by Spirit.
> Rush me around upon my spit."

Having implemented the effect by spitting on the ground, Sapo played her feet back and forth, watching them with her hands deep in her pockets. Slip Skate couldn't keep up with a Wood user's Sledding speed, which meant that it would take them longer than anticipated to reach Mink's parents on Rift Ridge. Water users couldn't have prolonged contact with

Wood, as it sapped their energy. So it wasn't as if the twins could give her a lift.

"Ready," Mouké confirmed to Tralé.

Standing on the board, Tralé placed his hand atop the curved portion of his scooter, right in front of Mink's face. He watched as Tralé's thumb and pinky turned to Wood and slipped into the crest. Simply being connected to Tralé's power, Mink could tell that the scooter felt lighter, as if it were Imbued with an Air user's Featherweight effect. That couldn't have been the case though, because it was Tralé's touch that seemed to cause the change. Mink racked his brain for any possible way to explain the sensation with only one of Tralé's hands connected.

"Mink," Alré called. "I will give the directions until we get through Etersna's western gate. Once we reach the forest, you'll continue in the same fashion. Listen and learn."

"Yes, ma'am. I'm just along for the ride at the moment."

Alré guided them to the main road, heading west out across the Eternsa Prefecture with the rest of the groups following in order. They traveled uneventfully for some time. The Penbik twins struggled to stay slow enough to avoid pulling away from the group. Alré forced them to match Sapo's speed, while Sapo entertained herself by Slip Skating backwards.

Mink watched the rolling pastoral hills of Eternsa's landscape slide by, pondering how the next few days would go, and imagining what it would be like to see his parents again. His reverie was broken about an hour into the trip by the cacophonous sound of Blin, Nylki, and two other Lightning users running by on Flash Feet, presumably on an errand to the next checkpoint. Tralé and Mouké traded quiet smiles, giving Mink the sense that they wanted to play catch-up.

"Are we going to have a problem?" Alré asked, noticing the exchange.

"No, ma'am," they replied together, returning their attention to the stretch of road ahead.

By the time the border gate came into view, Sapo looked a little worn out. The twins had both taken a knee on the flatboard of their scooters, propping their chins on their free hand. Mink yawned and looked over at Alré, who was engaged in a Silent Signal Fire chat, chuckling. Mink thought it unfair that she was allowed to jabber away in her mind while the rest of them had to ride in silence.

She directed them through the gate and off to a grassy field where temporary bleachers sat beside a long table covered in white linen. From an assortment of glass serving containers, Mink could smell the floral sweetness of typical Eternsa fare. At this point in the day, anything fresh would whet his appetite. Alré pointed out a spot for the twins to park. They wasted no time pulling up and yanking their hands free.

"Go make yourselves a plate and find a seat on the front-right of the bleachers." Alré dismounted and stretched before speedwalking to the food. Mink followed suit, passed by Sapo, who was Slip Skating toward an overdue lunch with a vengeance.

"That wasn't too bad, was it?" Tralé asked Mink as they got to the table.

"Uh, no," Mink admitted. "My buddy Dreh could take a few lessons in comfort from you."

"Dreh Hoy?" Tralé smiled broadly. "I know Dreh. Comfort's not the only thing I could teach him." Tralé laughed while Mink puzzled over what he found so funny. "I like Dreh." Tralé grabbed a plate and handed it to Mink before taking one for himself. "It's a shame I couldn't show you some real speed. What a snoozefest."

"Yeah, well. Thanks for the lift anyway, I guess." Tralé snorted. "Not like I had a choice."

Mink filled his plate with a flavorful assortment of flowery rice, boiled root vegetables, sweet soufflé, and crispy dried fruit wedges before taking a seat beside Sapo and Tralé. The bleachers were hastily made and rather uncomfortable, facing only open fields and the Great Barrier Range beyond. Mink tried hard not to stare at a big guy tending to Alré's scars. Typically, healers made Materialized prosthetics more resistant by adding wet sand to the parts as they formed. But, prolonged use of a Spirit effect was bound to start canceling the repair. The use of Silent Signal Fire must be taking a toll on her Body effect.

"Don't eat those," Sapo grabbed Mink's attention back to lunch, pointing out the vegetables on his plate. "They're nasty."

Lieutenant Jannri and Sergeant Makunam walked out in front of the stands, accompanied by a woman who was introduced as Sergeant Holph, head of the Extraction and Transportation Unit. Sergeant Makunam received some brief applause as the head of the Support Unit, and Lieutentant Jannri announced herself as leader of the Command Cell to oversee both Units that made up the overall Tear of God Team.

The top brass detailed the days ahead for the group, seated according to their Cells, and Mink got to hear the upshot of the High Council's deliberations. The Team sent to get the geode would be led by a small contingent of military personnel, but not in a military capacity. The youth camp facade and slower pace were employed to avoid any Machinist surveillance misconstruing their actions as a declaration of war.

When the Lieutenant finally announced that a Tear of God was the target of their mission, a mixture of reactions circulated in the bleachers. It seemed Mink knew more about what they were doing than did the rest of the 'campers.' Tolrin signaled for him to come forward. As he approached the front of the stands, some voices in the crowd started to sing "As the Falling Rain" in an exaggerated off-key. The Corporals barked them back to silence.

Mink forced a laugh and shook his head as the embarrassment flushed in his face. By the time he finished confirming what he knew and where they were headed, nearly everyone was in a heated conversation with the members of their Cell as to the veracity of the information. He felt as if he had lost their attention, but at least they had found resolve.

CHAPTER
31

THE LAST time Mink traveled the wild, grassy plain between the western gate of Eternsa and the forested mountainside, he had sprinted across in minutes. Quick Legs coupled with boost bar had made it feel like one simple step of the journey. This time, wrapped around the back of Tralé's scooter and digesting three helpings of a military banquet, the forest seemed to remain a distant goal despite their progress. The slower pace also emphasized the roughness of the terrain over which they traveled.

Uneven ground posed no problem for most of the Team, but Alré kept ordering halts to allow the Soil users time to make the way passable for the bulky wagon, which carried the gear and a week's worth of provisions for seventy-eight people. After a few of the contents bounced out, Tolrin had encouraged extra precaution, adding hours to the duration of their trek.

The twins had slowed their scooters to a crawl and were tediously watching the wagon lumber up behind them. Alré dismounted, stretched, and shielded her eyes to check on the wagon's progress.

"Is there anything I can do to help?" Sapo offered.

"Not your job," Alré responded dismissively.

Sapo huffed and Slip Skated a couple of yards ahead to a small basin, probably formed by an ancient sinkhole or crater, covered in tangles of a short runner grass. Mink watched as Sapo circled the edge of the basin, looked it over, and then slid gracefully in. The center was barely three feet deep, and the whole thing couldn't have been more than six yards wide, but she made the best of it. Mink loved how smooth and poetic her movements were. For all her height and the shallowness of the dip, Sapo managed to get some great hang time Slip Skating up the sides.

"Sapo!" Alré repremanded. "Get back in formation! Now!" Sapo twirled down to the ground and came back between the scooters with one graceful kick. "We need to be ready to start moving the second I say so. This is no place for frolicking."

Alré's raspy voice made anything she said come off like admonishment, and she did seem to be reigning Sapo in; still, Mink couldn't take anyone seriously who used a word like frolicking in her reprimand. He made eye contact with Sapo and quietly applauded her demonstration of skill. She half-smiled appreciatively and rolled her eyes in good humor. Turning around, she got into an exaggerated ready-to-go pose. Alré had already turned her attention back to the wagon.

"Okay, kids. Let's keep going," Alré said, climbing back on Mouké's scooter.

It wasn't until they got moving again that Mink felt the stillness of the Air around them. Why an Air user or two weren't creating a breeze was beyond him. It's not like the extra hit to the Lightning users' power mattered on this stretch. Keeping at this pace over dry land in the middle of the afternoon on a full stomach felt horrible, and they weren't even permitted the simple distractions of conversation or music.

"Sapo? Could you get a little mist going, please? I don't feel so well," Mink said, breaking the code of silence.

"She is not under your command, Mink!" barked Alré. "If you have a question or complaint, you will address me and I will tell you to be quiet. Understood?"

"My bad. Sorry. I just don't feel so good."

"Understood?" Alré practically yelled.

"Yes, ma'am. I understand perfectly."

The next hour seemed unbearably long until at last, they reached the edge of the pergnut forest. Mink half-expected them to camp there for the night. A few more good hours of daylight remained though, and after waiting in formation while the army communicated via Silent Signal Fire, it became obvious they were going to press on. The prospect of shade improved Mink's morale. Still, considering the wagon's trouble getting over the field, the forest would prove an even greater obstacle.

"All right, Mink," Alré addressed him, once she had received the order to continue. "Where did you cross over the range?"

Mink scanned the mountaintops up ahead and spotted the large tree with its branches bent to one side. It was some distance south of where they were currently facing. The tree looked so small to Mink now without the benefit of Tunnel Vision. Without a way to gauge how much forest stood between them and the tree, Mink had no idea how much longer they had to go.

"That tree up there. The big guy with all its branches to one side. That's where I came over. It also has a yellow cloth tied around it."

"Good," Alré said to herself. "A marker tree. That makes it easier."

Judging the distance left to travel, Tralé gave a long whistle. Sapo slumped, and Mouké cracked his neck. Alré went silent, likely making her report and awaiting instructions.

"Everyone agrees that's too steep to take the Team," she spoke after the pause. "Would you be able to find your way if we cut through a lower pass along the range?"

"I wouldn't bet on it. I've only been through this way once by myself."

"Ma'am, if I may?" Mouké said, not waiting for permission to continue. "The side of the mountain lends itself well to switchbacks. Tralé and I can easily clear a path wide enough for the Soil users to flatten it out for the wagon. Probably with room for Body users on either side to help with cornering."

Alré held her hand up, indicating that she was either having trouble hearing or being heard via Silent Signal Fire. Mink tried to guess the length of time it would take to travel the path that the twins proposed. They were already running behind schedule, and this was only the first day of the journey.

"Apparently, our best approach to the base lies ahead at a fifteen degree angle to the right," Alré reported to her Cell. "The Soil users sense a natural incline there that we can use to save some time and give them a grade to work with for the rest of the path. I hope you can move fast. Our first campsite is fifty feet below that marker tree."

The Penbik twins uttered their Animation chants, low and deliberate,

> *"Wood appears to have life with me.*
> *I make it move, fight, bend, and dance.*
> *My hands implement my intent.*
> *I use the target like a tool.*
> *It remains separate from me.*
> *I cannot kill my Element.*
> *I control as Atriarb does.*
> *Animate as soon as I reach."*

Controlling their scooters with one hand and using the other to perform effects, Tralé and Mouké demonstrated more Elemental skill than Mink had ever witnessed. The two of them reached ahead with their free hands and moved the trees one at a time, trunks gouging deep trenches in the dirt as they slid to the side. Once they had cleared a path about ten yards wide, they moved their scooters forward.

Mink could hear the soft grinding sound of the Soil users behind them smoothing out the road, while the twins wove around the troughs ahead, not waiting for the ground to be restored. There were some miles to clear and everyone wanted to set up camp in time to get some good sleep. Mink felt relieved as he listened to the twins' chants mixed with the creaking of moving trees. They were making better time than they had all day, with the Soil users filling and flattening the path a good distance ahead of the wagon. By now, the sun hung low on the far side of the Great Barrier Range, blocked by the bulk of the mountains.

CHAPTER

32

I NDEED, THEY reached the base of the mountain and the anticipated grade in less than an hour. There were fewer trees to move on the mountainside which should've meant faster progress, but it turned out to only be favorable for the twins. Even with their Manipulation effect, Shape Land, the Soil users had a harder time making a flat road ten yards wide on the incline, and many large rocks had to be physically cleared out by Body users.

The third switchback brought them high enough for Mink to easily look out over the trees below. That the western gate of Eternsa was still visible after traveling so long discouraged him. Then, thankfully he heard Sapo and the eliding flow of her adapted Area of Effect chant, Washout,

> *"One cloud of mist descend from high.*
> *The greater area be soaked.*
> *Water swirling relentlessly.*
> *All things become saturated.*
> *Cloudless, the mist hangs forever.*
> *Eternsa's essence be my fuel.*

The wrath of Floth herself take form.
Cover with mist upon my spit."

Sapo spat and moved her hands in large arcs with her fingers tickling the Air. The area around them humidified with a light mist. Tiny droplets hung in clouds that rippled in swirls reminiscent of Sapo's own flowing movements. The cooling effect of the mist collecting on Mink's arms and face refreshed him.

"Thanks, Sapo. That feels awesome," Mink said.

Sapo shot him a quick glance like she had forgotten he was even there. Tralé looked back at Mink with a humored grin.

"Thank you, Sapo. I feel better now," he emphasized between Animation chants. "Don't you, Mouké?"

"Thank you, Sapo." Mouké said monotonously.

Mink felt a little foolish forgetting that Sapo was just doing her job of keeping up the twins' energy with her Water effect. His own responsibilities were proving to be a cakewalk compared to everyone else's. He made a mental note not to make any more complaints. His sole contribution of the day was to point out a marker tree that the army already seemed to be acquainted with.

Fortunately, the Guide Cell received permission to move forward, leaving a path for the rest of the Team to follow. That meant no more stopping, and the promise of more time to rest at the campsite. Powered by Sapo's mist, the Penbik twins got into a rhythm lining up the trees like a natural colonnade along the road.

Despite their progress, twilight came down upon Alré's Cell with a few more switchbacks still to carve out until camp. Scanning the horizon out across the plain, Mink saw that none of the moons had yet risen to illuminate their way. Without the sun's heat, Sapo's mist began to give Mink a chill. His clothes and hair had become very damp and now clung to him. Alré's raspy voice chanted the Fire user's Materialization effect, Candle,

> *"I bring Fire into this world.*
> *My power makes it manifest.*
> *Newly formed flowing from my palms.*
> *I can change its shape with my hand.*
> *My Fire burns with warmth and light.*
> *My creation ends with a fist.*
> *Create Fire upon my snap."*

She snapped her fingers, then lifted her palms skyward and shaped a two-foot column of blue-white Fire, careful to keep it out of the mist. It hung high in the Air as she followed up with the Animation chant, Flame Ghost,

> *"Fire has a new life with me.*
> *I make it move, fight, bend, and dance.*
> *My snapping implements my intent.*
> *I use the target like a tool.*
> *It remains separate from me.*
> *I cannot kill my Element.*
> *I can control just as Symg does.*
> *Animate as soon as I snap."*

After a second snap, she reached for the Fire column and moved it along ahead of them. Mink looked away from the light, his eyes having adjusted to the dark. He could see a greater distance now. Alré's Fire cast stark shadows throughout the Woods, lending a new creepiness to the trek. He was glad to be drying off in the warmth given off by Flame Ghost, but the process quickly became itchy and irritating. He shifted around a bit on the back of Tralé's scooter and distracted himself by anticipating which trees would be next to slide out of their path.

The Guide Cell finished the last few switchbacks in good time, and finally got permission to break formation once they reached their campsite destination. They wouldn't be able to set up camp until the wagon reached them, so the Cell members hunted out a flat spot for their tents. To stake a claim for their Cell, Tralé and Mouké Materialized some long-burning Wood logs which Alré Imbued with Radiate. This made them glow without any flames or excess light that might call unwanted attention in the night. Alré recited,

> *"Fire's power is mine to give.*
> *I grant my target extreme heat.*
> *The target feels comfortable.*
> *Touching the target will cause burns.*
> *Heat extends from around the target.*
> *Nothing can cool down the target.*
> *I may use the Fire of Symg.*
> *Imbue Fire upon my snap."*

She implemented the chant with a snap, and a wave of flameless heat reached Mink's face. He backed away a little farther up the grade, selecting a flattish area on the outskirts of the group. Mink tracked the progress of the rest of the Team by way of the other Fire users' Flame Ghosted Candles. They were still far enough away that he caught only one glimpse of the wagon through the trees below. That left him plenty of time to climb his way up to the marker tree, have a look at it, and be down before they arrived.

"I'm going up to the top. Be back in a bit."

"Suit yourself." Alré reclined by the Radiated logs and looked back toward Octernal. "I can't promise your spot will still be available when the Team arrives."

"Duly noted." Mink set off on his ascent, not particularly caring if he had to spend the night by the tree alone. He would have to reclaim his pack from the wagon, though. He climbed with hands and feet, gripping the trunks and roots of the pergnut trees. A moon was rising, giving Mink the benefit of some light as he hoisted himself from one foothold to another. Moss and shrubs peppered the slope, but offered no more reliable support for climbing than the soft dirt they clung to. Close to the top, the mountain rounded off and Mink was able to walk comfortably the rest of the way to the marker tree, seeing it up close for the first time with his natural vision.

The trunk itself was quite wide. Four people holding hands couldn't form a circle around it. Mink barely had room to stand under the branches that were bent and woven to the north. He ducked below them and tested the bed of dry needles on the ground for comfort. Looking up, the thick weave of limbs and their hundreds of thousands of needle-like leaves blocked all but the brightest of stars from view. The pergnut's branches swayed hypnotically in the breeze with a persistent rustling sound, revealing the random sparkle of distant stars.

Mink sat and leaned back against the tree, looking skyward. Though extremely tired, he enjoyed having this moment to himself to reflect upon the past week, clearly the most eventful of his arduous sixteen years. His parents beating him up, killing him, and finding what very well might be a Tear of God... Somehow, he had used effects to be the harbinger, until Blin Attacked him. Yet he still made the mission, only to be grilled by all the advocates running his country. Too soon after that, he managed to make a complete fool of himself at a party and, without adequate time to recover, got volunteered among his age group's geniuses to help rescue his parents.

Any one of these things was more than he had hoped or expected of the past week, but in combination... Mink didn't recall falling asleep, but he awoke abruptly to a swift kick in the ribs. Blin stood above him in just enough moonlight to illuminate the sneer on his face.

"Wakey, wakey, Blankey." Blin crouched down, cocking his head to make eye contact with Mink in the dark. "Let's have a chat."

CHAPTER
33

MINK CONCENTRATED on breathing steadily while shielding himself from another attack. He was at a complete disadvantage.

"A thrilling conversation to be had, I'm sure." He sat up straighter against the tree, clenching his teeth through the pain. "But can't it wait until tomorrow? Next year, maybe?" He didn't want Blin to gain any satisfaction from knowing how much his ribs hurt, let alone give off a sense of fear.

"Tolrin wants to talk to you, but I think we need to get some things straight first."

"Okay, Blin. What exactly do we need to get straight?"

Blin extended his hand for Mink to shake. "Truce? For now?"

Mink left Blin hanging. "You're kidding, right?"

"Listen, Blankey." Blin slipped into a more serious and vulnerable demeanor than Mink thought possible, which made him uncomfortable. "I need this gig. I'm only here because I'm the third fastest with Flash Feet in our age group. If I can prove myself, I might be able to get a courier job with the army. My grades the way they are, I could really use the help."

Mink laughed and the resurging pain in his side reinforced his doubt of Blin's sincerity. "Blin, Blin, Blin. Are your brains that rotten? Why would I care about helping you? You want a truce? Then leave me alone. You're the one always beating up on me."

Blin finally gave up on getting a handshake out of Mink and abruptly withdrew his hand. "If you don't help me," Blin sneered, pulling Nyam's flatwrap out of his jacket, "then everyone will know what a nasty habit your mom has. So, if your brains aren't rotten, I suggest you put in a good word for me."

Mink's mind raced to process this turn of events. Even if his mom denied the boost bars were hers, it wouldn't take long for a Body user to detect signs of it on her using Diagnosis. Her short-lived legacy of turning a self effect into a target effect would be tainted by criminal activity. Not to mention the charges brought against Mink for possession.

"What do you mean 'put in a good word' for you?"

Blin quickly shoved Nyam's flatwrap back inside his jacket. "Tréa has been making reports from your Corporal, and Tolrin keeps asking about you. Now he wants to talk to you in his cabin. If you get me in his good graces, I'll give it back to you."

Mink had a bad feeling about making a deal with Blin, who had far from proven himself trustworthy. If he gave Blin any leverage, he might not ever let it go. "Well, what do I do, make stuff up? What makes you think you've given me anything nice to say?"

"Thoy told me at the party that you were sorry I got hurt." So, Thoy had been Eavesdropping on him last night! "That you were just trying to get away. Even that you wanted to apologize. If that's true, this is your chance." Blin sat, folding his arms as if he just won an argument.

Mink shook his head, both amused and irritated by Blin's audacity. "You have a funny way of trying to make friends. Tolrin is a Spirit user, Blin. He's smart enough to be suspicious if I just name drop you randomly. When there's a chance, I'll 'put in a good word.' But if anyone ever hears about the contents of that flatwrap, you'll have to defect to find work. My uncle will see to that without any prompting from me. Deal?"

Mink extended his hand and Blin hastily shook it. "If I can get this job, I'll make it up to you."

"You can start by not calling me 'Blankey.'"

Mink trailed Blin back down the slope to find that the camp had been well-established. Some people had set up tents made of fabric, others had Materialized octagonal Wood cabins. A few groups encircled Radiated logs, but the camp as a whole was quiet and dark. The camping spot Mink had chosen earlier was still available, and he could swear it looked smoother and flatter than before, as though a Soil user had actually gone to the trouble of preparing it for him.

All the same, Mink avoided making eye contact with others as Blin led him through the camp to a small cabin, dwarfed by its proximity to the enormous wagon. Mink was sensitive to conversations that hushed as he passed. He couldn't get a sense yet of just how the rest of the Team felt about him. They reached the doorless opening to Tolrin's cabin and Blin knocked on the wall.

"It's Blin with Mink, sir!"

"Come on in, Mink. You are dismissed, Blin," Tolrin called from inside.

As Mink passed him to enter, Blin patted the chest of his jacket where he carried Nyam's flatwrap. The inside of the octagonal cabin was quite spartan. Tolrin sat on the ground in front of a low Wood platform covered in papers. A bed roll waited off to the side, suggesting that the make-shift desk doubled as a bed. A glow crystal hung from the ceiling, bathing the interior in a stark white. The walls were a grainless brown Materialized Wood.

"Sit here," Tolrin ordered, pointing to the floor beside him.

Mink settled in, sitting cross-legged. He could make out about a dozen maps spread haphazardly in front of Tolrin.

"You know, it's times like these I wish we had more initiative to map out this rotting wilderness. Does it ever seem to you like our country is oblivious to the world outside its borders?" Tolrin looked up at Mink poker-faced.

Mink knew from his father's work that a little dissent toward Octernal could make big trouble. He suspected a test of some sort. "I dunno. We have plenty of classes on the rest of the world. Other cultures, languages, and stuff. I think it's all right that we know ourselves better. We should be more concerned with our own, I think. The wilderness is what it is."

Tolrin smiled and nodded his approval. "You're all right, Mink. So, I understand that you are the one who beat my record on the Reactionary Strategies exam. I was proud of that record. Mr. Gusky told me about you. But now I see he didn't quite tell me everything."

Mink swelled with pride. "I loved that class. It was one of the things I could actually do."

"Well, from one champion strategist to another, let me run something by you."

Mink felt the blood drain from his head. Tolrin Makunam was about to ask him for advice?

"You've said this thing we're after is as big or bigger than the Main Cameral building, two miles below the surface, and underneath a very large ore deposit, right?"

"Yessir."

"Lieutenant Jannri and I came up with an idea that uses only forty-six people to get it out of there. If this thing is what you say it is, anyone in close proximity should become more powerful. That being the case, we estimated only four Soil users would be needed as follows: One on the geode to widen the opening from inside the cavern. One on the surface to widen the opening from above. And two to Materialize Soil under it, providing leverage for the Body users to lift from underneath."

Tolrin paused at this point to make sure Mink didn't have any questions or objections so far. Mink followed, nodding for Tolrin to continue.

"At the surface, two Wood users will build eight pulley systems, equally spaced, which will ultimately integrate with the wagon for transportation. Two Water users will be present to keep up the Wood users' strength and prevent any unwanted visitors from approaching too close.

"We will have four Lightning users, harnessed to the backs of four Air users, to Thunderstrike or Scattered Storm any uninvited guests the Water users detain. Also, four Fire users will support the Body users in the cavern. We assume your dad will be our fourth Spirit user, responsible for relaying information between the surface and cavern squads.

"There will be twenty-four Body users in all; eight to pull the Tear of God up from the surface, and sixteen if we include your mom, to lift it up while the Soil users make the next layer of support. The thing I can't figure out is what to do with all the ore in our way. It's too much for even four Fire users to melt away. What are your thoughts?"

Mink took a moment to consider everything Tolrin had just told him, referencing his experience from a few days ago. "I don't know about the Spirit users communicating from surface to cavern. My dad had to break off Silent Signal Fire because of some kind of interference from the geode. You might have different results, since my lack of an Element could have played a part.

"Anyway, you may want to utilize them with the Perimeter Cell to scan for potential hiding enemies using Mental Vacation. Any communication will probably need to be relayed to the Cavern Squad before they go down the hole. Would the Support Unit be available to help with getting the geode up?"

"Don't bet on it," Tolrin replied. "Our Unit is mostly strike and combat ready. At the site, we'll be stationed along the edge of Rift Ridge, looking for approaching Machinists. We can't let them get within weapon range, if they show."

"Then," Mink continued, "I suggest the Air users start in the cavern so they can put the Featherweight effect on the geode and any exposed ore. You're going to want them and the Lightning users empowered by it anyway. That will free up eight Body users from the lifting to remove the ore. My mom dug straight up through it."

"Good point." Tolrin was impressed. "Very good point. That settles it then."

"You did all the heavy lifting on this one, sir. I just stood on top of your plan."

Tolrin groaned at Mink's pun, then clapped his shoulder. "When it's just the two of us, call me Sneak," Tolrin said, using his thornball nickname.

Mink felt a rush, suddenly remembering he was in the presence of the man he wanted to become when he was a kid. He started to gush, "You know, I used to go to all your—"

"Don't lose your cool, man." Tolrin held his hand up in front of Mink's face. "We have a few more things to discuss."

Mink collected himself from the walls. "All ears."

"Can you make any sense of these maps? Enough to see which way you came back?"

Mink looked over the maps in turn. Some were drawn with landmarks only, and not likely to scale. Others suggested topography, but lacked enough detail to give him a sense of orientation. He saw several references to the same points of interest using different names. None of the maps covered the whole wilderness.

CHAPTER
34

A S A point of reference, Mink located the rocky outcroppings where Nyam had trained him on Quick Legs, west of the wilderness basin, along the slope that led up to Rift Ridge. From there, Mink started the process of overlapping the maps in a rough sketch of the area between their current camp and the Ridge. The foothill region took him a while to orient until he felt comfortable with his organization. Tunnel Vision and the rolling monotony of the hills skewed Mink's perception of the space on the page almost as much as the well-intentioned cartographers. The scales of the maps varied widely, but the shape of their passage became clearer as he worked.

"We are here." Mink tapped his finger on a group of topography lines meant to represent the Great Barrier Range forest in which they were camped. Then, on a defensive survey map of Rift Ridge, he circled an area a few inches away from the edge of the cliff. "This is about where we are headed. Somewhere around this area you will find the hole my mom dug out, just big enough for her and me to fit through. Directly below that is the geode. That means..." He traced to where he estimated that his family had set up camp eight days ago.

"I would have gone something close to this way getting back to the Capitol." Mink drew a line with his fingers down the plateau, through the rock formations, over the foothills to the forest line on the mountain's other side.

Tolrin indicated the area of the foothills and rocks. "Do you remember how visible Rift Ridge is from here?"

"Yeah. You can see it pretty well until you get down to these valleys. But, when you're high enough up, it's the horizon line."

"So, we'd be pretty visible from Rift Ridge if we were there?"

Mink caught Tolrin's drift. "That's true, I hadn't thought of that. One thing I noticed in my time on the ridge was how open and far the view was. I figured my parents chose that spot to get a heads-up on anyone coming that might interrupt our training exercises."

"We have this camping cover story, but I don't want to put all my faith in it," Tolrin explained. "Where's the closest line of cover along your path that we can move the wagon through quickly? Close enough that you can still keep your bearings."

Mink tried to remember what he saw that night as he blazed through the wilderness. "To the north of the foothills I remember seeing some lower, flatter land with some trees, but not like this forest. Should be right along here." Mink indicated an arc along the north of the slope approaching Rift Ridge. "We should be able to remain hidden from sight until we get just a few hours away from our destination."

"That looks like it would take us too close to the borders of Harvest. I'd rather not attract any attention from the Reeks."

"It's really not that far north. These maps don't accurately depict the scale. But that path will move through a valley, so we wouldn't be easy to spot from either Harvest or Rift Ridge. Coming at the site of the Tear of God from the northern plateau is probably a better approach anyway. By the time we're moving up the slope, any Machinist surveillance will just see a group of campers coming out of the Woods. Right?"

Torlin looked over the maps as Mink had them laid out. He seemed to focus more on the southern areas of the maps, looking for an alternative route to the one Mink proposed. Something that would take them by the Federation of Animalist Nations and still provide a suitable amount of cover. Mink didn't have to tell him that the best southern route would add a day or two. If Tolrin pressed, Mink was prepared to admit it would be safer, but he would still prefer the faster route, since they were already delayed.

"You're the guide," Tolrin declared finally, exhaling and gathering up the maps. "I'm going to trust your judgement. Hopefully we'll be able to make some faster progress tomorrow."

As Tolrin rolled up the pages, he looked at Mink. "Could you see any sign of your folks from the marker tree today?"

"Nope."

"Don't worry about them. I'll get you there as soon as I can."

"Thanks, Sneak. They knew they were in for a wait. They'll be fine." Mink tried to reassure himself more than Tolrin.

"You're welcome." Tolrin bound the maps with some twine and tucked them into a long leather sack. "And if you'd rather I use a different messenger when I need you, I can oblige."

Mink rose and leaned on the wall. "Nah. Blin's a good choice. He and I have a way of communicating efficiently, you know? Like shorthand."

"Really? Took him long enough to get you tonight."

"My fault, I guess. Heavy sleeper. He was a little too gentle trying to wake me up." Mink tried to be as convincing as possible, ignoring the residual tenderness in his ribs.

Tolrin got up and unrolled his bed, tossing Mink a knowing look. "You're aware I'm a Spirit user, right?"

"Yes, sir. I mean, Sneak. Yes. Just like my dad. He was so proud that a fellow Spirit user was the first to threepeat a championship. You shoulda heard—"

"Thank you. That's really enough for now. Oh, and, Mink." Tolrin reached up and grabbed the glow crystal that was hanging in the room. The stark white light it cast up to his face looked ominous. "Don't be too aloof. You should sleep near the group. Too many on the Team feel you think you're superior to them because of your parents' discovery and your chosen role as being the guide of the Team."

"That's not true!" Mink protested reflexively. "They all look down on me. Always have. They have no—"

"Don't interrupt me, please. I know better. They don't. Just make yourself more a part of the Team. When they saw that you had gone up the mountain to be by yourself, it started the kind of chatter I'd rather not have in my Unit. You'll be all right. Join with us, and in a day or two, they'll respect you."

CHAPTER
35

MINK HEADED back to his camping spot, making a conscious effort to hold his head up. When he made eye contact, he would smile and nod or even give a polite wave. He felt good about following Tolrin's advice, until he realized that now he appeared to be parading through camp after having just had a one-on-one consult with the Sergeant. This probably wasn't correcting his elitist reputation. A few chortles behind his back confirmed his suspicions. This was going to be harder than he thought.

Mink grabbed his lonely pack off the back of the wagon. He hadn't packed a tent and didn't feel right asking to have a cabin made. As he approached his Cell, he recognized the handiwork of Tralé and Mouké, having set up a nice cabin for Alré and Wood tents for themselves. Sapo obviously couldn't sleep in Wood, and she had her canvas tent softly lit by a muted glow crystal. Their sites appeared nicely settled in contrast to his barren lot.

Mink sat his pack down on the ground and rooted around for his bed roll and a music crystal. That should be all he would need until morning, at which time he would start the long and trying journey of leading everyone down the mountain and through the forest, to the northern foothills. He thought it possible to be in the valley before sundown. He wanted to believe that he could be with his parents the next night.

A pair of hands roughly covered his eyes and a low, grumbly voice said, "Guess who?"

Mink's heart pounded up into his throat. "Corporal Alré?"

Pulti's familiar and very welcome laugh broke through the night Air. "Corporal Alré? Oh, I got you good!"

Mink spun on his heels and stared eagerly into Pulti's face, glad to see her. "Pulti! What are you doing here?" He gave her a quick hug.

She pushed back and flexed both of her arms. He noted she was dressed in her usual baggy sweater and pocket pants with permanent wrinkles. "Fourteenth strongest Body user under twenty-five, thank you very much."

"That's great! Are you in my Unit?"

"I'm in the Extraction Unit, Surface Squad, Pull Cell. Cool people. Fun times."

"Trade ya."

"Yeah, right. So, is this what you and Dreh were doing in the Capitol?"

Mink realized that it was yesterday she spoke of, and yet it seemed so long ago. Was it really just the night before that he'd last seen Pulti? She seemed so different then, so much more feminine. And here she was, back to her regular tomboyish self. He could scarcely believe that it had been that morning when he woke up so hungover. Thinking about it all made him suddenly tired. However, before he fell asleep, he had to tell his friend about what had happened over the past few days.

"Yeah, Dreh had to give me a lift. My mom and dad are still out there at the site. To get me to the capitol in time, my mom put the Quick Legs effect on me."

"No way! Wait. You're lying. Dreh took you."

"I would have made it by myself, but Blin stopped me and Thoy canceled the effect. That's when I went to Dreh and had him take me the rest of the way."

"That's insane. How did she do that? I want to try." Pulti mumbled through the Quick Legs chant, counting syllables distractedly with her fingers.

"I wish I could remember. It would make me feel more useful." Mink's good humor started to darken, so he deflected the attention to her. "Do you have Quick Legs now? How do you walk with it active?"

"That's hard. I'm always concentrating on that. Part of the trick is not flexing your toes. That's where the big push comes from. If you lift from the heel and curl your toes before they touch, the effect is weak enough to maintain a walking pace." Pulti ran around Mink so fast that she caused his hair to spin around his head. If he blinked, he might not have seen her move at all. "I've had it going for six months. I'm maintaining about three effects right now."

"Yeah. My mom usually keeps several going..." Mink trailed off, marveling at how it would be to have effects like Quick Legs, Regenerative Cells, and Tunnel Vision be his normal way of being.

"What was it like for you? To have those effects?" Pulti's eyes twinkled in the dark of night, excited by her friend's break-through experience.

Mink smiled, brightening. "Incredible."

She nodded, sharing his enthusiasm. "Back to your story. What did you do to Blin? He seemed really upset at the party."

"I went to kick him off of me and Quick Legs must've sent him flying into the training equipment. I didn't stick around to see how bad it was."

"You kicked him with Quick Legs, huh? You must've gone flying yourself." Pulti laughed, clearly experienced with what Quick Legs kicks could do.

"Anyway, Dreh took me to the Capitol so I could get my dad's message to the High Council. They went all heavy with the politics and after I answered a few questions, they let me go. Dreh brought me straight to the party and I guess you know the rest from there."

The two of them sat down next to Mink's pack, facing each other. Pulti shrugged and cocked a smile at Mink. "I really don't remember much of the party. After you came down from the stage and we went inside, I draw a blank."

"You're doing better than me. I thought you Body users could handle the effects of nutty better than that."

"But that's no fun at a party. I Dispel my resistance to loosen up more."

Mink was hit with another wave of sleepiness, and decided to change the subject. "I'm glad at least you're coming on this camping trip with me. It'd be great if Dreh were here, too."

"Yeah." Pulti leaned back on her hands. "Rots that we're split up like this. What was it like talking to the High Council? That sounds like serious business."

As he chronicled the High Council's process, Mink caught sight of Gyov sitting by her Cell about twenty yards down the path. He struggled with words as he continued recounting his story to Pulti. He couldn't believe his luck! How on Georra had Gyov wound up here? She waved and then made a flattening motion with her hand before shrugging and alternating between thumbs-up and thumbs-down. So she was the one who prepped his campsite, and maybe even protected his claim. Dizzy with a flood of raging emotions, Mink gathered his senses enough to turn his shock into playing it cool. He smiled and gave her a thumbs-up. Pulti followed his line of sight and looked at Gyov for a couple of seconds before positioning herself closer to Mink and directly facing him.

"Continue," she urged him.

CHAPTER
36

THE NEXT morning, a layer of dew clung to Mink. Before she left for the night, Pulti had thickened his skin to help him tolerate sleeping without shelter, using a modified version of the Implant chant, called Scaling Shell. She had added specifications that made the Materialized skin grow in fat, overlapping scales that were waterproof, held heat, and lessened the blow of physical attacks.

Now he looked like a tikrut, a reptilian beast of burden. A wet tikrut. With hair. Pulti had offered to share her tent instead, but after Mink's talk with Tolrin, he thought it best to stick with his Guide Cell and start the day off with them. Pulti had promised to be back early in the morning to restore his normal appearance. But so far, there was no sign of her.

The aroma of breakfast being prepared wafted up the campsite and reached somewhere deep inside Mink's empty stomach. He stored his bedroll back inside his bag, stuffed his music crystal in his pocket, grabbed a couple more music crystals out of his pack, and sat in front of the Guide Cell's Radiated logs to try and remove the sheen of dew. Had he been hungrier when he left his house the previous morning, he might have thought to pack some of his own food.

"Festering piles of the grotesque!" Tralé emerged from his Wood tent, laying eyes on Mink's new look. "Good morning, Mink. What happened to you?" Before he could respond, Tralé knocked on his brother's tent. "Mouké, you have got to see this."

"Two seconds," Mouké called from inside.

"Morning, guys." Mink tried sheepishly to explain his condition, "My friend helped me out because I didn't have a tent. I'm just waiting for her to get back and Dispel the effect so I can go eat."

"Whoa!" Mouké stepped out, gawking. "That's a good look on you, Mink."

"Thanks. I could get used to it." He tried to keep in good humor as he scanned the now bustling campsite for Pulti. He had no choice but to roll with his condition.

"I could go grab you a plate, man," Tralé offered. "What d'ya want? Grubs, grasses, or beetles?" The three of them shared a laugh. "I'm just messing with you. I've seen Scaling Shell before. That hottie from last night did this to you?"

"Yeah, Pulti. She's a Body user."

"I bet she is," Mouké commented. "She didn't stick around until morning? Just like a woman."

"It's not like that," Mink protested.

"Why not? Not your type?" Tralé looked at Mink like he was crazy.

"I grew up with her, you know? She's like my sister."

"Same thing with me and my fiance. Those can be the best relationships," Mouké advised.

Mink wasn't sure how to respond.

"Ever have a girlfriend?" Tralé asked.

"No."

"Tragic waste of youth," Mouké exclaimed. "You don't go around looking like that all the time, do you?"

Mink chuckled and raised his hands, flexing his fingers and watching how the scales slid over each other. "No, it's just, you know, I don't have an Element. So…"

"So what?" Mouké pressed.

"It's not exactly a turn-on."

Tralé put his weekend bag over his shoulder. "You need to leave that up to her to decide. Whoever she may be. Don't reject yourself."

"Yeah, man. And get some moisturizer."

"Okay. Thanks." Mink felt better for his little talk with the twins, despite his embarrassment. The conversation happened without his even trying, and he felt closer to them for it.

"Just stay here. I'll be right back with some food. Come help me carry, Mouké."

"Yes, dear."

"Bring me a plate, too!" Sapo called from inside her tent.

The twins started down the camp toward the wagon, Mouké calling over his shoulder to Sapo. "We'll bring you food, if you dry Mink off."

Sapo's head poked out of her tent and she stared blankly at Mink. "I didn't do it. The dew, I mean."

"I know."

"It's the cold Air from the north. Now, close your eyes and mouth or they'll dry out."

Mink shut his eyes and turned back toward the logs. He didn't know how much of his conversation with the twins she had heard. He played it back over in his mind just to be sure nothing too incriminating was mentioned. Sapo began her elided Extraction chant, Dehydrate,

> "I remove the target's Water.
> Its moisture gathers before me.
> I continue to pull it out.

The target becomes very dry.
I can only take what I need.
The effect ends when I step back.
By Floth, I absorb all of it.
Extract Water upon my spit."

As soon as Mink heard Sapo's spit hit the ground behind him, he felt dry. Chapped, in fact. Without moisture, his thick, scaly skin fought the slightest movements. He could feel static build up in his clothes and the breeze blew his hair into tangles.

"You can open your eyes now," Sapo said.

Mink would have thanked her for her help, had his cheeks not threatened to crack upon opening his mouth.

"I don't think it's a problem, by the way," Sapo said.

"I'm sorry, what?" Mink managed to mumble.

"Not having an Element. It's not a bad thing, in my opinion. Most guys I've dated have been so focused on Elements, they can't relate to me as a person."

Mink twisted around to face Sapo, feeling very much the wrinkly, reptilian old man.

"Don't worry," she clarified. "You're too young for me. Just wanted to tell you that not having an Element can work to your advantage."

Mink and Sapo shared several seconds of awkward silence. As much as Mink appreciated her vote of confidence, he wasn't sure how to respond to her advice. Her demeanor was so dry and matter-of-fact that he wondered if she would continue. Would it be rude to express relief at their mutual lack of romantic interest? Or should he thank her for the encouragement, even though he felt a bit insulted by her presumption that he would never discover his Elemental affinity?

"Besides," she said at last. "You look like rot right now." And with that, she disappeared back into her tent and tied it closed.

Mink creaked back around to face the Radiated logs. Where on Georra was Pulti? Before long, he would have to lead the group forward, and he certainly preferred not to do it in this condition. Tolrin was a Spirit user, so he could cancel the effect, but Mink couldn't imagine walking through camp now to find him. If there was a plus side, it suddenly occured to Mink that no one was Eavesdropping on him, or else the Sheilding Scales would have already been canceled, since Spirit effects removed Body effects. He liked knowing he could think about whatever he wanted.

As he waited for Pulti and the twins to return, Mink thumbed a music crystal. His thick skin muted a noticeable amount of the mid-range frequencies, so he rubbed one facet after another, tuning to find a song that would play. Soon enough, the twins came hiking back up to the camp carrying plates piled with food on Wood trays they had probably just Materialized. Joining them was a guy Mink hadn't seen before.

"This is Theen," Tralé introduced Mink to the dark skinned, chubby fellow with short black hair who waddled up from behind. "Theen, somewhere under all that is Mink." Tralé gestured to the monstrous looking humanoid slumped over the crystal that he rubbed in his hands.

"Pleased to make your acquaintance," Theen lisped as he failed to smooth down a cowlick. Wide-eyed, he asked "Did you really see the Tear of God?"

"Yes. It's quite massive," Mink replied with effort.

"That's cool." Theen lost himself in thought.

"You've taken a turn for the worse, I see," Tralé remarked, referencing Mink's increasingly parched look, while handing him a plate off the tray. "Theen is a Spirit user in the Scout Cell. He's agreed to help you."

Mouké slid a plate through Sapo's tent flap before taking two to Alré's cabin. An older man opened the door and took them in. Theen nodded to the guy and waved without being noticed.

"That's my Corporal, I mean, Camp Counselor. Ankrim. He's cool. He's a really good Spirit user. After we get back, he's going to give me some private instruction," Theen beamed. "And he doesn't come cheap, I can assure you."

"That's wonderful, Theen." Mink grew impatient, unsure if he could manage to eat with his face still scaly. "You have an effect in mind for canceling the Scaling Sheild?"

"Uh… Oh. Right. I got one." Rehearsing his rhythm, Theen repeated vowels in the light, slow voice of a Spirit user. Mink wondered how someone with a lisp, who still needed to practice before chanting, could be ranked high enough to be part of this mission. He didn't even say the word Spirit properly. Finally, Theen started his chant,

> *"Believe in the lie I tell you.*
> *Open your mind unto me.*
> *Your bending will made mine then firm.*
> *Upon uttered 'truth' you know. Truth."*

Mink had no idea what effect Theen was trying to implement. It sounded like a custom version of a much longer chant. Inspiration or Persuasion, perhaps? Immediately, Mink's appearance was restored. Theen managed to acheive the effect with only thirty-two syllables and didn't even use any specification, limitation, or apostrophication! Shortcuts were frowned upon by traditionalists, and considered unreliable at best. Yet, the proof was right in front of Mink's eyes. Perhaps developing shortcuts was a way for Theen to overcome his speech impediment. Still, he would need a formidable amount of power to direct an effect without using the full range of syllables.

"Theen, that was amazing." Mink stood up to confirm that his whole Body was back to normal. "My dad's a pretty good Spirit user and I don't think he could have done a better job."

Theen's eyes glistened appreciatively. "Honest?"

"Absolutely." Mink crammed half a slice of sweet toast in his mouth. "And he's an Intelligence Operative. You need some serious skill for that."

CHAPTER
37

TRALÉ STOOD by, balancing trays of untouched food on his arms, watching Mouké Manipulate both of their Wood tents. One had been flattened out into a sixteen-by-four foot rectangle. The other, Mouké held on the far side while vying for Mink's attention.

"Mind giving me a hand with this?" Mouké called out.

"What do you need me to do?" Mink rushed over to the twins, still clutching his own plate.

"Take that end and help me flip this onto the middle of the big board there." Mouké indicated for him to take hold of the front of the tent.

Setting his plate on the ground, Mink put one end of the rope sausage in his mouth and chewed it hands-free. The Wood the twins had Materialized was much lighter than Mink was expecting. Mouké probably could have positioned it without any help. The two of them placed the top of the tent down on the other flattened tent.

Mouké directed, "Hey, Theen! Get the rest of your Cell and tell them to eat with us. Plenty of room."

Theen tottered off to gather his Cell as Mink watched Mouké open the floor of the tent and curl it up and over both sides. He folded the back wall down, cupping it tightly to the edge of the flattened tent, and then did the same with the front wall that Mink had been stabilizing. No longer needed, Mink reclaimed his breakfast, eating savory bulbs and watching the tent's transformation. Mouké systematically walked down the middle of the overturned tent, smoothing and contouring the curled floor into sixteen petals, eight on either side.

"Think I should have reminded Theen to use Silent Signal Fire?" Mouké mused, looking over his handiwork.

"He can't," Tralé answered. "I wanted him to try that on Mink from down at the wagon, but he said he can't find a way to change the phonetics to make it work with his lisp. He can only do about six effects because of it."

"Really?" Mouké shrugged passively, but Mink grew more impressed with Theen's ability. "All right, Mink. Wipe your hands and help me flip this over. I don't want you getting grease all over it."

Mink obliged, and as they settled it back on the ground he realized Mouké had just made a breakfast table. The top was covered with dirt and leaves, so Mink didn't know why Mouké was worried about a little bit of grease. Before sitting, Mouké cleaned the surface off with his hands, rubbing the dirt onto his forearms vigorously. Tralé wasted no time arranging the food around the table and playfully moving it away from each place Mouké sat. Mink waited until the plate of spicy meat chips had stopped moving and sat closest to it.

"Hey, Sapo! Wanna come eat at the table?" Tralé shouted over Mink's head in the direction of her cloth tent.

The seats Mouké had fashioned were remarkably comfortable, evenly distributing Mink's weight and encouraging proper posture without a chairback. Mink pulled his plate closer and gnawed on his bread while Sapo emerged from her tent and strode up to the table, holding her already empty plate. She wore billowy yellow pants and a light pink field jacket, its array of pockets and padding enhancing her femininity. That's when Mink realized everyone had changed their clothes, except for him.

"Sapo? Can I use your tent to change my clothes before you pack it up?"

"Uh, no." Sapo laughed at Mink in that way that telegraphed she hoped he was kidding. "That's my bubble. I don't let people in my bubble."

"You can use Alré's cabin before I Dispel it," Mouké offered.

Mink nodded his thanks and nursed his rejection by sopping up yolk with sausage. When Corporals Alré and Ankrim came to the table, they carried all their gear slung over their shoulders and empty plates in hand, looking less than excited to be joining the group. Alré settled her pack in front of her and laid her head down with eyes closed.

Mouké waved a come-on-over to someone behind Mink, reminding him that they were expecting company. He looked over his shoulder to see Theen struggling up the hill, leading the big guy who had helped Alré the day before, and a girl Mink hadn't met. And Gyov! Her chestnut hair had been braided on either side of her head, complimenting her golden complexion and nicely framing her face. She looked straight into Mink, setting his insides astir in a frenzy of drumming and dancing.

"I got everybody." Theen huffed as he caught his breath.

He introduced the pair as Obyr and Frèni. As they all said their hellos, Obyr sat to Mink's left and, much to Mink's delight, Gyov sat to his right. Obyr's massive frame took up more than his fair share of table space. He quizzed Mink skeptically about the mission.

"How can you be so sure what you saw was actually a Tear of God?" Obyr asked, paying more attention to his breakfast than Mink. "You don't even have an Element. What do you know?"

"Not much else it could be. It does have an—"

"We're all wasting our time," Obyr cut him off, chewing. He looked around the table, declaring, "There are no such things as Tears of God. It's superstition and rot." Mink knew he represented the attitude of a great many Octernalians, that common sense would say the Book of Origin was a made-up fable meant to explain Elemental relationships. Obyr rattled on, but Mink was too pleased by Gyov's close proximity to take proper offense.

Gyov rolled her eyes privately at Mink, unable to get a word in edgewise. She tried to contribute, but Obyr was on a roll. Mink acknowledged her attempts with a smile. He felt proud of how calm he remained while sitting next to the perfect girl, close enough to feel the warmth of her leg against his. Still, it took special effort not to spill as he poured himself some kwona, visibly shaking the drink from the pot into his bowl. At last, Tralé got up from his position at the table, sat directly in front of Obyr, and started a full-blown argument.

"I've always been curious about something," Tralé interrupted. "How do you guys completely dismiss the religious nature of Elementalism when you, Obyr, invoke Curpo or even Symg, in your apostrophication?"

"Elementalism is scientific. Not religious," Obyr countered. "The resonance of the affinity, chemicals generated by the brain while speaking certain words with specific syllables, and basic physics all make the effects happen. There's no magic. No God. No superstition. To hold on to such nonsense prevents growth. It keeps you from truly understanding the Elemental work you are doing."

Tralé took advantage of Obyr stopping for Air. "Wrong. By denying your God, you're underdeveloped. You can't reach your full potential because you don't understand where the true power is coming from!"

"I'm the best Body user in our age group! You think I don't understand true power?!" Obyr seemed to puff up an extra twenty percent in size.

The debate raged on, excluding anyone unwilling to shout to be heard. No longer a part of the audience, Gyov leaned in close enough that Mink could smell her shampoo. "Do you remember me?" she whispered in her seductive Pashmeetan accent.

Remember her?! The previous school year, he had memorized her schedule so that he could pass by her at least once a day. "I'm not sure what you mean," he said, feigning a protective nonchalance. "From the party the other night? I'm sorry, but a lot of it is a blank for me."

"I'm Gyov, yeah? We had some same classes together when I first moved to Floth. You were the first one to show me around and be nice to me. We used to eat lunch together. Kinda like this."

Mink was amazed that Gyov would remember him from when they were kids. When they first met, he had admired how she overcame being an outsider who barely knew the language. She inspired him to persevere in spite of his own feelings of not belonging. No matter how much she was ridiculed, her attitude remained cheery and optimistic. However, she grew quickly in the use of her Elemental skills. Over time, Mink felt less and less on equal footing with her.

"Oh. Sure, I remember. Third grade. In sixth grade we had Pre-Logistics together." Mink caught his jaw twitching involuntarily. Of course he remembered those days. By then he had only failed Elemental Affinities three times. There was still plenty of hope that he would function normally. But as the years passed, Gyov's attention drifted away, along with the likelihood that he had an Element.

Gyov knocked a fist on the table. "Right. Ms. Cruchlè's class. Oh! I hated that class. So boring."

Mink nodded and laughed with her, but his mind was trying to play catch-up on this trip down memory lane with his heart's desire. "Not one of my favorites, either. So, what happened to you? How have you been since then?"

"Oh! Busy like you wouldn't even believe. My Soil classes have been interesting because I have permission to go to instructors that speak Pashmeetan so I can learn chants in my native tongue. Only not so much of a need in Floth, so I have small class. No slacking in small class I can tell you. Big benefit is I get very good with Soil and now am drafted here. With you." Gyov leaned her shoulder into Mink's arm and smiled.

CHAPTER

38

M INK SMILED back and blushed. Gyov's attractive accent
and her struggle with proper Octernalian only endeared
her to him more. To maintain his cool, he acted like he was
checking in with the Obyr-Tralé debate, nodding in mock interest. Really, he was much more focused on how to capitalize on
this first conversation with Gyov in at least five years.

"Of all the tens of thousands of years of scientific studies
tracking Materialization on a vibrational level, not one shred of
evidence points to a God behind it." Obyr closed his argument
by popping a shred of cheese into his mouth that stood for the
lack of evidence.

"That's because the very act of Materialization through vibration is the evidence of God." Tralé held his head in disbelief
that he should even have to explain such concepts.

"All you faith-nuts say the same rotting thing. The vibration results in an Element, not a God. Therefore, evidence that
the Elements exist." Obyr leaned across the table with two fingers from each hand inches away from Tralé's nose. "Two plus
two will never equal brown."

"Regardless, if you want to dispute the evidence, it's just like Traucher Dowk said, 'non-existent proof does not prove non-existence,'" Tralé said, casually sweeping Obyr's hands out of his face. Obyr leaned back and laughed.

Mink's split attention divorced from the debate to focus fully on Gyov. Committed to taking a risk, he admitted, "I miss having classes with you. When I couldn't take any Elemental courses, I really felt like everyone went on without me, you know? I've just been filling up my schedule with all the elective classes I can. I don't have more than one class with anyone."

"Is that why you always look so sad?" Gyov's eyes locked on to Mink's.

"Excuse me?" Mink, suprised by her being so direct, leaned away from Gyov enough for Obyr to elbow him out of his space. "What makes you think I'm sad?"

"I notice. I have confession. Every day at school I walk by you, hoping you remember me and talk to me."

It was almost too much to hear, coming straight out of Gyov's mouth as if they were going over answers for a test. Mink's face reddened, then tears backed up in his eyes. She was hoping he would talk to her? Daily?

Mink wiped his face with both hands in a hurry. "Whew. That sausage is hotter than it looks." He looked back at Gyov, who now seemed so serious he had to smile big to snap her out of it. "I'm not sad. Maybe that's just how I look."

"Did my confession upset you? I don't want you to think I stalk you or something."

"No, no. Not upsetting. Don't worry about it. Just a little surprised is all."

"Oh dear. I have upset you. You think I'm weird now and won't like me." She gave Mink a playful pout and a huff, going back to eating and giving him sidelong looks.

"What?" For the first time, Mink was starting to think Gyov was a little weird. In a good and fun way, he had to admit to himself. "I do like you."

There it was, hanging in the Air like a Fire user's Flame Ghosted Candle, Mink's professed undying love for Gyov, only not in quite so many words. He watched her pout turn to a giggle. She pretended to tuck her hair, already braided, behind her reddening ear. Her eyes met his and then traced down his face to his mouth, watching his lips as he continued.

"I like you a lot, actually." Mink refused to let the moment slip away. She would not fade from him again. To have returned to him now, like this… "I went out of my way to see you at school."

"You should have said 'hi', or something."

"I should have. From now on, I promise I will."

As they ate in the comfortable silence that followed, Mink reveled at the recent developments of his life while Obyr, Tralé, Frèni, and Corporal Ankrim argued Theology and Science in the background of his awareness.

"Then, please," a debate-weary Tralé countered, "explain to me the scientific facts behind the Dedication Dream."

With this, both Alré and Ankrim, the only two at the table to have had a Dedication Dream, shot to attention. Obyr shrugged off Tralé's challenge with a smirk. "Simple power of suggestion. By the time anyone turns twenty-five, they've heard so much about the Dream, they're bound to have one." Tralé threw up his hands and continued to eat. Obyr went on, "A lot of people can't even remember their Dream. Even if memory of a dream was reliable. Everyone just keeps repeating what they've heard all their lives."

Ankrim leaned toward Obyr with an eerily calm authority. "Until you've had a Dedication Dream, you have no right to form an opinion on them."

Obyr's silence relayed his discomfort at challenging his direct superior, but Frèni offered up some defense as Alré plopped her head back on her bag. "I think Obyr has some good points. We Elementalists certainly aren't any better off holding on to echoes of bygone religions. And we aren't any worse off for abandoning them." No one seemed interested in responding to Frèni's late interruption in the debate. "After bringing the nations together, our founding mothers refused to build temples for a reason. Different Elemental types needed to get out of hiding and mingle for us to progress as a society."

Theen added his voice. "All of this debate is pointless. In a couple of days we'll have a Tear of God or we won't. Then we'll know."

Undeterred by anyone else's doubt, Mink held his own opinion on the Tear of God. He had seen it. Now he was preoccupied by more relevant matters. Mink's whole attitude toward life seemed to have changed drastically, even just in the last minute. Food tasted better. He, the boy with no Element and a loser by such standards, had unburdened his heart to its desire, and here she remained beside him. A few inches closer, even.

"Hey, Mink," Mouké called from the end of the table. "I'm going to get a head start on cleaning up camp. Wanna change clothes now?"

Mink went to rise and realized he was semi-erect, with no way of hiding the protrusion as he walked in front of everyone. "Uh… do I have time to finish breakfast?" he stalled.

"Well, be snappy about it. Can't have everyone waiting on the Guide Cell."

Mink engrossed himself in last of the debate. He repeated every word in his mind enough times to push out any echoes of Gyov's voice. If only Alré would wake up and join the discussion, he might be turned off enough to get up and change his clothes.

"I'm not saying I don't think massive power exists in the world." Obyr seemed to be calming down. "I just think it's limiting and even damaging to think it comes out of the ether. Out of our control."

"Really?" Tralé had grown much more concerned with his food. "I think it's dangerous to think it's something you can control."

Obyr shrugged and started talking more to himself than anyone else. "You're obviously not the best Wood user under twenty-five then."

Tralé shot a smile and a wink to Mouké, who raised an eyebrow and bowl of kwona in salute. Albeit slowly, Mink was less aroused, continuing to buy some time by picking at his plate.

"That's snappy?" Mouké complained. "Mink, I'd hate to see you in slow motion. Are you going to use the cabin or not? I want to get the camp cleaned up so we can start clearing a path." Somewhere in Mouké's pressing, Mink's crisis was averted. He scraped the last of the food off his plate and into his mouth. He chewed while he hurried to fetch his clothes from his pack, and headed into the cabin.

It was more spacious than it looked on the outside. Vent holes for Air and light were situated high on each of the eight walls. Under each vent, the wall was adorned with the Elemental symbol that correlated to the direction the wall faced. Devoid of Alré and Ankrim's belongings, there was only one four-post bed pushed against the far wall, complete with a latticed headboard. This was just how Tralé and Mouké operated.

It felt so good to wear fresh clothes. Mink brushed his dry, tangled hair as best he could with no mirror or glass. This was perhaps the first time he was thankful that his face only managed to grow hairs on his lip and chin. Not having shaved for at least ten days was making him scruffy. His obsidian razor had been chipped slightly, but retained enough of a workable edge to get the job done. A quick rub of leaf oil on his face confirmed that he hadn't cut himself, and left a lingering spicy, sweet scent.

He wanted to appear the handsome suitor when he emerged from the cabin for Gyov to see. People had told him this shade of blue on his jacket was particularly flattering to his complexion. The pockets on his arms made them look bigger, even if they were useless for storing anything other than small crystals. The chest pockets had a similar effect, especially when he left the top three hooks unfastened.

He also wore a flesh colored mock-turtleneck and his only pair of zip pants, which were a gift from his parents for his sixteenth birthday. Zippers, fashioned from natural Wood, were rare on clothes, and these pants had eight of them. The pockets were internal so all that could be seen against the burnt-brown pants were red Wood zippers. Upon close inspection, the growth rings, indicative of natural-grown Wood, lined up perfectly when zipped up. His parents had spared no expense.

After lacing up his boots, Mink felt quite attractive indeed. If only he had some bronzer to darken his skin to a manlier shade like his Uncle Durren's, but no matter. Chin high and chest out, Mink strode from the cabin with his winningest smile.

Mouké was the only one to see. The table had been Dispelled and everyone was settling into formation down the trail. Impatiently, Mouké tossed Mink's pack to the ground by his feet.

"Man, Mink. You take all day for everything, don't you?"

"Can't rush perfection." Mink shrugged off the disappoinment, still high on his conversation with Gyov, and stuffed his old clothes into his pack.

"Well, Mr. Perfection, Tralé's waiting for you down on his scooter. I'll be the last one ready because I had to wait on you before Dispelling the cabin. Perfection..." Mouké continued to mutter to himself sarcastically before he chanted the Wood user's Dispel effect, Unroot,

> *"Atriarb undoes the effect.*
> *Take back the power which you gave."*

He reached out to the cabin, which subsequently vibrated only a couple of seconds until it had completely disappeared. According to the order in which each aspect vanished, Mink observed that the twins had built the roof first, raised it with walls, made the bed an extension of one wall, and then finished with the floor. "Sorry for holding you up, Mouké. And thanks for letting me use the cabin." Mink shouldered his bag and set off down the the slope to the trail.

"Don't worry about it. And don't forget to put your pack on the wagon!" Mouké yelled after him.

CHAPTER
39

MINK WOVE his way down the trail toward the wagon. The rest of the Cells were Dispelling their campsites, packing their bags, and falling back into formation. He got a sense that some of the looks he received were positive and some negative, but it only mattered to him now what one person thought. And she seemed to like him. The realization was so freeing.

Bag secured on the wagon, Mink jogged up to the front of the procession. The sun had risen well over Octernal on the eastern horizon, having burned off the cool morning mist that fed the mountain trees. He waved and caught Pulti's attention as he passed her cell. She did a double take and looked him over, probably shocked to see him wearing his better clothes on this kind of a trip. She waved back, giving him a thumbs-up. Mink welcomed her endorsement, figuring if Pulti was impressed, Gyov surely would be too.

It occured to Mink as he came up on Gyov's Strike Cell, that he had no idea what decorum applied to passing by her after their breakfast confessional. He wouldn't ignore her as he might have done two hours ago. It couldn't hurt to wave like he had to Pulti, but he felt like he should do more for Gyov. He caught sight of the back of her braided head on the edge of the path as she looked out toward their country. Instead of calling out, Mink saved it for later and caught up with his Cell.

Mouké reached his scooter a few seconds before Mink made it to Tralé's. Alré was looking down the line of campers, likely reconnecting with Silent Signal Fire. Sapo slid restlessly behind Alré, noticing Mink as he got situated on the scooter. She smiled at him and nodded approvingly, and then she spun a tight circle, fanning out her pants in style.

"Looks like you found your energy, at least." Tralé looked at Mink with a half smile.

"Yessir. I'm awake now."

"Too bad it took so long. You and I might have crested the moutain by now." He turned around and started chanting to Animate the pergnut trees ahead using the March Root effect,

> *"Wood appears to have life with me.*
> *I make it move, fight, bend, and dance.*
> *My hands implement my intent.*
> *I use the target like a tool.*
> *It remains separate from me.*
> *I cannot kill my Element.*
> *I control as Atriarb does.*
> *Animate as soon as I reach."*

Tralé resumed yesterday's work, reaching toward trees with solid intent and pushing them out of the way to the left, branches knocking against each other and roots cracking their way through the land. Mink, still distracted by thoughts of Gyov, looked over his shoulder to see if she might be looking at him. Gyov and Frèni were positioning themselves in front of the wagon, readying for the continuation of the procession. She winked as soon as he caught sight of her and mouthed the words "nice pants." Mink signaled his thanks and smiled. A dozen of the Scout and Strike Cells members tightened up their formation, blocking Gyov from view.

He turned his attention once more to the gouging of trees through the dirt. Alré watched the progress impatiently from a couple of steps behind, waiting for enough clearance to allow them to move on. She glanced back at the wagon and finally made her way forward to Mouké's scooter.

By the time Alré positioned herself on the back, the twins had moved all of the trees within their range. Sapo slid slowly backwards and side-to-side up the hill until Alré called for her to wait on the order to move. Tralé drummed his three gloved fingers impatiently on the crest, directly in front of Mink's face. Mink resisted looking back at Gyov again, not wanting to seem overly eager.

"I'll give you this much," Tralé squatted down on his scooter and looked at Mink eye-level, still March Rooting a tree off to the left with his free hand. "You've got exquisite taste in women."

Mink about lost his hold. "What are you talking about?"

Tralé smiled but didn't have a chance to answer before Corporal Alré commanded, "Let's go!"

Had he been listening to their conversation during the debate? Maybe Mink was being obvious. Ultimately, it didn't matter much, but he had hoped his personal feelings would be a little more private. Still kneeling while creeping his scooter forward, Tralé reached to the ground and plucked up a dirt clod, which he rubbed into the forearm of his driving arm. As they set off up the path, he reached for the next group of trees and dragged them off to the side. Mink remembered Gyov's face after he told her he liked her and the goofiest, head-over-heels, smitten smile spread across his face. Now that he thought more about it, he felt confident that she would be his girlfriend and everyone would know.

In a celebratory mood, Mink dug out a music crystal from his pocket and thumbed over the facets, looking for some perfect riding music. He settled on one of his favorite upbeat songs by The Thundersticks, "There's No End to Me," and resumed his grip on the handle of the scooter. The Wood must've picked up on some of the vibrations embedded in the crystal, because Tralé immediately glanced at Mink's hand.

"My, my, Mink. You've been holding out on me." Tralé used his free hand to slide open a hole by his submerged Wooden thumb. "Drop that bad boy on in there."

He dropped the crystal in and Tralé slid the opening shut. Holding onto the handles, Mink could hear the music as if he were touching the crystal directly. The songs started switching quickly from one to another, and Mink guessed that Tralé was able to move the crystal around from facet to facet with his submerged thumb. If Dreh had a way of listening to crystals in his sled like this, Mink didn't know about it.

"Here we go," Tralé beamed, settling on one of The Thundersticks' ballads, "Break it Off." He stood and continued his work of tree-moving with a cadence complimentary to the tempo of the music. "Exquisite taste, Mink. Exquisite." He felt validated by Tralé's approval. Maybe he did have some things in common with these people.

Tralé's pick wasn't a song Mink would've chosen, but it matched his mood all the same. The landscape danced for the rest of the climb. Trees swayed and shook their leaves. The grasses rippled on the plains spreading to the western wall of Eternsa. A few enormous clouds hovered to the north, aglow with sunlight that set them in stark contrast to the softening teal of the sky. They made some significant progress along the mountain beyond the steep incline Mink had climbed the previous night. Eventually, they reached a flatter approach to the top that lent itself well to the last switchback.

After the final turn, they approached the marker tree in no time. The trees closest to it had apparently been moved long ago to further isolate the chosen pergnut tree and help travelers find it. The cool morning wind refreshed the group as they summitted the mountain and looked out over the expansive wilderness below. Mink's Cell rested next to the branchless side of the marker tree. Sapo leaned against the trunk, pants flapping in the wind, as Mouké parked his scooter next to his brother's. The immensity and depth of the land stretched out beyond their sight. Mink could barely see or recognize the area where he last saw his mother during his training.

Clutching the back of Tralé's scooter, Mink slipped into one daydream after another about how he might spend some time with Gyov over the course of the journey. There would surely be at least one more stop before they made camp for the night, which could afford him the opportunity to get close to her. Lost in thought, Mink suddenly recalled that they had made it to the exact spot where Blin had so rudely awakened him the night before. He pressed up against his ribs and was satisfied that they were far less tender, thanks to Pulti's healing. It was very comforting to know that she, too, would be around.

Mink squinted, but couldn't make out any specific features of Rift Ridge without the aid of Tunnel Vision. In the distant haze on the horizon, somewhere in the cavern beneath the plateau, his parents guarded an enormous crystal of formidable power. While there was still so much distance to cross before he could reach them, Mink took comfort in being able to guess where they were. His daydreams took a turn toward returning home with his parents, and finding a reason for Gyov to come with them.

CHAPTER
40

S ERGEANT MAKUNAM says you know which way to go."
Corporal Alré appeared beside Mink, taking in the view
and breaking his reverie. "He says you talked to him about it
last night."

"Yes'm, a valley ahead to the north." Mink studied the
slope of the wilderness from their vantage point. The jagged
line of the range's shadow cut the valley in two as the morning sun rose behind them to the east. Their destination sat in
enough darkness that a potential path was difficult to see.

"So, Blankey, you lead the way." Alré challenged rudely,
adopting Mink's unwanted nickname and causing him to cringe.
He caught Tralé sending a sidelong glance of disapproval to the
Corporal, encouraging him with the show of support.

Once Mink gained his bearings, he could tell that the angle of the slope heading down the opposite side of the mountain was much less steep than what they'd just traveled. It fa-
vored a long, straight downward trip to the northern side of
the basin below. The valley was difficult to see through all
of the trees surrounding it on both sides. That should make
it easier for them to go undetected. As an added benefit, the

smaller mountains to their west would soon block the view of their descent.

He indicated a line down to the left of them that hugged along the mountain. "We should head down in that direction. It'll be okay to take a direct path, don't you think?" Mink did his best to come off as someone working with others to reach a mutual agreement. The members of his Cell looked and nodded at each other, and then down at the rest of the group still making their way up the trail.

"As long as they can keep that wagon from barreling down on us, I'm cool with it. It'll be nice to head downhill for a change." Mouké stretched his back, limited by one hand partially embedded in his scooter. He and Tralé scanned their pending route to account for the number of trees they would need to move.

"So, bro, wanna race?" Tralé pressed.

"Don't I always?" Mouké looked back at Alré. "Corporal Alré, do you give us permission to get off this rotting mountain as soon as possible?"

Alré checked the distance to Rift Ridge once more. "Please do."

Without further delay, Tralé and Mouké started their scooters down the hill. They couldn't speed up their chants without rendering them ineffective, so they added specifications to March Root that would move multiple trees at once,

> *"Wood appears to have life with me.*
> *I make it move, fight, bend, and dance.*
> *My hands implement my intent.*
> *I use the target like a tool.*
> *Touching root or branch move as one.*
> *Trees stay together in a group.*
> *My reach extends through their contact.*
> *I move Wood through land like Water.*
> *It remains separate from me.*

I cannot kill my Element.
I control as Atriarb does.
Animate as soon as I reach."

Mink's hair blew on his brow as they sped down the mountain. On several occasions, he felt sure that Tralé wouldn't finish his chant in time to move the trees before they crashed into them. The speed and uncertainty added a welcome thrill to contrast with the monotony of the previous day. Mouké wove around the trenches cut by the trees as best he could, while Tralé opted for jumping them in a more direct route. Mink flinched, worried that the landings would jar him loose.

Tralé lost a bit of ground to Mouké when he got distracted searching for different music instead of March Rooting trees. Settling on "Best Step Aside," Tralé resumed his pace. Mink became personally invested in beating Mouké. He bobbed his head to the song, and helped to steer by shifting his weight on the scooter. Tralé, visibly pleased, pulled his steering hand free. They couldn't listen to music anymore with Tralé's hand detached, but the exhilaration of free falling down through the forest had a cadence all its own. The needled pergnuts became more scarce as the forest shifted to become predominately comprised of rolled-leaf specklenut trees.

Mink steered the scooter on his own by leaning left and right, past Mouké, Sapo, and a couple of trees Mouké had missed as they rushed into the forest. Using both hands, Tralé moved trees in front and behind them simultanously. They had such a commanding lead, Tralé slammed his steering hand back into the scooter, slid it to a sideways stop, moved the couple of specklenut trees he had left behind, Animated a couple of his brother's trees for him, resumed play of the music, and sent a big smile to a fuming Mouké, still sixty to seventy yards uphill.

Continuing their downhill race, Tralé further orchestrated the trees to shake to the music as he cleared them from the path. He looked back once to check his lead on Mouké and gave Mink a satisfied nod. For his part, Mink couldn't be more proud. They were going to win the race because of his contribution. This kinship with Tralé felt like the closest thing he had to his friendship with Dreh.

When they reached level ground, Tralé arranged two dozen trees into a ring which he called the Winner's Circle. Thousands of wild specklenuts littered the area. Mink guessed they would never be made into nutty like their cousins in Octernal. Sapo Slip Skated in a slalom fashion through the trees Mouké had yet to move, slowing to a stop in Tralé and Mink's circle.

"Cheaters," Mouké complained as he pulled up with Alré, who seemed to be enjoying herself for the first time. She actually seemed happy. Everyone caught their breath and laughed while they looked back up the mountain at the path they had created. Mink couldn't believe the ground they had covered and cleared. The rest of the group seemed so small making their way down with the wagon. This easily stood out as the most fun Mink had had since the party. Tralé held his hand out to Mink for a high-five, which he gladly obliged.

"We make a good team," Tralé panted, wiping sweat off his forehead. Then, with a sideways glance at Mink, he asked, "Hey, Corporal Alré? I hate to admit it, but I'm exhausted. I didn't sleep well last night and might have overdone it on the way down. Sapo's mist is nice and all, but I think I'll need some Soil, too. There's a Soil user in the—"

"Can you get to the point?" Alré barked, easily slipping back into her gruff demeanor.

"I'd like to change my scooter into a two-seater and have that Soil user in the Scout Cell help keep my energy up. Please."

"Hold on. I have to go through a few people to ask Corporal Ankrim." Alré held her hand up for everyone to be quiet.

Tralé leaned to Mink, uttering under his breath, "Don't say I never did anything for you." In anticipation, Mink backed off of the scooter while Tralé chanted the Manipulation Wood effect, Bend Form,

> *"Wood is subject to my control.*
> *I can change its shape with my mind.*
> *My power molds its destiny.*
> *Respond to me upon my reach."*

Tralé split and expanded the back of his scooter using smoothing motions with both hands. After the back had doubled, Tralé opened it up to create two adjacent seats. Then he balanced the front and back by bulking up his board and tapering the connection from the crest up to the nose. Lastly, he dropped two smaller runners under each seat.

"Okay," Alré affirmed shortly. "After they make it down here, you can borrow the Soil user until you get your strength back up."

Mink's heart leapt. He couldn't believe his luck held out, and now he would be able to ride beside Gyov! Looking up at the rest of the group, he urged them along faster in his mind. Seventy-three Team members still marched down the slope alongside the wagon, a dozen or so in front and the balance behind. Mink couldn't see Pulti, and assumed she was holding the rear bumper, while Obyr braked it from the front. Everyone except for the wagon driver still traveled on foot.

They were close enough now that he could watch Gyov and Frèni Manipulate the ground into a smooth, flat slope for the wagon by waving their hands in sweeping motions over the ground. He admired her skill and revelled that she was recognized as one of the six best Soil users of the Flothian youth. It would make him so happy to be known as any kind of Elemental user. He couldn't imagine the joy such high regard could bring.

Mink gazed down the valley to gauge how quickly they might progress through the forest there. The deep shadows played tricks on his eyes, and he found it difficult to see just how dense the Wooded area might be. It took the better part of two hours for the rest of the Team to catch up, and the sun had not yet climbed over the mountain to illuminate the valley. The Team as a whole didn't get a chance to rest more than five minutes before receiving the order to move on. Gyov had just enough time to skip her way up to Tralé's scooter and sit next to Mink with a smile that he knew meant she was as happy as he was for the new arrangement.

Riding with her right beside him turned out to be a mixed blessing due to Alré's strict adherence to silence. At least Tralé was able to play music for the three of them. While Mink would've preferred to hear Gyov's voice, sitting with her felt great all the same. They made awkward eye contact several times. If only the seats had been made so their hands could touch, but alas, there was Tralé's steering hand in-between. Besides, it was necessary for Gyov to maintain direct contact with the scooter so her energy force could transfer over to Tralé. After all, this was business, not pleasure.

The rhythmic pace of tree moving, music, and the company of Gyov all had a placating effect on Mink. Before he knew it, they had traveled deep into the valley. The passage of time showed itself in Gyov's fatigue as she continued to energize Tralé at the expense of her own vitality. It must've been getting close to lunch…

A strange smell assaulted Mink's nose and quickly grew in intensity. Try as he might, he couldn't see anything beyond the shadows of the specklenut trees clustered along the valley walls. The others made faces and noticed it, too.

"Mouké? That sausage acting up on you?" Tralé commented while waving his head, trying to avoid the onslaught.

Mink looked back and saw that their whole group was recoiling now. He thought to himself that it smelled like death when suddenly, the grim and terrifying reality struck him.

"Reeks!" Mink shouted.

Everyone froze in fearful acknowledgment. Instinctively, all Cells circled the wagon tight with eyes scanning out toward the forest. Had they passed too close to Harvest after all? To gain the attention of the Reeks was a notoriously fatal mistake. And Mink knew as well as anyone that Reeks wouldn't move upwind until they had their prey surrounded.

CHAPTER

41

THE SMELL of decay struck terror into Mink's heart like he had never known. The fact that he had experienced mortality a week ago intensified his fear, since he now knew how easily death could come. The important difference here was that if he died, he wouldn't be coming back. Embarrassingly, all he could do was sit and clutch onto Tralé's scooter. Everyone tightened up around the wagon. All eyes searched the Wooded slopes on both sides of their valley path, dreading the first sighting.

"Mink, Gyov," Tralé forced himself to speak in a soft, calm voice. "Please get up off my scooter."

They stepped down and Mink glanced up at Tralé, who stood up slowly, looking over his shoulder into the trees beyond. Mink reached out for Gyov's hand. It felt warm and sodden. He pulled her close and they scarcely breathed. Side by side, they inched away from the scooter. Tralé sat down on the footboard with his back against the upward curve. He chanted the Elemental Armor effect, Impenetrable Bark,

> *"I wear Wood just like it's clothing.*
> *Petrified, it stops all attacks.*
> *Knocking back with its own hardness.*

Attacks bounce off with no harm done.
It cannot block attacks I make.
My armor protects only me.
Atriarb holds me in her grace.
Protect me from harm when I reach."

In a smooth, whirling motion, Tralé skillfully wrapped the Wood of the scooter around himself until it fit him like a big suit of armor. It covered his arms and legs in a swirling pattern of silver and black. He extended the armor of both arms into Wooden blades, and then curved claw-like Wooden spikes around his feet. With his left hand, he pulled a helmet over his head, made of Wood extended from the upper back and neck.

Mouké had already Manipulated his own scooter into armor, his with barbed Wooden spikes on the elbows and knees, the new-growth green banding the outside of his limbs and spine. He and Tralé backed up against each other, rotating to scan the surrounding forest.

Readying her attack, Alré chanted the Shooting Star effect from behind Mouké's position,

"I punch a ball of flame with aim.
From my closed fist to my target.
My power creates the Fire.
With hit or miss, my attack stops.
Fist-sized orbs hover, burning hot.
My attack cannot do me harm.
With all the blessings from Symg.
Burn my enemy when I snap."

She snapped her fingers and five small balls of yellow flame came to life in a semi-circle before her. It took some impressive power to produce five Shooting Stars at the ready. Mink had mistaken Sapo for the defensive type, but here she was, readying her Attack chant, Waterjet,

"I blast a forceful stream with aim.
From my mouth upon my target.

> *My power creates the geyser.*
> *With hit or miss, my attack stops.*
> *Pressurized force, compressed to pierce.*
> *My attack cannot do me harm.*
> *With all the blessings from Floth.*
> *Douse my enemy when I spit."*

Sapo withheld the implementation of the chant, which Mink knew meant she was waiting for the proper time to use it.

"Mink!" Tolrin's agitated voice boomed through Silent Signal Fire inside of Mink's head. "You assured me that we wouldn't pass too close to Harvest."

"We're still way south of the border, sir. These Reeks must have already been out here for some reason."

Looking into Mink's eyes, Gyov could probably tell he was engaged in Silent Signal Fire. She backed up and started chanting in exotic Pashmeetan,

> *"Jehbayo Groocks ahtima.*
> *Kah sarillmeett dazztasho.*
> *Oongsidata baengtamee.*
> *Shodari dazztasho tisi.*
> *Kah tipatcha dazztashoma.*
> *Engsa brrisoma ahtima.*
> *Sagga ahtima Grahcks engsi.*
> *Engsa dasho ahtima uhll."*

She stomped to implement the chant, and the top Soil curled up around her like a flower bud, hardening to a dark brown clay.

Tolrin's voice returned, taking on an unfamiliar edge and putting Mink on the defensive. "'For some reason?' Hunting for more puppets, perhaps?"

"I doubt it," Mink asserted. "If they were going to hunt us, they wouldn't be holding back in the shadows. They'd have tried to disrupt the chants by now." Reeks, unlike Machinists and Animalists, were able to learn and use a few basic chants, and he would wager they understood the importance of preventing an Elemental user from implementing.

Still surrounded by the Team, the wagon in all its bulk now stretched and bent into a low fortress, with four ramparts on either side. A Wood user climbed over the pile of gear to Manipulate the structure into its new, protective shape. Even before it was completed, members of the Tear of God Unit's Perimeter Cell positioned themselves inside. The driver jumped to the top of the wall behind her, removed her gloves and helped finish the Manipulation.

Tolrin's voice pulsed inside Mink's head, making it difficult to think. "I have Jannri to answer to, Mink. I have to assure her we didn't just march everyone into a death trap."

The driver, in a continued display of impressive skill, March Rooted trees downward two at a time in a wide arc around them to increase visibility, leaving only a couple feet of the top branches protruding from the ground. Not enough for a Reek or puppet to hide behind. Tolrin stood in front of the wagon-turned-fortress with Lieutenant Jannri beside him, both of them looking furious.

Mink did his best to sound calm in his explanation. "It depends on how we greet the puppets they send. That's how they'll determine our willingness to talk. Stay with me, Sneak. I can talk us through this. I've studied as much as we know about the Reeks."

Mink saw that most of the Team had finished putting up their Elemental Armor effects, and the Team as a whole was abuzz with the chanting of Attack effects, saving implementation for the first sign of trouble. The paranoid situation had degraded from bad to worse too fast for Mink to track what was happening. Everyone must have either assumed that the Reeks were going to attack, or planned on Attacking anyway out of hatred for the Reek's abhorrent nature. The window for a peaceful resolution looked closed and locked.

"There's a time and a place, Mink. This isn't it. I am not asking for input. We are implementing a contingency plan." Tolrin's tone was distant and cool, giving Mink the feeling that he had to come up with some idea to avert disaster and regain his advisory capacity.

The Air users, each with a Lightning user harnessed to their backs, positioned themselves several feet above the Team via Sky Step. The Lightning users, having spotted the puppets all over the slopes on either side of them, chanted and then pointed, sending Thunderstrike Attacks. The Thunderstrikes served well to let the rest of the Team know where the Reeks' puppets were coming from by way of their arcing Lightning bolts.

Puppets began to show themselves to the Elementalists from the shadows, approaching en masse from all directions. At least Mink assumed they were all puppets, since Reeks rarely accosted strangers in person. Reeks were alive, with clean eyes and pink mouths but, just like their puppets, they wore masks and gloves made from the flesh of their kill. There were easily a hundred cloaks, moving slowly, hoods drawn, the edges of their thick black coats gliding along the ground. The stench grew more intense as they drew near. Puppets were far from harmless, but Mink knew it would be a waste of energy to Attack them.

The group went silent, except for two campers huddled next to the fortress. They shoved another camper around, shouting, "Now Rénys. Do it! Come on, Rénys." Whoever Rénys was and whatever effect they were after, he wasn't obliging. Jannri and Tolrin shouted for everyone to hold their effects, but all the horrified faces worried Mink. No one felt like holding back now.

CHAPTER

42

MINK WATCHED the cloaks creep down the slopes of the valley walls toward them through the tops of the submerged trees. Were they moving so slowly because the Reeks controlling them were wielding too many? Or were they strategizing to bait the Team into attacking? The Elementalists backed tightly together and Mink stood fast against Gyov's Clay Pot, but there was nowhere to go. The puppets would be on them in less than a minute.

Hoping Silent Signal Fire was still connecting him to Tolrin, Mink pleaded, "We can see how many puppets are here, but we need to figure out the number of Reeks behind them. They'll back off if we know there aren't enough of them to attack."

"And how do you suggest we do that?" Tolrin boomed back at Mink. "They're all moving the same way to prevent us from counting repeats."

If only Mink could think of a way to group the puppets, they might have a better understanding of who they faced. Since Reeks were only human after all, it made sense to Mink that they wouldn't be able to hide their thought patterns. They all looked the same on the outside, but each puppet shared the consciousness of the particular Reek controlling it.

Mink figured it'd be worth a try. "Have the Spirit users Eavesdrop on as many as possible to see how many unique thought patterns there are. Tell Soil users to use the Tracking effect to trace the puppets' paths to the point of origin."

"That would be hard for me to do under these conditions, let alone these youth. But, I follow what you're saying. Now, I need you to let us work."

The overwhelming smell of decay made it difficult for Mink to sort out just what felt wrong. There was something about the way the Elementalists were backed up against each other... He was positive that they were still too far south of Harvest for their group to have been surrounded. Since they had come down the visible side of the mountain that morning, these rotheads must have already been here. Did Reeks make a habit of wandering through the wilderness?

"Something's not right." Mink hoped thinking it out with Tolrin might dislodge his mental block.

"Oh really, Mink? You think there's something wrong here?" Sarcasm wasn't Tolrin's strong suit. "Please don't bother me. I'm trying to get a Reek count."

The cloaks were close enough now that Mink could see their faces in the shade of their hoods. They formed a wall of stench and menace three-deep. The Penbik twins went shoulder-to-shoulder, protecting Sapo and Alré. Mink knew he should have something ready, but he was weaponless and couldn't perform effects. Reeks went out of their way to disguise themselves so that no one could differentiate them from each other, or identify their gender. But, they could never disguise the dead gray of their reanimated corpses' eyes. Mink checked the faces of the figures now surrounding him and confirmed that all he could see were puppets.

Mink could hear Tolrin yelling to the Spirit and Soil users from a distance. "I need my count! Where's my count?"

The puppets took their time now, turning three rows into five as they closed in and ran out of elbow room. Their unfocused eyes and slow, random movement almost gave Mink the sense that the Elementalists were invisible to them, and yet they were specifically surrounding the Team. Suddenly, it dawned on him what had been bothering him.

"We need to separate!" Mink practically screamed into Tolrin's mind.

"Not now, Mink."

"Listen, please! Tell everyone to mingle with the puppets. Put at least one between them and the closest Team member. It will buy us some time and give us the advantage."

"Sorry, Mink. Dispelling Silent Signal Fire now."

"Tolrin Makunam! Sneak!" Mink shouted in his mind, but got no reply.

They were all sitting targets. The only way to level the field was to integrate with the cloaks. This would confuse the Reeks' vision, possibly even drawing the real ones out of hiding as they tried to regain a visual.

"I'm waiting on my count!" Tolrin reminded everyone aloud.

Tréa's voice could be heard from across the Team. "Working on it. I'm between sixteen and forty."

Another voice called out, "I'm thinking thirty-two."

"Is that confirmed?" Tolrin pressed.

"No. Give or take five."

A succession of loud cracks and flashes made Mink flinch, and his heart sank as bolts of Lighting streaked randomly into the gathering puppets. Effects reflexively went off all over the place, risking chaos. Alré rushed the group closest to her, punching balls of flame, causing minature explosions of Fire whenever they struck upon contact, and sending three figures up in flames. The Penbik twins stabbed and cut with the sharp and pointy edges of their armor.

Waste of energy! Puppets were already dead, only their movements could be disabled. Sapo spat out a sharp stream of Water straight ahead, bisecting every rotten head and torso in her range. Effects happened so fast that by the time orders came to stop Attacking, the first row of puppets had been successfully maimed.

Still, the horde held its ground. Those that could walk continued their leisurely pace towards the Team. Others pulled themselves along with their arms. Mink counted twelve puppets that had been completely immobilized. He didn't bother counting how many of them were damaged in the Attacks, but he could tell there were plenty as yet untouched. Not one had so much as lifted a finger in defense.

Mink couldn't keep quiet any longer. After that kind of reception, the chances of avoiding an onslaught from the Reeks were slim. He had to act. He rushed into the ranks of puppets yelling, "Everyone mix in! Now! Put at least one between you and the other campers!" Those close enough to hear him regarded him skeptically. "Just do it! Before they attack. You have to split up and get in their groups!" Mink brushed his way into the thick of the mob, who didn't turn a lifeless eye his way.

The cloaks had crept near enough now that there wasn't much choice for the outer Cells. Tralé was the first to comply with Mink's orders. That was enough for Sapo and Mouké to follow. Alré didn't move, and Gyov's Clay Pot wasn't going anywhere but she was safe enough inside.

Some of the Scout Cell repositioned themselves in the throng, but Obyr rebelled by kicking a puppet with his Demolition Attack effect. The top half and its cloak sailed high over the trees, falling somewhere back in the forest while the lower half dropped to its knees. Obyr scowled defiantly at Mink.

"Mink!" Tolrin reconnected Silent Signal Fire. "You are not in the rotting chain of command! Don't you dare make orders!"

"Sergeant," Mink responded mentally. "If you want to buy some time for a Reek count, tell everyone to get in with the puppets. We'll confuse their vision so much they won't be able to coordinate an attack. Trust me."

"You have not yet given me reason to do so."

"They aren't attacking! Either the Reeks are trying to position themselves, or they don't intend to."

Mink's response was honored by way of Tolrin ordering every Team member to take up positions in with the horde. Jannri joined in, and soon all who were not in the fortress had complied. The plan seemed to work in a matter of seconds. The puppets stopped moving and turned their hooded heads every which way. Mink grinned, relieved. Everyone must realize by now that he had made the right assessment.

A cloak in Mink's vicinity staggered beside him and, sending a shiver of terror up his spine, put an unwelcome arm around him. Its flesh-gloved hand clutched tightly upon his shoulder. The reek of rotting flesh became so powerful, Mink felt bile shoot up his throat and he almost lost his breakfast. Leaning in close, the puppet smiled at Mink. The mask made of dead flesh curved unnaturally around the places where it had been sutured to the face. The eyes and inside of the mouth were a dead giveaway, discolored gray and dull with black splotches of decay. Definitely not a Reek.

"Yous fascinates us, boy," the gravelled voice hissed in broken Octernalian. "Yous performs no effects, mixes your peoples in with ours, and seems satisfies with yourself. Are yous insane?" Its grip around Mink was surprisingly strong, and despite the friendly gesture, felt hostile.

"I can't do any effects," Mink groaned through held breath. The head rocked back and its gray eyes widened. "I don't have an Element."

At this proclamation, a scattered group of eight cloaks burst into crackly laughter. All of them sounded exactly the same, like someone squeezing fistfulls of dry leaves. They must all be controlled by the same Reek. Try as it might, a Reek couldn't disguise its laughter, sending it out through each of its puppets.

Mink had to test out his theory. "Tralé! What's my nickname back home?"

Tralé looked over at Mink as if he didn't exactly appreciate having attention drawn to him during this horribly precarious crisis. "B-blankey," he stammered.

More puppets laughed. There were four distinct styles and yet many around him were still silent. Mink specifically identified the various sounds of hollow, crackly, staccato, and drawn-out whine. He needed to include more so he could track all of the Reeks.

Mink looked over to Theen on the far side of the group. Theen couldn't stand still, appearing to make himself dizzy as he whipped around fearfully. "Hey, Theen! What do you call an Elementalist with no Element?"

"This is no time for jokes," Theen said in his trademark lisp, setting off a new wave of chuckles, including more puppets. Now, he had all of their attention.

Mink had to capitalize on this opportunity. "A dead weight," Mink answered his own self-deprecating riddle loud enough for everyone to hear him. The Elementalists were visibly upset by his apparent lack of seriousness, but he had played into the Reeks' dark sense of humor perfectly. The laughter rolled for many long seconds. The cloak embracing Mink clapped him on the shoulder while cackling, its flesh glove making a horrible flapping sound. It was difficult to distinguish the separate laughs at first, but as they died out, the sounds became clearer. Mink managed to double check his count.

"Fifteen Reeks!" Mink yelled in the direction of Tolrin and Jannri. "There are fifteen of them." Puppets and Elementalists gazed in unison at Mink while Tréa confirmed his count.

Grinning, Mink felt like he had just proved himself in the presence of geniuses. The puppet squeezed him a little tighter and tilted its head closer to Mink's face, which caused him to pull away, revolted.

"Prouds of yourselfs, boy? I would loves to extinguishes yours exuberance."

Knowing that Reeks respected resistance to taunting, Mink put his own arm around the puppet and patted its rigored shoulder. "Not today, friend," Mink replied.

So few Reeks against this many Elementalists would be a suicide mission. As much as the Reeks celebrated death, they never needlessly pursued their own end. Their careful approach to the Team must have been to disguise the fact that the Reeks in control wielded too many at once, and therefore weren't capable of much dexterity. That made their ambivalence to having puppets destroyed more understandable. Had the Elementalists taken out enough of them, the Reeks might have stood a better chance of coordinating an attack, using their remaining forces more deftly.

Now that the conflict had eased up, Tolrin spoke inside Mink's mind, "I got a puppet talking to me. Asking what we're doing here, and how we plan on paying for their losses."

Mink remained silent, not sure how to respond. The cloak clung to him, completely inanimate, although Mink knew it could see and hear him. Gyov maintained Clay Pot, but the rest of the Team had calmed down quite a bit.

Tolrin continued after a pause, "Jannri is talking to them now. What you did was really foolish. I'm glad the big gamble paid off, but I was pretty close to killing you myself." Mink flushed with a mix of embarrassment and frustration. Tolrin went on, "That said, impressive strategy. I don't think I could have ever come up with that. You may have saved us all."

"Thanks, Sneak." Somewhat relieved, Mink's thoughts now turned toward his parents. He may not have discovered his affinity yet, but he wanted to tell them how, probably for the first time, he actually felt in his Element.

CHAPTER
43

THE REEKS' negotiation process essentially amounted to looting the Elementalists' belongings. Cloaks stood lifeless as the Reeks controlling them shifted focus from one to another, exploring through dead eyes what the Team had on hand. The Reeks never did show themselves, preferring to handle everything through their puppets. Much to everyone's dismay, they insisted on escorting the Elementalist "campers" safely to their destination, seeming to accept the group's cover story. Even though the Reeks agreed to maintain a distance, it was clear that the Team wouldn't be rid of them any time soon.

Gyov finally Dispelled her Clay Pot. The Penbik twins hurried into the dust cloud it produced before completely dissapating, taking what energy they could from the Soil. Everyone was exhausted, especially Gyov. Mink worried that she had spent too much time on Tralé's scooter earlier, leaving barely enough energy for her Clay Pot effect. The guilt of his selfishness at the expense of her safety sank his heart, darkening his joy of having her travel beside him.

If Obyr still had his Demolition effect active, he could fully restore Gyov with one punch, considering how well Body augmented Soil. But he didn't seem the kind of guy to do favors, despite his tending to Alré's Materialized skin. Mink would have asked Pulti to replenish Gyov's energy, but she still wasn't anywhere to be seen. He wanted to hold Gyov and apologize, but the couple of rotheads between them had their eyes locked on Mink and were leaving her alone. He figured it best to keep it that way until the negotiations were concluded.

In stark contrast to their slow en masse approach, the puppets rushed back up into the northern forest individually once each of their bartering requests had been honored. The Elementalists scarcely moved, and only spoke briefly when necessary. Just because the Reeks hadn't fought back, didn't mean they felt any better having them around. As far as Mink was concerned, everyone should be extremely glad affairs hadn't gotten any worse. From his studies, he could count on one hand the number of Reek encounters survived in the past hundred years.

By the time the last of the dark visitors headed up the slope of the valley with their pilfered provisions, the Team had Dispelled their Elemental Armor and Attack effects. The Penbik twins returned their Impenetrable Bark armor to scooters. Clearly fatigued, Gyov hung close to Mink with her head down and hadn't made eye contact with him since she Dispelled her Clay Pot. Mink wanted to engage her in some way, misconstruing her exhaustion for resentment toward him. But nothing he could come up with sounded right in his head. A simple apology didn't seem like enough.

"You," Gyov began, halting to maintain her composure, "were great. All I could do was hide. I was so afraid."

"Trust me, I would have rather been able to hide." Mink gave her shoulder a squeeze. "I'm glad you were safe."

Gyov looked away from Mink and watched her Scout Cell gathering around Corporal Ankrim. "I should get back. Let me clean up and regain some strength. We can talk later." She shuffled away.

"Yeah. It was nice to be able to ride with you for a while, I'm sorry it took so much out of you," Mink called out to her back before rejoining his Guide Cell.

As the sun rose high over the hills, an uncomfortable heat settled heavily over the group. It certainly didn't make the residual stench any more bearable. The trees of the surrounding area were no help, still submerged in the ground up to their tops. No one looked up as Mink came within reach of Tralé.

"I have never been more embarrassed by anyone in my command," Alré brow beat Mink upon his arrival in the angriest version of her raspy voice. "There will not be a next time. I will take you out myself. Do you understand me?"

The twins and Sapo sent looks of disbelief and insubordination to Alré, but all of her attention was aimed at Mink. "I understand, Coporal Alré, ma'am. There will not be a next time."

"This is exactly why we shouldn't have brought kids out here." Alré wouldn't let it go. "You have no idea that what you do affects the rest of us. Kids only think about themselves. It costs lives." Mink couldn't help but take another look at Alré's Materialized skin on her right side, which only made her angrier. "Eat your lunch quickly, silently, and then be ready to move out. All of you." Alré spun on her heel and marched alone along the trail toward the bend ahead, fists clenched.

Tralé led Mink by the shoulder over to his scooter. "Come on, Mink. Let's—"

"I said 'silently'!" Alré roared without looking back.

Having a quick lunch was not a problem. With the lingering stink and emotional hangover, no one could find much of an appetite. Corporal Ankrim fully restored Sapo with Spear, so she could pay it forward to the twins using the Area of Effect chant, Washout,

"Torrents of rain descend from high.
The greater area be soaked.
Water falling relentlessly.

All things become saturated.
Cloudless, the rain falls forever.
Eternsa's essence be my fuel.
The wrath of Floth herself take form.
Cover with rain upon my spit."

Sapo spat and managed to keep the rain isolated to the Guide Cell. Mink could have stepped away to stay dry, but he wanted the Water effect to snuff out the Silent Signal Fire Tolrin had put on him. He closed his eyes and enjoyed the warm rain, relieved to know his thoughts were all his own. Apparently, everyone was angry that he had talked directly to the puppets. Was Gyov upset with him too? She did compliment him, but what did she mean by "talk later?" Mink knew it was partly his fault that she got so worn out. He rested his chin on the back of Tralé's scooter and worked on his apologies.

Using Quick Legs, Pulti finally made a much appreciated appearance beside Mink. "Can't stay long. Sergeant Holph is being a real rothead about everyone keeping with their Cell right now." It only took a second for Sapo's rain to drench her.

"I can understand that," Mink admitted, wondering how she planned on explaining her sudden soaked appearance.

"Just wanted to congratulate you on saving everyone's hide. After lights out tonight, I'll find you. We can spend some time together then."

Mink smiled. "That would be awesome. We might even join my parents, if we can make it to Rift Ridge."

Pulti shrugged with a half-smile. "We'll see. Gotta run." Just before she disappeared, she kissed his cheek.

Sapo's Washout canceled all at once, leaving Mink feeling suddenly quiet and still. Alré returned to the Cell from the path ahead without a word and sat on the back of Mouké's scooter. No one looked her way, instead focusing on the valley ahead to the west, all still dripping.

"Move out. Quickly," Alré said in an eerie calm. "We are going to try to make camp at Rift Ridge tonight."

Mink's heart lept in anticipation of their imminent arrival. Perhaps the encounter with the Reeks put a Fire under everyone's feet to complete the mission. A clear sign of their somber focus, Tralé removed Mink's music crystal and handed it back to him.

"You're some kind of genius, Mink. I like the way you handled yourself."

Mink appreciated the endorsement and tucked his crystal away as Tralé embedded his thumb and finger, Sledding them away on his scooter.

Not a word was uttered the rest of the day other than the chants necessary for removing obstacles along the valley floor. They made good time, and ascended the slope to approach the northern plateau before the sun completely disappeared behind the ridge. There were fewer trees at this elevation, but still enough to feel adequately hidden between the valley walls. The occasional waft of the Reeks' puppets were the only indication of their dark escorts, hiding among the trees to the northwest.

Alré held up a hand and whispered hurriedly, "Stop, stop, stop. Halt!"

The twins and Sapo froze and looked at her. Alré held a finger to her lips and put her forehead on the back of Mouké's scooter.

"Mink," Tolrin's voice came so soft at first through Silent Signal Fire that Mink thought he imagined it. "First, let me say your parents seem to be all right." Mink's throat tightened and his heart skipped a beat. "But scouts on the hilltop report that it looks like the Machinists have surrounded the opening above the cavern."

"What?!" Mink involuntarily shouted in his mind.

"From what we can tell, your dad has most of them under the Hibernation effect and your mom is preventing the rest from entering. We're formulating a plan to help them."

Mink's mind went into overdrive. Hibernation wouldn't last long, and although the effect might be reapplied, any Machinist with an Elemental affinity for Body and Water would be immune.

"Furthermore," Tolrin continued with more bad news. "there are hundreds of cloaks mixed in with their forces. The Machinists appear to be working with the Reeks."

Mink caught another waft of death. It made sense that the Reeks controlling the puppets moving ahead of them would also be in communication with those on Rift Ridge, making the illusion of the camping trip that much more important. Mink shared his suspicions with Tolrin by thinking, "Those puppets we encountered must have been sent to gather information about us. I think we were spotted coming down the western slope of the Great Barrier Range."

"Way ahead of you there, Mink. The only way they could have surrounded us like that back there would be if they knew which way we were headed to begin with."

Alré lifted her head and kept her voice to a whisper, announcing what Mink already knew. "We're going to camp here tonight. Sapo and I will take first watch."

CHAPTER
44

UNDER THE inching dark of night, each Cell established its
own cabin one by one down the valley path from whence
they came. The persistent call of insects helped muffle the
sounds that might give away the position of the Team. Knowing that the puppets were likely watching from the shadows of
the surrounding trees above, great care was taken to maintain
the guise of a educational camping trip. Extra precaution was
necessary, and Cell members had to bunk together.

The twins fashioned one large octagonal cabin that could
house the Guide Cell and their scooters, plus give whoever
was on watch an elevated and protected position on the roof.
Sapo used her canvas tent as a barrier between herself and the
Wood, lest her energy be drained overnight. They each had a
simple platform bed extending out from one of the eight walls,
partitioned for privacy. Mink stowed his pack on the floor next
to his head, reclining fitfully. Knowing his parents were at a
stalemate against Machinist forces, he doubted he would sleep
before watch.

A knock came on the door, followed by Blin's voice. "Mink,
Tolrin wants to see you."

He had expected to be called, but had about given up on it by the time the second moon rose. "Be right there." On his way out, he nodded to the twins, who were already climbing into their beds.

This night seemed darker than the previous one. If anyone was using a glow crystal, Mink couldn't see it. Aside from the people on watch, everyone had holed up in their Cell's bunk. Blin walked beside him in silence.

"Mink?" Blin started as they neared Tolrin's cabin. "Just want to say I hope your parents are okay."

"Then hand over my mom's flatwrap."

Mink startled as Blin stepped in front of him and raised an arm. To his surprise, no blow followed, but rather an earnest squeeze on the shoulder.

"When we're headed home, I'll hand it to her myself," Blin offered.

Mink didn't feel like he understood anything or anyone anymore. "Fine, then. Thanks."

Blin headed off, and Mink knocked on the Command Cell's door. He heard Tolrin's voice come from outside, around the back. "Over this way, Mink." Following the sound of low voices, he discovered Tolrin engaged in conversation with some members of the Strike Cell under Corporal Counkrat's command, including the Water user Rénys. Squaring up, Tolrin addressed Mink. "It seems Rénys here has a massive effect loaded up. He chanted specifications for eighteen hours after we left the briefing yesterday morning."

Mink looked at Rénys, who gave a silent nod. "Will it harm those with Water affinity?"

Rénys shook his head, remaining quiet to keep the effect ready to implement.

"Anyone know what kind of an effect it is?" Tolrin questioned the rest of the group. "Some kind of A.o.E.? Waterjet?"

Crali, a Body user in the Strike Cell, spoke up, "I don't think it's either. The specification he kept repeating was—" Crali paused to make sure he got it right. "the target's Water expanded."

"Rénys," Mink said, facing the silent Water user. "Do you think your effect can give us an advantage against the Machinists?"

Rénys nodded, smiling slyly.

Turning his attention to Tolrin, Mink wasted no time in laying out his idea. "I can believe that Rénys stands a good chance of eliminating a large number of the Machinists and Harvest forces, except for those with Fire, Water, and Wood affinities. I would suggest that your Air and Lightning users of the Perimeter Cell sneak around the cliff side of the Ridge and take care of as many of the remaining as possible. If we strike first and thoroughly, the only ones left to deal with will be those who are hidden."

"But most of them will be dead or asleep... Much better odds!" Tolrin finished. "A+ on Mr. Gusky's exam... I believe it." He grabbed Mink by the back of the neck approvingly. Then he conceded, "We aren't a battle-ready army. There's no way we can get reinforcements. But we cannot go back empty handed. And I'm not going to stay here and wait to see what happens. We have the first twenty seconds of the battle planned.

"Our priority is to distract enemy forces from the Tear of God, clearing entry for ourselves. The Guide, Scout, and Strike Cells should form a Decoy Unit pulling them to the north, away from the site. My Relay Cell can help the Extraction Unit sneak around to the south and make for the hole while the Machinists' attention is on the Decoy Unit."

Mink cleverly added, "Same way you won the National Thornball Championship against the Tad Stormwings."

Tolrin smiled, amused. "Against heavy defense, the best strategy is to make them defend the wrong area. They had some monstrous layers of defense in front of the Grax goal. Too bad we already scored on that one." He allowed himself a chuckle.

"And," Mink's resolve strengthened, "we'll catch any remaining Machinists between the crossfire of the Decoy Unit and the Tear of God Unit's defensive Cells." Approving nods of agreement circulated among the group.

"What about the Reeks?" Crali apparently voiced a concern of the others. Either the odor of rot had lessened, or Mink was getting used to it. The Reeks disturbed Mink as well, but he knew that Machinists posed a greater threat, since they had weapons that shot metal. And metal damaged all Elemental types.

"I don't think the Reeks will miss out on the opportunity to acquire puppets," Mink answered. "They'll have their hands full reaping all the dead bodies from the battlefield."

Lieutenant Jannri finally spoke up, her voice soft and warm. "Which Unit would you rather go with, Mink? You would reach your parents more quickly with the Tear of God Unit."

He hadn't considered this. Although Mink wanted nothing more than to be reunited with Nyam and Juré as soon as possible, he felt a greater obligation to stay with his group. "I'll move with the Guide Cell and find my parents after we've pushed through to meet the Tear of God Unit," he decided. "I'll just need a paddle."

Jannri approved. "Have the twins make something up for you. Whatever you need."

Dismissed, Mink rushed back to his cabin, feeling excited and optimistic about the newly hatched battle plan. The prospect of getting a new paddle made by the twins and using it to fight Machinists also energized him. En route, he spotted Gyov standing outside the door of the Scout Cell's cabin. Mink approached her at a walking pace, trying desparately to remember the apology he had come up with.

"Gyov, I'm so sorry for putting you in danger. And it was selfish of me to let you drain your energy just so I could sit by you. Please—"

Gyov cut Mink off by shoving her hand over his mouth. "Are you going to let me say something?"

Mink nodded, bewildered.

"But not here." Gyov led Mink by the hand off into the misty Woods to the south. He almost suggested they stay close to the group, but the prospect of having some time alone with her under the blanket of night was too tempting. He inhaled deeply to be sure no puppets were in the area, and instead got drunk on a noseful of her sweet, floral perfume. They snuck down into a vale low enough to be completely hidden from sight, Gyov insisting they lay down on the warm Soil. After they settled side by side, Mink studied the moons now obscured by the wide leaves of the almany trees. He waited for her to speak.

"There's a song," Gyov said at last. "Back at Gynsgade, that was my favorite song when I was little girl. It's all I could think of earlier when those puppets were coming at us. It played over and over in my head while I sat closed in my Clay Pot."

Mink propped up on an elbow and listened while she spoke, her eyes fixed on the sky.

"'Oongk Ggyoriah Ahtima,' translated as 'The World I Have.' About a princess who knows only of her safe world and yet the man she loves lives a life of hardship and disappointment." Gyov continued to elaborate in the accent Mink found so endearing. "She tries to bring the man from his harsh world into her luxury, but the love suffers. Only when she leaves her easy life to share his difficult one, then she becomes strong enough for them to have sustainable love."

Gyov paused and bit her lower lip, blinking rapidly. Mink rolled onto his back, giving her space. The night insects sang over the silence.

She continued, "I wish to believe that I could be strength-ened by your world, Mink. I want to be strong enough. All that time I tried to bolster courage in safety of my Elemental Armor, only made me feel weaker and without courage."

Mink's eyes traced the braid along the side of her head as he tried to understand what she was getting at. Too weak for him?

"Then you took charge of the situation and truly showed everyone how strong your world has made you. I don't de-serve to be with you." Gyov rolled to face him, her expression sullen and hands folded protectively on her stomach.

"You need to leave that up to me to decide," Mink echoed Tralé's advice from the morning. "Don't reject yourself, Gyov."

"You're strongest and bravest person I know, Mink." she stared into his eyes. "I can't imagine your daily struggles not knowing your Element. Yet, you remain so sweet and positive and sure."

Mink smiled, returning her gaze. "That's funny. You are the one who inspired me to be that way." Gyov gave him a dubi-ous look. "Really. I was always impressed by how cheerful and playful you were when you first moved to Floth, even when ev-eryone made fun of you for being different. I decided that's how I wanted to be. Like you."

Gyov rolled her eyes. "You wouldn't want me once you got to know me better."

Mink had heard enough. He moved closer and firmly set his lips against the warm tenderness of hers. She recoiled slightly, but not enough to break away from him. She relaxed into it, grabbing the back of his head. Her lips were soft, soon stretching thin in a smile of pleasure and relief. Mink leaned away and returned her grin. At last, he had kissed the girl he longed for all these years. The moment did not disappoint, and when it fully hit Mink that this was his first kiss, he beamed. Perfect. Absolutely perfect.

"Sing it to me," Mink coaxed.

"What? 'Oongk Ggyoriah Ahtima?'"

"I want to hear it."

Gyov laughed and cleared her throat. "You may not laugh at my singing."

"You didn't laugh at mine, so it's a deal."

"Oh..." Gyov gave Mink a little kiss. "Okay. I only know in Pashmeeta. I will translate later." She began,

> *"Uhertcha o sogreng yota*
> *Jehdati sa Ggyoriah ri*
> *Yoriah oo meeckseng brooba*
> *Kah oongk Ggyoriah ahtima*
> *Baengo engllti sio – "*

Mink listened, captivated by the soft lilt of her voice in the night. The singing of her language was somehow even more lovely than when she spoke. Her lulling of the tune was cut short by the crack of splitting Wood, making them both jump, searching to find the source of the sudden sound. The echo made it more difficult to pinpoint, but Mink was sure it had come from the direction of the camp.

"We should get back." Mink scanned the shadows.

"Good idea," Gyov agreed nervously, helping Mink stand. They walked up out of the vale holding hands. As the camp came back in view, Mink could find no reason for the sound they heard, but it was a sobering reminder of the dangers they faced.

"Do you feel better?" he asked.

"Do you still want to be with me?" Gyov countered his question with her own.

"Yes. Very much so." Mink gave her hand a reassuring squeeze.

"Then, yes, better. But I still think you are crazy. In good way." Gyov gave him another short, comfortable kiss before they split up toward their respective Cells.

Mink reached his cabin and took two steps inside before turning on his heel. He suddenly remembered that Pulti wanted to meet up with him after everyone got settled. Did he have a story to tell her! He walked with a purpose as if he were on his way to meet with Tolrin. The Pull Cell's cabin had to be near the rest of the Tear of God Unit's cabins, but other than that, he wasn't sure how to find Pulti. No one stopped him, which was a good thing. Mink pretended to be on a patrol and nodded amiably to the people standing guard atop their cabins. With any luck, Pulti would be on watch.

He found her, shaking by the side of her cabin. He sped up his pace, careful not to draw attention. The unmistakable stench of puppets had returned.

"Hey, Pulti. So glad I found you..." He suddenly realized she was crying. "What's wrong? What happened?"

She shot him a pained and angry look, tears streaming. "Go back to your cabin, Mink," she said through clenched teeth. Mink reeled. Did something happen while he and Gyov were out of sight? What did they miss?

"Just tell me —"

"I swear by Curpo, if you don't leave right now, I will throw you back home." Pulti broke down in quiet sobs again and clutched the wall.

"All right," he relented, hands raised and backing away. "I'll come find you at breakfast."

Pulti slumped to the ground, sobbing and shaking her head.

Mink hurried back to his cabin with his hands shoved in his pockets, both elated and worried, convinced that he knew nothing about women. He and Theen had last watch of the night, which naturally meant no more sleep before battle. Relentless thoughts of his parents' fight, Gyov, Pulti, and everyone's safety contorted his emotions. He tossed around in his bed until somehow, sleep finally caught up with him. When

Tralé tapped Mink for his watch shift, adrenaline kicked in and cold kwona did the rest.

CHAPTER
45

JUST AFTER breakfast, Mink spent some enjoyable time practicing with the balance and weight of his new paddle in the vale where Gyov had sung to him. It was a beautiful thing. He had requested that Tralé carve grooves for Air flow, just like he had asked Dreh to do after winning the party contest. But Tralé went one better, braiding the Wood to act much in the same way as a bird's feather. The angle of the braids helped the paddle thrust and slice with remarkable speed and accuracy. When fanned, it really grabbed and pushed the Air forcefully. Tralé assured Mink that even if he were to free fall, he could steer and glide by riding on the paddle. After spending fifteen minutes with it, Mink believed him.

Satisfied with his paddle practice, he rejoined the Guide Cell. Everyone had been told to wear neutral-toned clothes to help them blend into the landscape. Mink's pants were the color of green mud, and his pocket jacket was mossy brown. Alré had packed enough of the official camouflage to lend a raincoat for Sapo to wear over her pastels. Mouké had plenty of tan to wear, but Tralé, by defiance or lack, chose to wear a forest green jacket and goldenrod pants.

By order, breakfast had been with Cell members only. There was more food than anyone could stomach on the cusp of battle, even without the odor of decay. Mink really wanted to find out what happened to Pulti last night, but it would have to wait. Tolrin's Relay Cell had already set off to escort the Tear of God Unit, including Pulti, south across the grasslands toward the spot where Nyam had given Mink her flatwrap. They had precious few hours to get into strike position. To ensure that their timing was right, the Support Unit would need to head out shortly.

"Will that work for you?" Tralé asked, nodding with casual confidence to the paddle slung across Mink's back as they mounted the scooter.

"If I knew they could be made like this, I'd never have owned another." Mink clapped Tralé's back appreciatively.

"Okay then." Tralé winked. "That's a yes. Glad you like it." He stretched and twisted nervously, waiting on the word to move, thumb and pinky embedded at the ready.

The camp was nearly Dispelled, and everyone had already stored what they wouldn't need that day on the long-since departed wagon. After the Guide Cell reestablished formation, the Scout Cell fell in close behind. Within arm's reach of Mink and Alré, Gyov and Fréni stood side by side, Obyr behind them, and Ankrim and Theen tucked into his flanks. Corporal Counkrat's Strike Cell lined up in three rows of five behind Rénys, who was being harnessed to Crali's back, only steps away from the Scout Cell. Game-face time.

"Here. For you," Gyov discretely extended a music crystal to Mink.

"What's this?" He took it and looked it over quickly before stashing it in an interior pocket of his jacket.

"I never got to finish singing my song to you. So I recorded it and the translation. For good luck."

Mink patted the pocket. "Thanks. That makes me feel better." He gave her a weak smile. In truth, not much could comfort him, as the reality of their fateful morning weighed on his mind. The Team was about to set off for battle, veritably breaking a truce among countries that had lasted nearly 16,000 years. All for the immense purpose of acquiring a Tear of God and, in the process, saving his parents' lives. The well-crafted paddle strapped to his back seemed a mere trinket against the dire forces they were about to face.

The gravity of the moment burdened Mink's heart, and he barely registered Gyov squeezing his hand before back-stepping to her position behind him. Tralé and Mink turned their attention to Rénys being brought up to Sapo. Apparently, Rénys hadn't thought to chant Slip Skate before loading up his massively specified effect, so he had to be carried in order to make good time. Mink truly hoped that Rénys hadn't uttered a single sound since finishing his chant, or they were all in for a very bad day.

The newly purposed Decoy Unit made use of the shrubs and almany trees for cover until they got into position. Mink and his group moved up the grade toward the plateau north of the Machinist Army at a speed three times faster than they had traveled yesterday. It impressed him that Sapo was able to keep pace, especially uphill. He hoped each of them were conserving enough energy to play their part in the battle. Fortunately, travel was made much easier by not having to create a path, or wait on the wagon.

Under Corporal Ankrim's command, the Decoy Unit halted just before they reached level ground. The shrubs that surrounded them now would not provide adequate protection, and their current position was still too far away to stage their attack on the Machinists. Mink recognized the grove of hudlew trees that stood out about two miles beyond them, the same red fruits showing vividly that he had chosen from just days ago, under very different circumstances. Taking shelter in the grove would position the Unit conveniently due north of their enemies. A couple of miles felt like a long distance to be exposed, but since the Decoy Unit's mission was to provide misdirection, it was decided that detection could only advance their cause.

A bluff rose to their right as they continued west, providing just enough cover for travel. It took some minutes to reach the hudlew grove, and every second felt too long for Mink, who kept expecting bedlam to loose from the Machinist camp. They reached the sanctuary of the fruit trees without incident, welcomed by the thick, bittersweet smell of overripe hudlews. As Rénys unharnessed himself from Crali, Mink dismounted Tralé's scooter and tried to get a visual on the Machinists surrounding his mom and dad.

The thickness of the foliage protected them better than anticipated. Mink peeked through the bushes and felt a deep pulse of adrenaline. Machinists and vehicles crowded Rift Ridge a few miles from the edge of the grove where they hid. It barely registered for him that the vast majority of the masses slept, as he had never seen such throngs outside of a thornball stadium. More than half of the wakeful enemy was crowded on the far edge of their forces, serving as Mink's only clue to where his parents might be located. If the opening Nyam had dug remained there, Mink certainly couldn't make it out from here.

Dozens of vehicles every bit as large as the Elementalists' Wooden wagon scattered the area like moving houses, closed off with thick metal doors, and mounted with turrets that had long tubes sticking out of them. There were also scores of smaller vehicles similar to the one the scout drove. Hundreds of infantrymen wore metal armor and carried weapons the size of Mink. Thousands more milled about in green uniforms, bearing more compact weapons. Several hundred black cloaks mingled among the Machinists.

Behind Mink, Alré climbed a tree and held a spy glass to her eye. Ankrim sat against the trunk, squinting through the bushes as he chanted the Mental Vacation Movement effect of a Spirit user,

> *"My mind can go where I can see.*
> *Leaving my Body where I am.*
> *My eyes select the place I go.*
> *Instantly seeing from that spot.*
> *I perceive everything around.*
> *Threatened, I return inside me.*
> *Spirit and Air empower me.*
> *Travel by mind when I say, 'There.'"*

Ankrim motioned for Obyr to come stand guard for his Body. When he was close, Anrkim fixated on a spot in the heart of the Machinists' forces, saying, "There." His Body went limp, and Obyr gingerly propped it against the tree trunk. The rest of the group was hiding just out of sight in the grove. Gyov came up behind Mink, beckoning him back from the shrubs.

"What can you see?" she whispered in his ear.

Mink spoke softly back. "I've never seen so many people. I hope we know what we're doing." Gyov looked worried. She craned her neck, but couldn't get a view of what Mink had seen from where they stood.

The hudlew fruits fermenting on the ground gave off a dizzying sweet smell in the heat of the day. Corporal Ankrim sat up suddenly, having returned from his reconnoiter. He winked at Mink, stood, and knocked on Alré's boot, indicating for her to climb back down. With Obyr and Gyov in tow, they approached the group in the shadows of the fruit trees. Alré signaled for the Decoy Unit to huddle up.

Ankrim addressed everyone in a low voice. "Just about all of those button pushers down there are asleep. We should only have to deal with Body and Water affinities. Rénys will take care of the Body users, leaving the Water affinities for our Lightning users who will be brought over the cliff by Air users."

"You make it sound so easy," Obyr whined.

"There aren't that many of them," Alré countered, expressing confidence that their Elemental powers trumped the limitations of weaponry. "Just a small contingent of the Machinist's total forces. Our earlier reports were obviously exaggerated by those who haven't seen what Freeland is capable of. They won't even have time to call for back up."

"You're dad is really something else," Ankrim directed to Mink. "Most of our work has been done for us." He continued to address the group. "Tréa tells me they're just about in position. I need Lightning users to mount up. It's show time."

CHAPTER

46

THE AIR users Imbued the four Lightning users with Featherweight, chanting breathily,

> *"Power of Air is mine to give.*
> *I grant my target weightlessness.*
> *The target is easy to lift.*
> *Carrying is not a burden.*
> *The slightest breeze can move it far.*
> *No lack of strength experienced.*
> *I may borrow the Air from Hewl.*
> *Imbue Air as soon as I clap."*

After clapping to implement the effect, the Air users grabbed the straps on the harnesses and slung their riders onto their backs like they were empty sacks. Mink flashed to the strength Nyam had displayed hauling him single-handedly upward, pounding through two miles of dirt and ore, mysteriously empowered by the Tear of God that the Team would momentarily fight to acquire.

"Wait until your Cell is on the cliffside to chant the Sky Step, Corporal Thol," Ankrim instructed his comrade. "Maintain cover until Rénys' chant takes effect, then come up and have the Lightning users implement their A.o.E., Scattered Storm."

Corporal Thol Ramink nodded and tucked her thumbs under her shoulder straps. "See you on the victory rendezvous. May God's grace be your keep." Ankrim nodded. Thol drew a circle in the Air with her finger, signaling for her Cell to move out.

As the eight of them left, Mink counted only nineteen who remained in the hudlew grove, himself included. This, against thousands of armored, gun-toting Machinists. A swallow got stuck in his throat. They all watched in silence until the Perimeter Cell was out of view. Obyr and Alré took deeper cover for him to fortify her with a fresh application of Materialized Body.

The next half hour of waiting was anguish. They remained silent, Mink and Gyov holding hands. He vascillated repeatedly between believing everything would be okay, and deciding this was a huge mistake.

When the time came, Ankrim and Alré simultaneously held their hands overhead in the shape of a triangle, indicating formation. The twins positioned their scooters about ten yards apart, where they could easily push through the shrubs. The other sixteen filled the space between, with Rénys positioned strategically in the middle. Mink took his place in the line and weilded his paddle with unfelt fervor, but he was far from prepared to engage the formidable sea of Machinists and puppets that awaited them on the ridge. Everyone on the line looked at Ankrim.

After a few very long seconds, he pumped his left fist up and down. Ready or not, they burst forth through the shrubs. Out in the open, the sense of exposure and vulnerability churned Mink from the inside. Rénys rushed ahead of the group, waving his hands back, indicating for all of them to stay behind him. As they ran in a V-pattern, Mink scanned the field in front.

He immediately noticed that not one Machinist, Reek, or puppet faced their way. Not one. "Corporal Alré, they're not looking at us! They are specifically not looking in this direction."

"And we are taking advantage of that fact, Mink. Shut up!" Alré jogged, eyes focused hungrily on the impending battlefield.

"I think we should pull back. We might be moving into a trap." Mink made great effort to keep his place in the line, but his reluctant legs felt heavy with dread.

"Mind your place, Mink!" Alré barked. "Everyone advances. That is an order!"

The momentum of the day's fate reached a point-of-no-return as Rénys implemented his secret, massive Water effect by unceremoniously spitting on the ground, still at a full run. He collapsed in exhaustion, but before his limp Body flopped to a rest, screams could be heard from the Machinists. As Mink thrust his paddle forward, its grooves grabbed the air and pulled him unwillingly ahead. He feigned the enthusiasm he saw in the others, hoping that it might foster some deep-rooted war cry.

Torrents of Water gushed out of every orifice of the Machinists' bodies. Those without armor bloated visibly. Within seconds, the swarms of soldiers and puppets across the battlefield were ankle-deep in Water, as it collected quickly on top of the hard cracked Soil with nowhere to go. Obyr hoisted Rénys over his shoulder and kept advancing.

The flood continued to build under the glare of the relentless sun, revealing that the surface of the plateau above the Tear of God's chamber was a shallow basin. The rushing Water carried dead and sleeping bodies alike toward the opening Nyam had dug up from the geode. The force of the whirlpool began eroding the Soil of the hole, widening the underground access. Bodies eddied and dropped through the center like bubbles getting sucked down a drain. Wails and curses echoed across the field from those Machinists who still had dry throats.

"Anyone harmed by Water or Lightning, stay on the out-side of that flood!" Ankrim ordered. Now that they were nearly a hundred feet away from the Water's edge, Mink slowed down. It was a scene unlike anything he had imagined. He understood now that Rénys' effect was going to increase the strength of the Wood users making the pulley systems, with an added bonus of softening the Soil for the extraction of the geode. Very smart. Mink only hoped that the Water rushing down into the vortex of the flood wouldn't weaken his dad.

Hovering now over the cliff's horizon, the Lightning us-ers wasted no time finding a place to point, implementing their effects. Instantly, four cores of Lightning appeared in the Machinists' camp. Several Lightning bolts per second shot throughout the remaining forces with a deafening roll of thun-der, raging an electric war-storm in broad daylight. The Scat-tered Storms effects arced violent flashes toward every metal object within their range, and crackling sparks danced atop the Water over smouldering bodies that the receding Water left in the muck. Still, Mink counted hundreds of Machinists and cloaks as yet unharmed.

Before Mink's group could reach the Water's edge and engage in battle, several dozen puppets sprung up from un-der the dirt in unison, like corpses rising from their graves. Unlike those they had encountered before, these puppets moved quickly and with dexterity, rapidly surrounding the Decoy Unit. Five of them swarmed each member of the Unit, possessing affinities specific to the individual, which would keep the attackers safe from harm. The Elementalists fought for their lives.

Obyr dropped Rénys, punching and kicking at the pup-pets grabbing him, to no avail. They all had Soil affinities! As a Body user, he could only make them stronger. In an instant, Obyr went from a man of intimidating stature to a four-and-a-half foot boy, no more than ninety pounds. All of his Body effects had been canceled. In a flash, it came to Mink that the Team had revealed their Elemental affinities to the Reeks in yesterday's encounter. They desperately needed help, but the Extraction Unit was just now cresting over the slope of the plateau, entirely on the opposite side of the battlefield.

Mink fought off five puppets with his paddle, but their evasion was so well-timed that he couldn't break their bones fast enough to slow the onslaught. Since he hadn't shown an Elemental affinity, nor displayed any prowess with his weapon, how were they prepared to counter him so well? Sapo could clearly be seen towering over the black cloaks with Wood affinity that held her fast. She screamed and screamed for help, the sound barely carrying over the thunder of the persistent Lightning. Mink's paddle suddenly split into three pieces, shot by a distant Machinist. Before the shards struck the ground, the five hooded figures grabbed his arms and head, immobolizing him.

Amid the chaos, Mink heard Ankrim and Alré yelling, but couldn't make out their words. As if the thunder wasn't loud enough, all the puppets now hissed their foul breath in everyone's ears. Theen went limp. The twins' armor was canceled. Gyov twisted and turned, unable to break free of the cold, dead grasp that held her fast. They all had been subdued, two cloaks clutching each arm and one holding the head. In unison, the captors rotated and stretched the Elementalists, putting them up on display for the three Machinists wading toward them.

Straining, Mink heard the distinctive tones of chants coming from those members of his group still able to speak, but they were soon interrupted. Much to his disgust and horror, the puppets began to shove their flesh-gloved, rotting fingers into each of their mouths, including his own. Mink threw up everything he had, the taste of decay and bile blurring his vision as his eyes teared. He fought through the haze and struggled to free himself in vain, watching powerless as the twins,

Sapo, Alré, everyone, including Gyov, got caught in the same foul death-grip.

Mink hoped to God that Alré was somehow still connected via Silent Signal Fire to contact the rest of the Team for salvation. Choking on the repulsive claws pressing down on his tongue, amidst the constant daystorm of thunder and Lightning, Mink watched as puffs of blood-red mist exploded all over his people. The Machinists had opened fire.

CHAPTER

47

THE PUPPETS holding Mink kept him upright while the others were being laid down, their blood darkening the dirt. A dozen more black robes hurried toward them from the shrubs where Mink and the rest of the Decoy Unit had burst through only moments ago. The timing of their appearance and the urgent movement of these figures led Mink to believe that the Reeks had finally arrived. If ever there were a time for rescue, this was it.

The Machinists who shot Mink's friends lowered their weapons to the ground and rushed at him from about fifty yards away. Their heavy boots sloshed through the Water that remained from Rénys' effect. A bolt of Lightning lashed out at them, silhouetting their uniforms, but not slowing them in the slightest. The hundred or so Machinists remaining on the field either took shelter in vehicles, or advanced to engage the Extraction Unit moving in on the muddy, expanded opening above the Tear of God's cavern.

One by one, the Decoy Unit members stopped struggling. Crali stared at the sky and convulsed. Sapo lay motionless with her eyes shut, held firmly to the ground, the puppets still clutching her lower jaw. Alré stared at Mink without emotion, the Materialized skin over half her face dull in the sunlight. Tralé's muscles stopped tensing and his breathing quickened.

"Leave her alone!" Mink tried to yell at the puppets holding Gyov, his voice muffled by the fingers in his mouth. She could only stare fearfully back at him, caught in the puppets' grasp, blood oozing from her clothes, tears streaming down her face. "No! No, no, no!" Mink's garbled protests went unheeded.

The Reeks reached the maimed and helpless group before the Machinists, and crouched down beside Mink's unconscious, vulnerable comrades. Each Reek pulled a pair of wire-thin metal wands from their sleeves and began carefully inserting them into the Elementalists' eyes through their tear ducts. Pressing the upward tips of the wands into their ring fingers, the Reek's blood ran down the wands and into the eyes of their prone, wounded prey. They chanted in an evil hissing language Mink had never heard before, and hoped to never hear again.

In a remarkable display of strength and determination, Gyov kept struggling and bit off the fingers in her mouth. She spat them and her blood into the face of the puppet holding her right leg. It flinched enough for her to kick her leg free and try to fend off the rest of her foes. Her kicks were weak demonstrations of how much pain she felt and blood she had lost. The puppet holding her left arm set its knees on her shoulder and elbow and punched her head until she was unconscious.

"Leave her alone! Get away from her! No! Gyov!" Mink bellowed unintelligibly. He was completely powerless as a Reek crouched over her and inserted its wands into her eyes, chanting.

Mink went limp in the arms of his captors, sobbing. All of his comrades were dead or dying. What role had he played in killing the people who had come to respect and support him as friends? Tralé, Mouké, Sapo, Gyov, Theen, Crali, Rénys, Ankrim, Frèni, Counkrat, Aprèl, Proth, Jaog, Byth, Gibby, Sèplè,

Alré, and Obyr. The geniuses of his generation lay lifeless on the ground in their own blood.

Just last night he had kissed Gyov for the first time. Now their mouths were violated by the claws of death. He had assured her that she was strong enough and that he wanted to be with her. Yet, here they were at the merciless hands of Reeks and Machinists because of a plan he helped create.

The three soldiers rushed in, fingers on triggers. The Machinists were so pale that Mink couldn't immediately recognize them as men. One sprinted straight for Mink, pale white with blond stubble showing under a mirrored visor. In its glass, Mink made himself out amid the curved silhouettes of the puppets, reflecting the hopelessness of his situation. The Machinist fixed a weapon inches from his chest. Mink's devastated heart welcomed the gun. He wanted him to shoot. No one should have to survive this...

From between the cloaks and uniforms, Mink caught sight of the Extraction Unit making victorious headway over the opening over the Tear of God, and the memory of his mission bristled in his bones. He struggled and bucked with renewed determination, fighting for the chance to see Juré and Nyam again. All was not lost. Three flashes spat out of the barrel of the Machinist's weapon.

Mink was unharmed. How had he managed to avoid all three shots? The puppets clutching Mink's arms and head laughed and spoke in Machinist gibberish to the shooter. In response, the Machinist turned the weapon against a hooded face and three more flashes took the puppet's head off. It remained standing and maintained a forceful grip on Mink's left arm.

The Machinist barked some orders and Mink was laid on his back down in the dirt. Two of the puppets that had been holding his arms each took a leg. The Machinist unsheathed a ten-inch knife strapped to his tactical jacket while he spoke unintelligibly to Mink. Gripping it with both hands, he held the knife high above Mink's chest. He shut his eyes.

Now all he could think of was Gyov. Having experienced the expansion of consciousness after death once before, Mink hoped that she could see him and understand his thoughts. He wanted her to know how much he loved her. How long he had been loving her. If only, after he died they could remain together...

Anticipating certain death, having every other option stripped from his control, Mink rolled his head back and relaxed in surrender. He felt the pressure of the knife blade pushing into his ribs. There was no pain. He felt no fear. In fact, he felt... fine. A pulsing vibration spread from his heart, setting him at ease.

He opened his eyes and looked at his chest. Embedded up to the hilt, the knife remained there, rising and falling with his unlabored breath. The Machinist, confused, first twisted it sunwise and then counter-sunwise. Mink's emotions calmed and the blade felt like it belonged there, firmly embedded in his chest!

For a second, he saw Juré's face looking at him from the glass of the soldier's helmet, until he realized it was his own. How could he be so unrecognizable? His reflection showed a confidence and wisdom that had eluded him his whole life. It was as if he were seeing himself for the first time.

The Machinist removed the blade and stabbed Mink several times out of frustration, causing no more harm than rips in Mink's clothes. The Machinist stood, staggering and shocked, barking frantic orders to the puppets and pointing off somewhere on the battlefield. The puppets lifted Mink up in time to watch as a black robe was lowered over a free-standing, lifeless Gyov. She withdrew the hood and gave Mink a sinister smile.

Then a familiar, crackling voice came out of her mouth. "How's yours exuberance today, Blankey?"

"You?!" Mink couldn't believe it. He fought and struggled against the five puppets carrying him away, to no avail. This was not the way he wanted to remember Gyov, as a puppet laughing at him.

The Scattered Storms were over and all that remained of Rénys' Water effect was mud. A few hundred charred and smoking corpses lay unattended to, probably too badly burnt by the Lightning to be made into puppets. Regardless, several dozen Reeks emerged from the larger of the vehicles and poked about, seeing what they could use. Presumably, most of the Machinists and puppets Mink had spied through the bushes had been washed away. More than a mile away, the Extraction Unit was setting up over the hole to the chamber, maintaining a tense cease-fire with the remaining hundred Machinists still stationed on their side of the battlefield.

Mink barely had the energy to cry as the puppets dragged him to one of the larger vehicles. They shouted something and a door lifted from the back. The inside of the vehicle was walled with a dizzying array of screens, lights, and switches. Mink was forced into a seat and tied down with rope. The puppets left him alone, exiting the rear of the vehicle. A hatch opened in the ceiling near the front and a pale, white-haired man climbed down a short ladder. He brought a swivel chair in front of Mink and sat, holding a Wooden handle and a ten-inch knife.

As he talked in broken Octernalian, he whittled away at the handle. "Name me General Stroud." He looked up, expecting a response that Mink wasn't going to grant. He cocked an eyebrow and muttered to himself, spinning in his seat to touch one of the screens on the wall. As he tapped it, the displays changed until a three-dimensional image appeared of Mink standing with Nyam and Juré. "You?"

Mink couldn't believe what he was seeing. It was most certainly him with his parents on Rift Ridge, clear as if it were happening in the moment. But that was over a week ago. His baffled expression seemed to be the only answer the General needed.

Shaking his head, the General continued, whittling. "Of all the people... I think you victim here. Never I see parents abuse children this bad. So sad for you."

Mink set his face in defiance. He wasn't abused. Ten years of watching everyone around him progress while he stayed on the level of a toddler was abuse. But, how could he make a Machinist understand that his parents were helping?

His Element? That knife! The way the blade resonated with him while it was stuck in his chest. The way his blood flowed right through the blade. Could it be? Did he have an affinity for metal? Metal wasn't even an Element.

"Weeks ago," General Stroud continued. "We work deal with you people to check out possible source for ore in wilderness. We watch by satellite and send a scout. You send representative from your country. Everybody up-and-up." A representative? From Octernal? Could he be referring to Juré? "Everything go to plan. Then this."

General Stroud pressed another screen in front of Mink. "We all see. Even scout family." A video playback taken from the scout's dashboard showed Mink how Nyam had ripped the door off the vehicle and crushed the sleeping scout's neck in both her hands. His head flopped down as if the only thing holding it on was skin. Knowing his mom had killed the scout was one thing. Watching her do it made Mink feel sick.

He looked away and started to cry again, moved to misery by watching his mother kill and knowing that man's family had seen the same thing. The General turned off the screen. The scout had to die. Mink knew in his heart that there would have been no other chance for the Elementalists to win the Tear of

God. He felt bad that Machinists had watched the whole thing happen, but they would have done the same thing if the roles were reversed.

A woman's voice came through speakers into the cabin of the vehicle. The General replied and turned to Mink. "You do this for a rock?" He arched his brow in inquiry, his voice insistent.

"Not just a rock. It's a Tear of God." Mink clarified.

"That word has no meaning for me." Irritated, the General wiped his face and resumed whittling, shaking his head. "A rock. We lose too many good people over a rock."

"I lost friends. I lost my girlfriend."

"That word has no meaning for me. You people start this battle. No sorrow for your loss. You seem to me a good kid. Better than your people. Make you offer. Leave your culture of violence. Come with us back to Freeland. Live in culture of peace where discrimination is illegal."

Mink's head shot up. Live with the Machinists? Why would he ever go with the people who killed Gyov? Who killed the few people that started to recognize him? The General called it a culture of peace. They certainly had a strange way of showing it and an impressive assortment of weapons, considering.

"Think about it. Don't have to answer now. But say to you this. Our bullets and knives don't kill you. Bet we know what can. If you say no." General Stroud pressed the point of the handle he had been whittling against Mink's neck.

CHAPTER
48

MINK LOOKED the General straight in his steel blue eyes. Where he had hoped to see an enemy, he saw condolence, resolve, and a strange understanding. Looking away, Mink shrugged, exhausted. The General sheathed his knife and slid the sharpened handle through a belt loop.

"You think about offer. Myself go settle our survivors. Your people will have their rock." With that, he climbed up the ladder and through the hatch.

Mink sat and stared at the three-dimensional picture of himself with his parents on the screen across from him. Would he ever see them again? Were they safe? He wanted to believe the General would tell him if he asked. They lied to him, his parents. They weren't just there to work on his Elemental affinity. His dad was coming here anyway, on assignment. He knew about the scout and the potential ore deposits. Everything except for the Tear of God.

That was the game changer. No one would have ever expected a Tear of God out here. Its mere existence was reason enough to justify everything that had happened. It didn't make Mink feel any better about Gyov and the rest of them being gone. But, if Octernal was going to have a Tear of God resting in the Cradle once more, that was more important than anything that could ever happen to Mink.

Still, he wondered… If he did have a metal affinity, what could he do with it back home? There weren't any classes in metal. No chants. No history. Octernal rarely used metal with all the petrified Wood they could Imbue. Freeland and the Machinists had tons of metal. The best chance for him to explore his discovered affinity would be to defect to Freeland. It made sense. It also made Mink ill.

He stared at the faces of his parents, small and suspended before him. More than anything, he wanted to join them again. To tell them about Gyov, about the knife, and his affinity for metal. And to ask them why they had lied about the nature of their trip to Rift Ridge. Mink didn't expect Juré to divulge classified information, but why not admit he knew about the scout?

Mink sat tied to the chair for an hour or more. No sound other than the constant buzz of an engine or generator and his own breath to listen to. Hopefully, that meant the battle was over and the killing had stopped. He knew in his mind that he must go with the Machinists to Freeland, or else have a pointy stick jabbed in his throat. It made logical sense to go explore his affinity. But it took every minute of that hour to convince his heart that it was the right thing to do.

The initial image went away and suddenly a diminutive holographic video of the Tear of God being situated, in all of its immensity, played in front of him. The wagon merged with the eight pulleys, clutching the rock like prongs holding a jewel. It morphed into a huge land barge, dwarfed by its cargo. Seeing the whole geode out in the open, Mink was awestruck by its size, despite having seen it up close just a week ago. It's dull brown and gray surface was pocked and uneven, rather like a moon from a distance. How the Machinists were capturing this image eluded Mink, but it had to be from a position high above the battlefield. Squinting, he couldn't quite make out who was who among the Elementalists congregating, but judging by the numbers, it didn't appear that the Extraction Unit had lost many people.

The hologram shifted to reveal a lower angle as the Machinists in the foreground pointed their weapons down in front of them, but kept a vigil on the Elementalists. Mink watched as the Team began to head home, somber with a heavy victory. First, he noticed Tolrin by his shaved head. Then he traced his line of sight to finally see his parents once again. They looked weak and careworn, as if they may have aged years over the course of the last week. Tolrin came up to each and hugged them. They collapsed in tears. Pulti suddenly appeared by Nyam and held her, both of them mourning. Tolrin assisted Juré to a seat on the wagon.

Mink wondered if Tolrin had told them he was captured or dead. He supposed it didn't make much of a difference. It broke his heart that he had no way to assure them he was okay, but he felt relieved to know that his parents, Pulti, and Tolrin were safe. His thoughts drifted to Pulti. It was just going to be her and Dreh now. He wished them well.

He imagined how much stronger everyone was, being that close to the Tear of God. Remembering how he felt when Nyam had touched the crystal, Mink wondered if the needle sensation was metal growing out of his bones. Did Nyam have an idea? She had given him a curious look. Now, Mink would probably never know. The sound of the hatch opening and General Stroud descending the ladder broke his reverie.

"So?" The General began. "Have we made mind up?"

Mink didn't look at the General, but kept watching the floating image of the Tear of God leaving on the barge. "I will go to Freeland."

"Good, good." The General put his hand on Mink's shoulder and watched the display with him. "That's recording of half hour ago. Thought you would want to know."

General Stroud placed the pointed handle on a ledge beside Mink and unsheathed his knife. "Excuse me. But, must see for myself." He quickly slashed at the ropes binding Mink's chest and wrists, passing part of the blade through Mink's Body. The severed ropes fell to the floor and Mink's jacket bore a long slash, but he was unharmed. "Amazing," the General breathed, putting his knife away and untying Mink's ankles.

For a fleeting moment, Mink thought about making a break for it. He could knock out the General and escape. The Machinists would shoot at him, but that wouldn't matter. He had no chance of outrunning their vehicles. The offer to defect to Freeland would certainly expire the moment he fled. Instead, he stood up and thanked the General for freeing him.

"Follow me." Stroud led Mink to the rear door.

Outside, the Machinists busied themselves cleaning up and getting ready to go under the eerie quiet of post-battle shock. The perfect amount of breeze to cut the midday heat blew wisps of clouds through the endless sky. It felt out of place that the weather was so nice.

Perhaps as a means of reestablishing the peace, the Elementalists offered the Machinists all the ore they removed. Soldiers were placing Body bags into a couple of large vehicles. Other machines were piling ore beside the gaping hole that birthed the first reported Tear of God in sixteen thousand years.

"You take time need to adjust," Stroud offered. "A few hours from now, leave for Freeland. Stay close here." With that, the General left Mink and joined the troops gathering their dead.

The Reeks led their newly claimed puppets north toward the hudlew grove in a cluster of several hundred black cloaks. Good riddance, Mink thought. He vowed never to forget the voice of the Reek that took Gyov. At least one of the Machinists had to know his name. It grieved him to realize that he actually knew some of those puppets. Gyov's haunting smile invaded his mind when he remembered that her Body was among those walking into the forest leading to Harvest. He suddenly recalled the music crystal she had given him that morning, which he quickly pulled out of his pocket.

Mink ran his fingers over the surface of the crystal, but each facet he checked in turn was blank. Finally, on the fifth facet of its eight sides, he heard her dulcet voice. She sang the whole song of Oongk Ggyoriah Ahtima to him and then translated it. He was so grateful to have her voice preserved. Closing his eyes, he put his hands in his pockets and visualized her face in front of his, her voice in his head. He listened through the whole translation.

It was the story she had described. A princess loved a man who had to work very hard for very little. Once she opted to struggle with him, they were happy and finally able to marry. What Gyov hadn't told Mink was that after their marriage, their life got easier. She became a queen, and he her king.

Mink almost put the crystal away after the translation, but before he let it go, her voice continued. She had recorded to him, "Thank you for making me feel better last night. I have been scared about what might happen, but now I know I only need to stay by you. You make me feel safe." Mink hung his head with remorse and let tears flow.

The recording continued, "I am so glad for you that you get to see your parents and hope you introduce me to them. Maybe you already have. If not, then shame on you. Hmph. But, I trust you are the kind that will have me meet them. You are a unique guy and have a warm heart. I'm rambling now, but I want to also say. You are a good kisser. I wasn't expecting that."

Mink put away the crystal. There may have been more to the message, but his heart couldn't hear it. Not yet. He watched as the last of the black cloaks slipped through the shrubs in the distant hudlew grove, imagining her form gliding among the puppets and recalling how he held her in the vale last night.

"Goodbye, Gyov. Thank you for the crystal. I love you."

The Elementalists had long since been in the heart of the wilderness and out of view. Mink couldn't even see the top of the Tear of God, despite how massive it was, over the great distance of what once were ocean depths. He folded his arms over the knife-cut slits in his clothes and walked over to the enormous hole that remained.

A few dozen Machinists had the unenviable task of surfacing and bagging all the bodies that had fallen into the cavern. It helped that the Soil users had raised the ground inside closer to the top and hadn't Dispelled the Materialized Soil. Hundreds of dead lined the ground between the opening and their transports. The clean up process lasted until dusk.

Separating himself from the morbidity, Mink ventured just far enough to the eastern edge of the plateau to see the line of the Great Barrier Range. He caught the last of the day's light glinting off the geode now cresting the horizon, a faint but discernable speck made visible across the expanse of the land. That the Elementalists were able to get the Tear of God so far in less than a day was all the proof Mink needed to know that it was real.

Awestruck, Mink squinted as his parents and former allies disappeared over the eastern range with one last shimmer of the geode dropping out of view. He took solace in the fact that they came to possess it. Would they forgive him for not joining them? For allowing them to believe he was dead? That was out of his control. More importantly, he had discovered his Elemental affinity.

DON'T MISS THE NEXT CHAPTER IN
THE TEAR OF GOD SAGA

BOOK TWO

MACHINES

BY RAYMOND HENRI

COMING SOON

ABOUT THE AUTHOR

Raymond Henri has enjoyed storytelling from an early age. After exploring a variety of other forms of writing, this is his first novel. His character-driven stories and intricate world building create a rich experience where multi-faceted lives collide and shape each other against a tantalizing backdrop.